BOOK ONE OF
THE SOUTHERN MAGICKS SERIES

ASHTON K. ROSE

Published by Geekaflame Publishing

geekaflame.com

Cover Design by Fantasy & Coffee Design.
Interior Design by EliottDesigns.

ISBN: 978-0-6453365-0-4

To my Grandma and Grandpa who always accepted me without judegment and encouraged my dream of becoming a storyteller.

Miss you

Although the locations in this story are fictional, I'd like to acknowledge the Ngoorabul/Ngarabal, Marbul, Bigambul, Jucumbul, Goodjinburra, and Minyungbal people, Traditional Custodians of the land that inspired the locations in this story and pay my respects to their Elders past and present. I extend that respect to all Aboriginal and Torres Strait Islander peoples.

This book is set in modern Australia and written in a combination of British English/grammar and Australian slang/contemporary language that I've tried to make as accessible as possible to non-Australian audiences.

Content warnings/Trigger Warnings can be found on the following page of my website geekaflame.com/tsm1contentwarnings.

1

I knew Nora Rowe had died in her home without anyone telling me.

I unlocked the door and my stomach dropped as I took in the sight of the small dim living room of her kit home, filled with books and old newspapers. The acrid smell of cigarettes and wood fire smoke filled my nose as I weaved my way through the stacks. Mismatched flatpack bookshelves that warped under the strain of thousands of books lined the walls. Her living room held no other furniture apart from an old TV and a worn leather armchair—the carpet covered by stained, threadbare rugs.

I flicked the first light switch I saw twice.

Why had I expected the power to work?

I walked over to the windows and pushed the dust-caked lace curtains aside.

My eyes watered as the sun poured into the room.

In the kitchen, the doors of the cupboards hung open. The only things left behind were a few cheap plastic items scattered across the scratched lino.

I stepped on a plastic cup on the floor. I wobbled on my feet for a few sick seconds before I grabbed the counter to steady myself. The sharp aluminium edge bit into the skin of my hand.

This place was a death trap!

She had over twenty library books I had to separate from the donations. My legs shook as I walked to the shelves closest to the door.

I ignored the erratic beating of my heart and the part of my brain telling me to run and pulled out my keys to flick the small key chain light on. I placed it between my teeth and examined the spines for library tags.

When the light hit the grimy glass of a small photo frame on the shelf, I saw something move behind me. I kept my eyes fixed on the glass and used my thumb to clear a spot of dust.

If it hadn't moved, I could have ignored the human-shaped shadow reflected in the glass.

As a kid, I'd been hassled about seeing things and having an overactive imagination. When I was seven, Gran told me the truth. I shared her secret ability to see ghosts.

I turned to look at the woman who sat in the armchair.

This Nora was a couple of years older than the one who celebrated her birthday in the photo. Her gaze focused on the TV, which would have been new the year Queen Elizabeth was coronated.

I kept my gaze locked on her, blinking one eye at a time.

I slowed my breath and took a careful step backwards to the door. The back of my calf hit something that drove several points of pain into my skin.

The stack of books I knocked over sliced through my composure just as easily as it did the silence in the room, the hard covers and spines slapping against each other as they hit the floor.

"What the fuck are you doing in my house?" Nora stood and turned to face me.

I knew I'd given the game away when I jumped out of my skin and almost dropped my keys.

I made a noise like a dying rat.

She knew I could hear her.

The first thing Gran had taught me was not to let a ghost realise you could sense them. It was dangerous—a trigger for the ire of a vengeful spirit.

"I'm sorry," I said. "Your son gave us the key."

"Worthless piece of shit. Letting strangers into my house. He stole my grandma's dinner set for drug money before my body was cold. I saw him put it in his car before he called someone to deal with the *mess*."

"I'll just be going now."

"Actually, I'll be going."

I felt a sharp pain in my chest.

I tried to breathe, but my lungs refused to move.

I couldn't breathe!

The edge of my vision went black as I gasped for air. I fell flat on my front. I was so focused on trying to breathe, I almost missed the presence pushing at the back of my mind. It started small, a hint of a suggestion. The temptation to give in grew. This was her body. I was nothing but a figment of her imagination. Dexter wasn't real. Nothing more than a thought exercise to see what it'd be like to be a man her grandson's age. With each second, it pressed harder, and the urge to give in grew.

Forget.

It would be easy to give in and never have another worry again. All the pain and pressure of life could vanish if I relaxed and let her take control.

No!

I shivered as I tried to move my arms to push myself onto my hands and knees. I focused on the door. It was only a short crawl. I had to do it. For a second, my vision went entirely black.

No!

I gathered all the strength I had and screamed. The remaining air expelled from my lungs. I took a sharp breath. I moved my stiff arms and pushed myself onto my hands and knees.

I was Dexter; I was real, and this was my body. Nothing would take that away from me.

I closed my eyes and pushed back the ghost. I wrapped a mental net around the invasive presence in my mind and forced it back through the hole where it had entered. A hole it had dug in a part of my mind I didn't even know existed.

One arm forwards, one leg forwards, and breathe.

Move. Breathe. Move. Breathe.

I made it to the threshold and pulled the door open. I slid headfirst down the concrete stairs to lie on my back.

The pressure in my mind slowly vanished as I fell.

I opened my eyes.

Pale blue sky, almost cloudless.

My eyes watered from the bright light.

The perfect day was oblivious to my plight. The mid-autumn day was hardly different from late summer. I could've laid there for hours, but the hot concrete felt like it was melting the skin off my back where my shirt had ridden up. I rolled onto the dead grass beside the cracked front path.

Sweat ran into my eyes as I sat up. I squeezed my eyes shut to clear my vision.

I could still feel the cold air wafting from the open door. I had to shut it. Mrs Gregory was looking for any excuse to fire me. I stood and walked to the threshold.

All I had to do was grab the handle, pull it closed, remove my hand from the handle and step back.

One quick movement.

I could do it.

As I stared, my eyes adjusted to the dim. She stood just inside, her hard eyes focused on me.

She smiled.

I stepped forwards and grabbed the door handle. Her hand shot out towards my arm.

Her pale, icy fingers clamped around my left wrist. I tightened the grip of my right hand around the door handle. I tucked my chin to my chest and threw myself backwards down the stairs, using the weight of my body to swing the door closed. My shirt ripped as I fell backwards; the sleeve stayed in her hand as my arm slipped free.

The air expelled from my lungs as I hit the ground.

I lay on my back and my lungs refused to work. Fixed to the spot in terror, I gasped for air as my body refused to perform. A function that was usually thoughtless had become my only thought, the pinpoint the world had narrowed to.

There was a dizzy relief as I breathed again, and after a few minutes I slowly stood.

Blood ran down my exposed arm, the only part of my body that had hit the thin concrete path.

Ghosts could touch me! Physically hurt me!

I closed my eyes and concentrated on my breathing, forcing back the panic attack that bubbled in the back of my mind. I knew about the possession, but the touch? Why hadn't Gran told me? I needed to call Gran, but I knew she couldn't help me. She hadn't talked to me about magic since her accident when I was seventeen.

I suspected the accident was magic-related, but she'd kept silent about it.

She'd looked at me sceptically any time I'd mentioned magic afterwards, as though I spoke of childish whimsy and needed to grow up.

So I had.

I'd left Dunn and become a librarian, a nice stable job for a responsible young man who liked books.

A normal young man who had resigned himself to a life of pretending he couldn't see the dead.

I'd somehow ended up with nowhere else to turn and ended up back in this town.

Now Gran was in America with Aunt Myrtle, so it was hard to get help.

I drove back to the library to pretend I'd been out for my lunch break.

As the masked men step through the crack in the painted brick wall, I forced myself to swallow the yelp that almost escaped my throat. I was transfixed. The crack grew from a few inches to large enough for a man to fit through. I was frozen, my dark eyes fixed on them through a gap in the shelves, the book I'd been about to place still in my hand.

The first of the two men touched the wall, and it slowly reformed. He was tall, pale, and wore an emerald suit. Every other aspect of his appearance slipped from my mind as soon as I processed it.

"Are you sure it's here?" the emerald man asked.

His black-suited companion pulled a list from his pocket. "The old families keep a stash of valuable spell books here. In case it all goes to shit," Black replied.

"When it does, we'll be at the helm," Emerald said.

"The Boss said this stash is checked often." Black focused on the wall a little way down from me.

"No one else comes down here?"

"Only the bookworms."

I took a careful step back and bumped into the book cart.

I needed to stop walking backwards entirely.

The squeak of the wheels echoed through the basement, cutting off the words Emerald was about to say.

Emerald looked straight at me. "Fuck."

"Stay away." I waved the heavy tome I held like a weapon.

Black walked up beside him and touched his shoulder. "That's Dexter."

"Really? They did a superb job on him. I must meet the Memory Mage who did it."

"Who are you?" I asked.

Black waved a hand between Emerald and me. "This is Dark Matter, and I'm Nox."

I backed into the shelf behind me hard enough to almost topple it. "Please don't hurt me. I can keep my mouth shut."

"We were never here." Nox forced me to meet his hard, narrowed eyes.

I nodded.

My legs gave way and my breathing sped up.

They turned away and Dark Matter opened a hole in the cream wall beside them. They started pulling objects from it.

My stomach dropped when I realised that was the safe.

No need to crack it when Dark Matter could make part of the wall vanish.

My head spun, my vision faded in and out and each breath was barely a hitch before I exhaled. The robbery seemed too easy.

Had they set off a silent alarm?

The old families wouldn't have left a valuable stash unprotected. I closed my eyes and focused. I could hear a distant high-pitched hum like tinnitus in the back of my mind. I ran both hands through my thick dark curls as the pain set in and burrowed its way into me.

"You better leave," Nox said.

The voice was a slap across the face. It flung me out of the nightmare world where only my pain and I existed.

They had walked back through the hole where they entered.

Nox poked his head back through the gap in the wall to look at me. He clapped then waved a hand towards the door in a shooing motion as though I were a cat or small child.

When had I stood?

It didn't matter. I had to put as much distance as possible between us.

I ran. The soles of my fashion boots squeaked against the faded mint lino as they tried to find purchase.

I broke through the disturbance that had overwhelmed all my senses.

I forced a breath out then in.

I felt every wobble of my legs and refused to give in to the urge to look back. I'd either trip or find they'd changed their minds and were behind me.

I bolted the steel door behind me at the top of the stairs and looked down at my pale, shaky hands when I felt something prick against my skin. I had gripped the edge of the door so hard pieces of chipped red paint had come off on my sweaty hands. I wiped my hands on my grey jeans and froze when I saw paint under my nails.

I couldn't lie about being down there.

I always stacked books on Tuesday afternoon.

If I'd gripped the shitty door hard enough to leave nail marks, I would have obviously been scared by something. If I told them what I saw, Nox and Dark Matter would hunt me down. It wouldn't be hard; they knew where I worked and could walk through walls.

I couldn't quit and hide in my bedroom until they were captured less than a month after my wedding. The people who said I was marrying for the money would think they were right.

It also wouldn't take a genius to figure out where the guy married to the Lacy family's eldest son lived. Even though Eli wasn't the heir anymore, we still lived with his family.

I locked myself in the staff bathroom and drowned my hands in the pearlescent pink soap. A chemical floral smell permeated the room. I turned the water as high as I could without soaking my pants and started removing several layers of garish paint from my nails. I imagined anything past the yellow paint under the red top layer had asbestos or lead in it. The door had been red and in need of a new paint job as long as I could remember.

I used my clean hands to splash cold water onto my hot, sweaty face.

If they had really wanted to hurt me, I wouldn't have been able to do anything to stop them.

Why was I such a pathetic freak?

I took another five minutes to collect myself then walked back to my office in a relaxed manner.

Two magical incidents in the one day.

No one could know what I'd witnessed even without the threat of revenge from Nox and Dark Matter.

I wasn't supposed to know about magic.

I'd been told plenty of horror stories about what happened to those who found out about magic when they shouldn't. My ability to compose myself after both incidents would mark me as someone who already knew. The group that controlled local use of magic would know it was Gran who told me. She and her father had been openly bitter about being frozen out of the inner circle.

June looked up from the front counter as I walked into the main room of the library.

The moment my brown eyes met June's green ones, she blew a strand of frizzy blonde hair that had escaped her ponytail from her face. "Is there a protocol for when I catch the head of the Ladies' Book Club stealing books?"

"The what?" I was surprised by the sudden segue from my own problems.

"Those expensive alarms the town council had installed, they don't work," June said. "Mrs Chastain dropped a pile of books as she was walking down the stairs."

"How did you know she was stealing the books?"

June placed a hardcover encyclopedia for the Victorian era on the counter. It was labelled as not for loan and had dented corners. I knew these books were expensive. I'd catalogued them myself after we'd inherited them as a donation from a university professor. A full set was worth a few thousand dollars second-hand. I sighed. "How many are missing?"

"Three."

"And the chances of them still being in Dunn?" I could already picture their online listing.

"Maybe not as bad as you think. Mrs Chastain writes erotic Victorian bodice rippers."

"So they're likely in her house?"

"Yes, but she claimed to have accidentally mixed this up with the books she borrowed." June clicked her tongue. "Called me a tyrant because I was accusing her of stealing because she couldn't research in peace with her kids home for the holidays."

I pointed to the corkboard by the door, which held flyers advertising the holiday programs. "School holidays don't start until next week."

"Not the point. We're not getting those books back unless we report this to the police. They ain't going to care about a housewife stealing encyclopedias," June said.

I grabbed a book from the cream-coloured steel shelf behind me and waved it between the large grey plastic alarms on either side of the entrance.

Nothing.

I'd just washed asbestos paint from my fingernails, and the council had wasted money on alarms that didn't even work. I looked around the library, but none of the other patrons paid attention to us.

I walked behind the desk and pulled the phone book from its shelf and flipped through the sticky notes poking from the side until I found the one that marked the page with the alarm repair and installation on it. As I stared at the number, I noticed the name above it: Mark Chastain. "Would Mrs Chastain know how to disable a security alarm?"

June turned the book around to read it. "Her husband owns the alarm company. This just gets worse."

At least someone hadn't used magic to disable the alarm. Mrs Chastain probably knew where to place powerful magnets to disable it.

The shrill ring of the desk phone silenced my next words. The red light next to the mayor's name on the extension list flashed. For a few seconds, June and I stared at each other, then at the phone, as though it was poised to bite the person who reached out to touch it. In a mad panic that we'd miss the call, I grabbed the receiver and pulled it to my ear.

"Dunn Public Library. Dexter speaking," I spoke carefully into the receiver, tangling the cord around my fingers. The action was a nervous habit I'd stopped trying to break.

"I'd like to see you in my office after you close today," Mayor Chesterfield said.

My hand stilled, fingers tightening around the cord loops. Why had he called me directly? Couldn't he have given orders through Mrs Gregory like normal? I used the bite of the ageing plastic against my skin to silence my worried thoughts. Was this about the theft or one of my actual misdeeds? Had Mrs Gregory found out about the books I'd saved?

"Are you still there?"

"Yes… sir." I gripped the cord tighter.

I heard foil wrinkle then a crunch. I could practically smell the peanuts Mayor Chesterfield ate.

"Arrive before five. I don't want to stay late at the office, my wife's got the in-laws coming for dinner."

"Yes."

"Good." Mayor Chesterfield hung up.

I ripped my fingers from the cord and slammed the receiver onto its cradle.

2

I waited as Mayor Chesterfield drank his cup of milky tea. After ten minutes, he put the empty cup down and looked me in the eye. I was about to speak when there was a knock at the door. Without waiting for the mayor to respond, the people on the other side walked in.

A stern man and woman, both in simple dark suits. I knew instantly the woman was in charge. She was at least twenty years older than the man, who was nearer to my age. She had hard grey eyes and sandy brown hair pulled back into a tight bun, which gave her a school madam look that aged her by two decades at first glance.

I recognised the man as one of the kids who had headed to the selective and private Dunn Academy after primary school.

Alexander Hawking.

At twelve, he'd been a spiteful, sour boy who'd always jumped at the chance to spy on other kids for the teachers. His favourite pastimes were kicking sand in kindergarteners' faces and knocking kids from the playground structure, and he and his cronies ruled with an iron fist. I'd married the guy who used to lead raiding parties to throw balls at them while the rest of us huddled in the garden, hoping neither group remembered we existed.

It wasn't a surprise Hawking had become a cop.

The woman looked straight into my dark eyes.

It felt as though she was looking through me and into my soul. She blinked, and in a second, the look vanished back into hard professionalism that predated her forty or so years.

If anyone had ever given me a 'you're fucked' look. I had to resist the urge to sigh like a petulant teen called into the principal's office.

Where were these feelings coming from? I had been upset when I'd entered the office, but this sudden anger felt like it had come out of nowhere.

As though it wasn't my own.

"You must be Dexter."

"Must? I have a feeling you already know." The words spilled from my mouth of their own accord.

God, that sounded rude.

What the hell was wrong with me?

It was like I'd completely lost my ability to keep my thoughts to myself.

Her raised eyebrow was the only change to her expression. "My name is Andrea Dominguez. I'm a detective investigating a theft from a store of rare books that were placed under the care of the library."

"Theft?"

"Yes."

"Why would someone steal from here?" A panicked retelling of the incident with Mrs Chastain and the door alarms sat in my mouth as I pressed my lips shut. That was the only theft I knew about if I needed a defence.

Anyone could have walked out of here with books and it wasn't my fault.

"That's what I'd like to know."

"I haven't seen any suspicious activity," I said.

"Why did you vanish for most of the morning?" Dominguez said.

"I was working in the basement as ordered."

"It took you twice as long as it should have."

"I was kind of slacking off. There's not a lot to do around here." I was stunned at the words. What the hell was she doing to me?

"What exactly were you doing?"

"Reading fanfiction on my phone." I felt her gaze burrow into my forehead. My cheeks reddened. I looked suspicious right now, but somehow my muddied mind had supplied a truthful lie. I'd been minutes from "taking a break" when the break-in happened.

"Fanfiction?"

"Stories people write about fictional characters."

"You have Internet down there?"

I forced myself to keep the smile. She knew exactly what I was talking about. "I downloaded it. I must have lost track of time." I had to focus; if I couldn't keep my mouth shut, I was done for. I needed to stick to one-word answers instead of blabbing my misdeeds. If she'd gotten me to admit that my *breaks* were slacking off, what else could she get me to say?

"And you saw nothing odd while you were down there?"

"No." I almost snapped the word.

"If I find anything to connect you to this, I'm taking you in." Dominguez fixed me with her gaze again.

My eyes slid towards her as though they were magnetised, and my head moved in a nod the moment I met her eyes again. She made a hum of satisfaction, smiled, then turned and left the office. Her lackey gave me a hard, narrow-eyed look before he followed her from the office. Hawking shut the door loudly but not quite hard enough to be considered a slam.

I felt the tension slide from my shoulders, the pressure that had pressed in on my mind and loosened my tongue fading.

Why were they suspicious of me?

I'd been there, but her tone made it sound like I was a suspect. Those men had threatened to kill me.

Mayor Chesterfield took his glasses off and rubbed the bridge of his nose between two fingers. "The only reason I'm giving you the benefit of doubt is because I respect your grandfather and Eli."

I closed my eyes and took a few calming breaths then nodded.

He pulled a small white business card from his desk drawer. "Call the number on this card if you encounter anything strange."

"Strange, sir? Like what? Possible asbestos?" I was instantly anxious over how stilted and awkward my attempt at obliviousness sounded.

"You'll know when you need the number. I'm not exactly allowed to tell you, but it will allow you to take anything dangerous over their heads."

My grandfather's main political rival was giving me a "get out of jail free" card.

I forced myself to smile and take the card from his long, pale fingers.

"Leave. I actually want to get home in time for dinner," Chesterfield said.

I nodded and left the mayor's office; my gaze focused on the faded grey carpet. I only let the smile drop from my face after I had walked down the first flight of stairs.

Did this man want to help me now I'd married into his family? The Lacys and Chesterfields had always been close, even before my husband Eli's parents got married. The Chesterfield family had been close to my own before the rivalry between Grandfather and Mayor Chesterfield.

Chesterfield had turned up at my wedding as Eli's doting uncle after he used the fact that Grandfather lived with a man against him during their last council election. Was I supposed to believe someone who sank that low had changed so dramatically in a little over a decade?

After I grabbed my bag from the library office and walked out to the street, I pulled the card the mayor had given me from my pocket. It was a fine, cream-coloured card with metallic green numbers. The card held only a phone number with a green border around the edge. I looked up the number; it had no history. I forced my heavy fingers to move and add the number to my contacts.

It couldn't hurt to trust him.

If he hurt me, he'd be indirectly hurting his nephew. Family was the only thing the man seemed to care about outside of the mayoral position. Before I knew him as an overbearing boss, I'd known him as my best friend's doting father who spoilt him rotten.

I'd give him one chance.

When I walked into the bedroom, Eli sat at the end of our bed, playing a shooting game. He wore a headset and chatted to someone. I didn't know why he needed a second console in the bedroom, but I wouldn't ask. Maybe he found the bed more comfortable than the couch. He narrowed his eyes when he saw me stumble into the room, my left leg still sore from the fall.

He looked at his watch then pressed a button on his headset. "You okay?"

"Just a long day, same old stuff." Plus I almost died twice. I gave him a warm smile and met his eyes. Eli was a perfectly normal guy, the exact person everyone expected me to marry. After their matchmaking with his sister and my brother failed, we were a second best.

I put a bottle of wine and two glasses on my oak bedside table. After the day I'd had, I needed to lie down with a drink.

"I think we'll have a night in." He examined the bottle, which, I realised with horror, was only three quarters full. Had I really drunk that much on my way to the bedroom? "Have those fish and chips tomorrow night."

Shit. I'd forgotten our date. I lay down on the bed, my head spinning.

The last thing I heard before I gave in to the pull of sleep was Eli saying something about my grazed elbow.

It was dark when I woke. The TV was off and the room was silent apart from Eli. He stood near the window, talking on his phone. I slowed my breathing to hear him speak.

"I have no idea why he didn't check in with you after the meeting," he said.

He listened to the person on the other end.

"Maybe something happened, June. You know he's not the type to drink like that." Eli turned around before I could close my eyes. "I've got to go."

I looked at him without speaking. There was just enough moonlight for us to see each other. My brown eyes rested on his hazel ones as we stared at each other. I loved looking into his eyes, always had. They were the prettiest eyes I'd ever seen on anyone, even when he was just the annoying son of our family friends before I'd had romantic feelings for him. I'd always noticed him, but he hadn't become dateable until I moved back after university, when he became this attractive man who asked me out after discovering I was bisexual.

"I could hear your breathing change. If you're going to eavesdrop on my conversations, maybe keep your breathing even."

I looked over at the bedside table to check my phone.

"What happened at work?"

"I fell down the stairs when I was collecting some books at a house."

"Did you go to the doctor?" His voice was laced with panic.

"No. I didn't want to worry anyone."

Eli raised an eyebrow. "You fall down a set of stairs and instead of going to a doctor, you what? Went back to work?"

And it had been a mistake. If I never went back, I wouldn't have been there when those books were stolen. I blinked tears from my eyes. I wished I could really talk to him. He was better with people than I was. He would know what to do.

The way he said it made me sound like an irrational idiot with a work addiction.

Was I an irrational idiot obsessed with pleasing my boss, the corporate drone I'd always promised myself I'd never become? I had to focus on work. I'd worked hard for my degree and had to make money. If I didn't, those people who called me a gold-digger for marrying Eli would be right.

Eli gave me a tight smile and sat on the end of the bed to pull his thick woollen socks off. "Mum said you have dinner in the fridge."

I looked him in the eyes again when he laid on the bed beside me. "I'm sorry about messing up our date."

"This family doesn't do secrets, remember. If there's anything you need to tell me, I'm here."

"Your mum's golden rule." I forced myself not to roll my eyes.

"Telling the truth is critical to good relationships."

"There's nothing to tell. I was stupid and tried to walk down the front stairs of a house with an armful of books. It was four stairs and my head missed the concrete."

"I'm allowed to be worried about you, Dex."

"I know." I smiled at him. "Love you."

"Love you too, goodnight."

I walked into the bathroom after I smiled at him.

I noticed it under the cold bathroom light as I brushed my teeth. A violent hand-shaped bruise was on the arm Nora Rowe had grabbed.

I took a couple of slow, focused breaths to still my panic. The bedside table light had been on when I first walked into the bedroom.

Eli had seen it.

Even though the light was low, I knew he had seen it. Knowing he knew I was lying felt dirtier than the act of lying itself.

Maybe that said something about me.

June was in the office when I arrived at work the next day. She looked up from my computer when I loudly placed my water bottle on the desk beside her. "What did Uncle Chaz want yesterday?"

It was still weird hearing Mayor Chesterfield referred to as Uncle Chaz.

"Just Mrs Gregory pissed I kept the diverse books she tried to throw away for no reason." I sat down at Mrs Gregory's desk and scanned the returns pile.

"Did you tell him about the theft?"

I dropped the book I held, frozen in place. My heart rate skyrocketed. "Theft?"

"Mrs Chastain? Are you sure you're okay? You're acting very jumpy."

"Yes."

"Eli said you hurt yourself. Fell down a bloody staircase and didn't tell anyone."

I picked up a pen to flip between my fingers. "I didn't want to worry anyone."

"I get you don't want me to babysit you, but I sort of assumed we were friends at this point. With you being married to my best friend."

I paused and looked up at her. "Sorry."

"Are you sure everything is okay?"

I swallowed the fear that bubbled in the back of my throat. I'd really let my guard down. I'd known June my entire life, and she was nice to me. I wanted her to be my friend, but she couldn't know about what had happened to me.

No one could.

"Things are a certain way and I need this job to keep up my part of the deal."

The colour drained from her face slightly. "Deal?"

I looked down at the dark wood table. I ran my fingers along the edge of the chipped varnish but resisted the urge to pick at it. I wasn't sure how to phrase what I was about to tell her. "Lacy Senior met with me before the wedding and made me promise I wasn't marrying into the family for money or power."

"Power?" June laughed. "Your family has more actual power than the Lacy family and plenty of money."

"There are rumours." I rubbed my finger against the chipped varnish and a brown crust formed on my finger. "He was only reacting to them, protecting his family."

"Barton Lacy Senior wouldn't hesitate to kill his own family to protect them from themselves." June's chair—my chair—squeaked as she leant backwards. "Why are you so worried about what people say suddenly?"

I'd come to work yesterday after being attacked by a ghost and falling downstairs onto concrete. Dominguez had implied the reason she had done nothing other than talk to me was because of my place in the Lacy family. I was married to the man who'd been considered the heir until he married a man, even though he had an older sister. Sometimes this town felt so backwards it was suffocating. Like I was in a warped version of the 1950s, where an idealistic nostalgic veneer was fitted over a foundation of utter terror and violence. *Lord of the Flies* in wholesome family movie skin. How had Grandfather survived here as a gay man in the sixties? I'd heard stories about my great-great-grandfather, and he was a lot like Eli's. The Arkwright family and their legacy within the town was all that mattered to him. He had tried to bury Grandfather, to get rid of him when he wasn't the perfect heir he'd been painfully carved into. I didn't have the backbone and strength Grandfather did to rise to power in a town filled with vipers.

I wanted to let out a bitter laugh. Lacy Senior had been best friends with Grandfather until he was forced out of the closet. Then was all buddy-buddy again when Grandfather became mayor. No one had told me, but I'd noticed an absence of him in photos. That was the man who was on about me faking a relationship with Eli for an advantage.

"My earliest memory of Lacy Senior was Harlan telling me to be careful around him because we were all tools for him to use."

"Harlan? That's your grandfather's partner?"

"Yes." Harlan had been around my entire life and had lived down the road with Grandfather. He increasingly felt like the only grandparent who'd spent time around me without an ulterior motive.

Grandfather had turned to me to become the next Arkwright mayor after my brother Ralph left. Gran wanted me to become a tool for her revenge. Pop had spent all our time together towards the end trying to undo the damage his wife had done.

Harlan saw me as a person, and he was reduced to just Grandfather's partner—or worse, boyfriend, like what they had together was just a shallow fling—by society. I only called him Harlan so it didn't confuse other people.

"Look, the best tactic with Lacy Senior is to avoid him," June said.

"You don't live with him," I said.

"If you let him get to you, it will consume you." I turned my attention to the day's schedule without another word. I'd always cared what other people thought. It was human nature, wasn't it?

I picked up the receiver of my desk phone and I found myself halfway through dialling Aunt Myrtle's number before my brain caught up to my fingers. I slammed the phone back on the receiver. I couldn't have a conversation with Gran about ghosts over the work phone.

All the phone calls were likely recorded.

I looked over at June, who now sat stamping a pile of new books. "I'm going to get us some coffee."

She nodded and I grabbed my keys then headed for the door. I made sure I shut the office door loud enough to wake up Mrs Gregory, who sat asleep at the checkout counter.

The shadowy girl always stood on the curb at the corner of Short Street and Main Street. Her fuzzy frame flickered as she watched the passing cars and people through dark, curious eyes. I approached her once when I was ten, but she acted like she couldn't see me. I knew she could. I'd seen her kill a crow; she was aware of her surroundings. I'd been crossing the street to avoid her since I could remember. Gran said it was a bad idea to look at her or even think of her. I have no idea what possessed me to speak to her at the time. One second, we made eye contact, and the next I was standing in front of her watching my breath move her dark hair. Rather than appearing human like the other spirits I'd encountered, she looked like she was lifted from a black and white film. I knew she was still there, even though I didn't look at her anymore. I could feel her waiting in the back of my mind. Had she slowly made the chink in my mental armour that Nora Rowe had tried to exploit?

Or had there always been a door into my mind?

I closed my eyes as I passed her.

The urge to look at her was intoxicating.

3

I stopped in front of an old weatherboard house. I put my headphones in and grabbed the book list.

I needed to collect three.

I let myself in with the key the son gave us. The house had been on the market for almost a year and hadn't been cleaned out.

The smell made my stomach roll.

I resisted the urge to shut the door and leave. A feral cat or possum probably just slipped into the house and couldn't get out.

I tried to breathe through my mouth as I walked down the dim hall. The hardwood floorboards creaked under my shoes. I wanted to leave and come back in a few weeks. Maybe someone would come clean the house, or the smell wouldn't be as bad once the dead thing aged.

I started to turn around when I walked into the living room and found myself flat on my back on the floor, the wind knocked from my lungs.

I dry heaved when I inhaled. I forced myself to take another rancid breath and hold it. The metallic smell of what I'd slipped in wormed its way through the stench.

I took a breath.

Out, in, out, in, hold.

I slowly let the breath out.

I pulled myself onto my hands and knees. I only slid once in the cold, wet puddle as I pushed myself upwards.

A woman lay on the floor, her dark tangled hair inches from where my shoes had been.

The room spun.

My vision faded for a second when I met her cloudy eyes. Her face was frozen in an expression of terror. Below her chest, she was a tattered mass of fabric and rotting flesh that didn't even look like it belonged to a person any more. I dry heaved as my gaze slid up her body back to her empty blue eyes. She couldn't have been older than eighteen. Her parents would have to identify her body.

I fell backwards as I tried to move away. My head spun. I felt like I was looking at myself from the outside in. I couldn't slow my short, panicked breaths.

I closed my eyes and took a deep, slow breath.

The edges of my vision were fuzzy.

Air, I needed air.

She was still there.

This was real.

In a heart-stopping moment, I realised what the metallic smell was. I'd slipped in blood.

I let out a gasp like a wounded animal. For a second, I looked around the room for an invisible enemy, not realising I'd made the noise. I was covered in her stagnant blood.

I vomited before I could angle my head away from my body.

I heard the scrape of cloth against cloth.

I wasn't alone. My limbs shook as the truth solidified in my mind.

The *thing* that did this was locked in the house with me.

Tears ran down my cheeks as I struggled to my feet, forcing my stiff legs to stop shaking and hold my weight.

Was it in this room, waiting for the perfect moment to strike?

I had to know.

I slowly looked around the room, then walked backwards and reached behind me until I felt the light switch. The empty click sliced through the silence.

The house had been empty for a year; there was no power.

My heart threatened to burst through my chest.

Was this a heart attack?

Why couldn't I breathe?

Why was this happening to me?

I wiped my hands on the side of my pant leg and pulled my phone from my pocket. I angled the thin light from the torch, illuminating what had been obscured from my vision.

She wasn't the only one! At least three others were scattered around the remains of a chalk diagram.

The bodies were in various states of disarray. Everything was covered in a layer of blood. Unidentifiable masses of decomposing flesh were strewn throughout the room from ceiling to floor. I almost dropped my phone when I noticed the burnt-out candles placed around the diagram.

The surviving chalk markings told part of the story. They were placed at significant points. Some had been knocked over in the struggle, but a few still stood.

How had the place not burnt down?

I slowly walked back into the hall. It had to be a thing that did this. A creature they summoned from somewhere else. No earthly being could have done it.

Gran's warning was a dark, little voice in the back of my mind. I had to get out. The demon was still in the house. The gate it had entered through was closed. If no doors were broken or windows smashed, it was still inside.

A pair of yellow eyes opened; they reflected the light from my phone.

Could it read my mind?

I would have vomited again if I had anything left in my stomach. I turned and bolted. Its claws slapped against the wood, an echo of my own footsteps. I ran into the bedroom at the end of the hall and slammed the door. I heard the glass in the bedroom doors break as I locked the en suite door. The open side of the bathroom window was covered with a security screen. I needed something to break the glass. I froze as I reached for the stainless steel and glass bathroom scales. If it got out, the whole town would be at risk. I couldn't shut a solid glass windowpane.

I pushed on the earpieces of my wireless headphones until they sat securely in my ears and paused my music. I unlocked my phone, dialled the number from the card Mayor Chesterfield had given me, and slipped the phone back into my pocket.

"Hello, Gain Solutions. How can—"

The creature growled as it broke down the bedroom doors.

The man on the end of the line had fallen silent.

Was it finally done playing with its food?

"Help me. That thing's going to get in and kill me. I can't break the window or it'll escape."

"Someone will be with you momentarily."

His cheery, singsong tone grated my nerves. I was about to die and he acted like I'd just ordered a pizza from the happiest place on Earth.

I struggled not to sob as the demon ran a claw along the wall as it made its way to the en suite door. It was fucking with me. "Please. Help me. I've only just gotten married; I don't want to die." I backed away from the door as the demon crashed into it. The wood bowed, and the hinges creaked, but it stood against the impact.

I yelped and took another step backward. The back of my knees hit the bathtub as the pain shot through my legs.

I lost my balance.

My head hit the sharp edge of the tiled brick windowsill when it broke my fall.

I slid sideways into the tub.

I landed on my arm as I instinctively tried to break the fall.

I closed my eyes, the lack of light and the cold porcelain relieving the pain for a few precious seconds.

I forced my fingers to move as my wrist throbbed; if I could move them, then they weren't broken.

If I gave into the darkness, I'd wake up from this nightmare. It was easy to let myself slip into the feeling of bliss that called to me.

It felt like I was waking from a long sleep. Relief washed over me; it was all a dream. I let myself slip into the embrace of the welcoming darkness.

The tendrils would carry me into the real world if I allowed them to tangle themselves in my brain and latch on.

End this nightmare.

I let them carry me into the darkness.

"Are you okay? Please answer me."

I was on my hands and knees, watching blood drip onto the porcelain.

Why was I here?

How did I get here?

I watched the red drops form a puddle on the smooth white surface.

Was that my blood?

The way the drops slid into the large red puddle was oddly relaxing. The rich dark red on white enthralled me.

"I need you to speak to me. Please."

The voice was desperate, pleading and right in my ear.

Something growled outside the door and crashed into it.

Terror gripped my heart and tears formed in my eyes as I remembered.

This was real.

I let out a sob of despair.

It wasn't some sick nightmare.

It was real.

My tears mingled with the drops of blood. The red swirled into a darkly mesmerising pattern as it mixed into the salty water.

My arms slid from under me as the pain shot up my wrist when I put weight on it. The crack my nose made as it hit the bottom of the tub cut through the room.

"Dexter? Dex! I need you to speak to me." The voice was like a slap across the face.

How did he know my name? The thing crashed into the door again as it played with me.

Did it enjoy my suffering?

Did it want me to beg for the release of death?

I wasn't going to give it that satisfaction. I gritted my teeth together to hold in an angry snarl.

"How do you know my name? Who are you? What do you want?" I said.

"Have you hit your head? Are you bleeding? Speak to me," the man on the phone responded.

It growled again and ran its claws along the door.

"It's going to kill me." My voice sounded hollow. A subconscious part of me had already come to terms with my fate.

Another hit. I heard two screws break free and roll across the tiles. The bells that tolled my death.

"Can it hear me?" he said.

"Yes." I pulled myself up onto my hands and knees. Warm, bitter blood slid down the edge of my face into my mouth. I spat it out and wiped my mouth on my shirt collar. I was sure the demon's newfound aggression was because it knew I'd called for help.

"I need you to stay with me," the man said. "Someone is coming. Take your mind off that thing. Let's talk about something else. Let me know you're okay."

"How do you know my name?"

"Your number is on a list."

I screamed hysterically as it broke down the door.

I slid down and curled into a ball.

I closed my eyes.

Maybe it would be better if I couldn't see it.

I braced myself for impact.

The gunshots caused my ears to ring. The pain drowned out the sound of the dying creature. I felt something warm splatter on me. I knew it was from the demon.

More body fluid...

I couldn't hear anything. As I opened my eyes, the sight of its black blood caused me to heave, but I swallowed the bile that rose in my throat. I closed my eyes again and rested my head against the tub, tears rolling down my cheeks. The cold surface under me now felt like an anchor to reality.

I let the tension fall from my body.

I was alive.

"It's all right, Dex."

I felt a hand run through my hair.

When had someone hopped in the tub with me?

My head rested on someone's lap. I knew the voice, but every time I remembered who it was, the thought slipped from my mind. I took a deep breath in then out.

Who was it?

I yelped in pain as the man who held me touched the back of my head.

The hand retracted as though it had been burnt.

"You're going to have to tell him if you stick around," another man said.

"I don't care about that," the man holding me said. "He needs to go to the hospital. Some of this blood is his. Pass me a medical pad; he has a head wound."

His hand pushed something soft against my head. It hurt. I tried to pull away.

"Love, it's okay. I need you to stay still. I'm sorry it hurts, but I'm trying to help." The man in the tub held me tighter.

Eli! I forced my eyes open. The light from the window stung. I closed my eyes again. It had to be Eli. I didn't need to see him. I knew I was safe.

"You need to keep him awake. He likely has a concussion," a woman said. "He could be in shock too."

"I know first aid as well as you." Eli pulled me closer.

I was safe now. I could sleep.

"Dex, love. You need to open your eyes. Stay awake while I get you to the hospital. You likely have a concussion." Eli shook me gently. "Please look at me. Let me know you're okay."

I opened my eyes and turned my head away from the window.

The other man stood beside the woman and they were looking down at us. He narrowed his eyes at me through his glasses while the woman gave me a forced smile.

"He's not ready for this. Non-magical people can't deal with this kind of shit." The man crossed his arms.

"He's from a magical family, Lionel," Eli said. "And married to me."

"He's not magical, though. Old Ed had him tested at six like everyone else, and he failed," Lionel said.

Old Ed? Grandfather knew about this! My head spun as I tried to sit up.

"Lean on me." Eli helped me to my feet and out of the tub. Eli frowned at Lionel. "I'll talk to him about it."

Eli held me in the back seat as the woman drove us to the hospital.

When I opened my eyes, Grandfather sat by my bed. He looked the part of the Arkwright patriarch. For a short man, he was intimidating. He had a harsh figure, sharp cheekbones, and defined muscles. His eyes were the bluest I'd ever seen on a person, and he used them to look at people as though he mentally pulled them apart.

I looked nothing like him.

I carried the looks of my mother's family Gran's curls and Pop's dark hair and eyes. I could feel Grandfather's eyes burrow into my soul.

When I was a boy, I thought he could see all my secrets if he looked at me long enough.

Was it implausible that he could read minds when Gran and I could see spirits?

This was the first moment I knew with one hundred per cent certainty that he couldn't read my mind, or he would know my secret.

He watched me for about a minute as he straightened his square, almost rimless glasses. "You have questions?"

"I was attacked by a monster. I have questions," I said. I'd had time to think about what Gran and Pop had told me about demons.

It wasn't a lot.

What we called demons were creatures from other dimensions. Them not overrunning us meant humans were amongst the few creatures that could open gates between dimensions.

"The Arkwrights have a strong history of magic. I was disappointed when Ben never inherited magical ability. When two of your brothers had magical abilities despite neither of your parents having them, I was surprised."

"I thought Eli was going to tell me about this," I said.

"You can't tell Ralph. He doesn't know about magic," Grandfather said.

"How would I tell Ralph?"

"I know you never lost contact with him. You were always his favourite brother."

"Does everyone know I still have contact with him?"

"Yes."

"Is this why my relationship with Viola is icy? Because she has a grudge against me staying in contact with my brother?"

"It hurts that he'd rather contact you instead of his own kid."

"That's hardly my fault. I gave him Megan's number and email and sent him photos and updates. I want him to care about his daughter."

"I'm not here to talk about my deadbeat grandson."

"No." I met his eyes. "You're here to shut me up."

"Don't phrase it like that."

"I'm going to talk to Eli about this. I need a practical explanation, not waffle about magical inheritance. Hell, I don't even know what his job really is. He lied to me, and you lied to me. Half the people I consider my family have lied to me my whole life," I said.

"I told Elijah not to come so I could be the one to tell you this," Grandfather said.

I shouldn't have been angry because I was doing the same thing. If it came out, everyone would give me hell for being upset, but I'd been isolated from this entire community of magical people. I swallowed my next words when I realised it wasn't them I was angry at.

It was Gran.

She'd been raised by a man who'd witnessed his father's murder and it had affected her. She was paranoid about an event that involved people long dead. Her whole life was warped around a grandparent she'd never met and the bitterness of being rejected from the magical community. Some people might still use mediums for their own gain, but surely the people closest to me could know. They would protect me.

"I'll talk to Eli about it. You've never been good at talking to less than a room full of people."

Grandfather let out a loud breath. "We were seconds from losing you yesterday, Dex. I needed this. I wanted to be the one to tell you." For a second before he looked away from me, I swore I saw tears in his eyes.

I'd never seen him cry before.

It hit me like a punch to the gut.

He stood up. "I'll see you at dinner on Tuesday. It's your turn to cook."

"I'm sorry. Please tell me what I need to know." I tried to meet his eyes. "What do you want me to know?"

But his eyes slid from mine. He walked out of the room.

He didn't turn around or say another word.

Tears formed in my eyes and I let them fall. We'd been so close when I was a kid. I struggled to breathe as the white walls closed in on me.

I closed my eyes and curled into a ball under the rough, hot pile of blankets and stiff sheets. The constant smell of disinfectant made me nauseous.

I needed to get out of here!

The room didn't even have a TV, and only Grandfather visited since Eli left me here yesterday. I spent the night snoozing and staring at the textured walls until I saw things.

When I couldn't find my phone amongst the things in my pocket, I used the hospital phone to dial Eli's cell, one of the handful of numbers I'd memorised in case of emergency.

"Hello?" Eli said. It sounded like he was in a crowded room. Was he in the office? Did he work from an office? What was his actual job?

"You need to get me out of here before I claw my way out," I said.

"Have you been cleared to leave?" Eli said.

"I don't care."

Eli sighed. "Isn't Edwin supposed to see you?"

"Oh, he did."

"And you got in a fight."

"The man tries to act like things like family lineage don't matter. In reality he is so far up his arse about Arkwright family importance he can't see anything else."

"I'll come and get you," Eli said. "I have plenty of sick days. I'm pretty sure people can take off sick days to look after spouses. There are benefits to signing that marriage certificate my family shoved in our faces."

I'd heard him joke like that before, but in that moment, it stung. A small part of me worried he'd only married me because his family had pressured him.

"Dex? Are you okay?" Eli said.

"Yes." I forced my mouth into a shaky smile, even though he couldn't see me.

"See you soon. Love you," Eli said.

"Love you," I said seconds before he hung up.

Eli rushed into the room ten minutes later and stood at the end of the bed for a few seconds before he moved into a deep bow. "I've brought my steed to rescue you my dear prince."

I looked down at the bundle he presented me: a set of clean clothes. He closed the door and I quickly dressed, grateful to finally relax into the soft cotton of a simple tee shirt and track pants. I'd scratched my skin where it had touched the seams of the rough hospital gown. My stomach did a little flip when I realised I could go home and have a bath. I was sure I couldn't wash my hair, but I could clean my body. They had cleaned me when I'd been admitted, but I still felt grimy.

I smiled and took Eli's outstretched hand to walk from the room once I slipped into a pair of sandals. The nurse who sat guard at the nurse's station had a sour look on her face but let us go without remark. "Dad convinced your doctor to let you go home," Eli said. "On the condition either he or Mum are there at all times."

This was where Eli's parents worked. Why was I surprised they were magic doctors after all I'd seen over the last forty-eight hours? Had they been asked to stay away from me? Neither of his parents were the type not to check up on me, even before I started dating Eli.

It only took the walk from the disconnected garage and four steps onto the house's veranda for my head to spin so violently I almost vomited on the white, black and gold geometric hall rug that protected the shiny red mahogany floorboards. My inability to hold my weight almost caused Eli to drop me as he adjusted his grip on me.

"How about I sit you in the living room?" Eli turned me left towards the living room door rather than past the entrance and down the hall towards the stairs.

I put all my effort into stabilising my legs so they could carry my weight when I heard the strain in his voice.

Once Eli left me alone to pour the bath for me, I grabbed the receiver of the modern landline phone from the vintage glass-topped gold end table.

I called Aunt Myrtle's house again.

I needed to talk to Gran. Privacy wasn't an issue; the house was empty in the middle of the day. It was the same message. I slammed the phone down on the receiver.

I heard a gasp behind me. I turned around. Cynthia, Eli's mother, was standing behind me, her arms loaded with a stack of paper. She must have taken a work-from-home day to mark essays for the medical students she mentored.

Eli's dad had promised one of them would be home with me.

She had keys in hand. The strap of her black leather handbag sat so close to the edge of her shoulder, it looked like one wrong move would cause it to slide off. If we arrived five minutes earlier, I probably would have missed her. Now she'd seen me angrily trying to make a phone call.

"Eli wasn't supposed to leave you alone until I got home," Cynthia said.

"He's getting a bath ready. I couldn't stand another minute in that place," I said.

Where I'd been recovering hadn't been a hospital but a small private clinic for the magical community. I still had no idea why I'd been given staples over magical healing. Now I started to feel like a prisoner. Part of my brain had caught onto the idea that it was more than medical necessity and someone had told them not to leave me alone. No one had seemed keen to keep an eye on me when I was at the clinic. I hadn't been seen by a doctor since I'd woken up.

"Are you okay?" She touched my shoulder gently.

"I don't know. Every time I close my eyes, I see that dead girl." I realised what I'd said too late. Fuck! They would never trust me.

Thankfully, I could see in her eyes that so closely matched Eli's: she knew what happened.

She worked at *that* clinic.

I'd called the people Gran had warned me about for help. The people who would use my abilities until there was nothing left. Mediumship was rare, a branch of Death Magic. Practical application of Death Magic had been almost entirely banned in her father's lifetime.

How had I spent so long fooling myself into thinking these people were normal? This wealthy, powerful founding family couldn't be anything but neck-deep in magic.

Grandfather walked through the door like he owned the place. He stopped when he saw me. "What… are…" He shook his head. "I don't even want to know."

"What are you doing here?" I said.

"The clinic called me before you even left the building. They said they couldn't stop you from leaving, but they wanted me to check on you. I assumed no one would be home to look after you," he said.

"Yeah, well, I'm fine. You didn't need to take time out of your busy day to hunt me down." The drugs were wearing off and my head was pounding. The pain increased with every word. I didn't realise I was shaking until Cynthia rubbed my back between my shoulders.

He pointed at the chemist's paper bag I crushed in my grip. "It's time to take your pills."

I felt dizzy.

"It's time you got out of my house." Cynthia gave Grandfather a glare that could only be described as a death stare until he relaxed under her gaze and left the house without argument.

When I woke from a nap, I was alone. Late afternoon light streamed in the windows of the third-story corner room. I thought the location was once the old sandstone house's attic. Ceiling low, the walls were covered with off-white painted wooden panelling reflecting the light in a way that gave the room a warm glow. The room smelt like intoxicatingly fresh air with a hint of the eucalypt forest surrounding the house and freshly ironed sheets. The scent of linen was collected from the reed diffuser on the windowsill by a cool breeze as it travelled into the room. I took a long breath of the fresh air. The combination of the idyllic moment, medication and sleep-clouded mind made me feel like I was in a dream. A spike of fear and disappointment stabbed into my chest. I looked at the clock on Eli's bedside table.

The numbers were clear and easy to read.

I wasn't dreaming.

I was experiencing my first moment of peace since Nora Rowe's ghost had attacked me.

I lay my head back on the light blue silk pillowcase. I could enjoy a few minutes where I wasn't needed or had somewhere to be. It was only going to get worse from here.

I could email Gran; she used a screen reader, so I could contact her directly.

I turned my laptop on, but the Wi-Fi didn't work. Instead of trying to fix it, I took five extra minutes to use my phone to email Gran. I revealed nothing in the email, just that I needed to have a phone conversation with her. I'd learnt not to write anything I didn't want someone else to read at a young age. My oldest brother had always been on the hunt for things to get me in trouble.

I needed her.

I didn't know what to do.

I didn't want strangers to know my secret, but I was sick of keeping it from the people I cared about, especially now they would understand.

I needed her to tell me what to do.

I used the glass of water on Eli's table to take my medication, which were a sedative and antibiotic. When I started to turn off my laptop, I noticed a second browser window open.

It was Eli's inbox.

I saw an email with the subject, "Thought you'd want to read about your precious husband."

I was reading the open email before I realised what I was doing.

Subject DA294 was witnessed trying to contact Subject EG346 before the incident.

Possible involvement?

Gate testing went wrong?

Are you sure there was no one else on site at arrival?

He is connected to unregulated activities through Subject EG346. Is Subject DA294 an illegal magic user? Any contact DA294 makes with EG346 must be reported. EG346 reported to have passed through customs at 8 a.m yester—

I slammed the laptop closed when I heard someone walking down the hall.

Eli's eyes widened when he saw me holding the laptop. The words he was about to speak died in his mouth.

I slowly tapped the laptop with a finger. "Movie?"

"Who do you keep trying to contact?" Eli said.

I let out a long, slow breath. "Gran."

"I'm sorry you had to wake up alone. I had to yell at someone on the phone."

I waved a hand towards the laptop. "About that?"

"You need to sleep."

"Why are you acting so weird about me contacting Gran?"

"You know you can tell me anything," Eli said.

"What do you think I need to tell you?" I said.

Eli looked down at the blue quilt for a few seconds. When he finally looked at me, his eyes were damp. "I don't know. People keep trying to push their way into my private business, as though they think they're protecting me when they have no idea."

"I'm tired from the pill I took." I laid down and turned my back to him.

"It's like you're holding your breath and I'm not sure how to convince you it's okay to let go."

"I know your mum's big on the whole 'no secrets in this house' thing, but after what you hid from me, none of you have any ground to stand on."

Eli sighed, leant over and kissed my forehead then laid down beside me.

Subject EG could be Gran, as her first name was Evelyn and her maiden name Gristle. Had they tracked the call I'd made at work?

Passed through customs? Where? Did they mean Australia? Why would she be coming to visit?

4

The room was dark when I woke and the laptop was back on the desk in the office next door. I grabbed my phone to check the time. I had an email from Aunt Myrtle. It was a quick message; they had just driven into Tallow. She wanted to meet me for brunch. The message ended with, "Gran is well and looking forward to seeing you." I walked through the open French doors that split the two rooms and over to the desk.

Did someone suspect Gran and I of having magical abilities? Is that why Eli was so keen on knowing who I contacted and why? I turned on my laptop and logged out of my email. If I put a password on the computer, it would look suspicious next time Eli tried to use it, like I had something to hide. I could easily claim my email login had expired. They couldn't know I was going to see Gran until I was able to talk to her. I needed to know what to do next; if I acted on my own, I could put myself in danger.

Danger Gran could have steered me from.

The next morning, I snuck out of the house and drove into Tallow. I shouldn't have driven with the painkillers in my system, so I didn't take the sedative.

I met Gran and Aunt Myrtle at an Italian restaurant that Gran liked. She used to tell me stories about the building of her favourite diner when she was growing up just outside of Tallow. It once housed an ice cream shop that closed when I was fifteen.

Three places Gran liked.

She was sure there would always be an eatery she loved in this building. She enjoyed telling stories about coming to the diner with her friends when they had leave from their boarding school.

As we ate, Aunt Myrtle told me about Uncle Jorge's new job in Hong Kong, and I knew what was coming before she asked. Gran had been vision-impaired and a wheelchair user since she was in a car accident a few years ago. It would be hard for her to go to a new city in an unfamiliar country. With my parents on their second world cruise, there weren't many places she could go.

"Can you take care of Gran?" Aunt Myrtle asked.

"The Lacy's house isn't exactly wheelchair accessible," I replied.

"I thought I'd ask you before Mason because he and Ariella are expecting again."

I choked on my water.

After my coughing fit subsided, I had a headache and a lot of questions. "How do you know before me? I live just down the road from them."

"Ari and I talk occasionally."

"It's Ari now? I thought she reminded you too much of the girls who bullied you in school."

"Viola does as well, and I adjusted to her. So why not Ariella? They both gave me the nieces I desired."

"Thanks for that."

"I love you and your brothers, but I always wanted a niece to spoil."

"I'll take care of Gran. It will be good to spend some time with her."

Gran was eating her pasta and had been quiet since I hadn't ordered wine with my meal.

I saw her frown when I ordered water. She knew something was wrong.

"The rest of her things will be sent in a few days. I have her essentials in the car. Are you okay? You look pale."

"I'm fine. I just need the bathroom."

In the bathroom, I splashed cold water on my face. My head was killing me. Maybe I should have asked Aunt Myrtle to the house. I closed my eyes and leant against the sink. I heard someone walk into the bathroom, but I didn't look up to see who it was.

I moaned in pain when my phone rang. The loud ring echoed through the bathroom.

I pulled it out of my pocket.

It was Eli.

I slid my finger to the right and refused the call.

"Did you just hang up on me?"

I looked up as Eli walked into view of the small mirror above the sink. "How long have you been standing there?"

"Long enough."

"If I answered the phone, you'd know something was wrong with me." My voice shook.

"If a coughing fit puts you in this state, then maybe you should be at home resting."

"Why wasn't I healed with magic?"

"Healing Magic is not something that gets thrown around. It is very exhausting for the caster," Eli said. "The doctors decided you had the time and ability to heal on your own. It's not good for a person's body either. Do you think mages would let mortals die if they could heal any wound with magic?"

"Mortal. Is that how you see me?"

"It's just a term for non-magic users."

I looked away from him. "The only reason you even know me is because I have magic in my family. Without that, I'd just be another mortal to you."

He reached out and touched my arm.

"Have you been following me?"

"I want to protect you. A colleague saw you walk in here by yourself and she was worried."

"I rejected that call because it would make you right." I looked back up at him.

"Right?" Eli said.

"You would have told me not to come. If I said anything, you'd have been right."

"Dex, you can't be mad at me for something I never did! I know you have plenty to be mad at me about, but don't direct it in the wrong direction."

"Myrtle can't take care of Gran any more. I already said yes."

"Can I take you home before you faint?"

I gave him a smile.

Eli put his arm around me as we walked from the bathroom back to the table.

Aunt Myrtle smiled at him, "Eli. I didn't realise you were around. My nephew should have invited you to join us."

"Dex came here by himself. He should be at home, resting. He fell in the shower the day before yesterday and lacerated his scalp."

Myrtle looked at me. "I noticed the patch on the back of your head, but I didn't want to say anything until you mentioned it. We could have come to the house, or you could have come with someone."

"I just needed to get outside. I was at home or in a hospital room all of yesterday and I needed some fresh air." I rubbed my clammy forehead as a fresh bout of pain hit me.

"You're lucky I brought these." Eli pulled a sheet of my painkillers from his pocket and popped them into my hand. "Take a sedative pill when you get home."

I took the pills and left to sit in the car while Eli talked to Aunt Myrtle and Gran.

"Where's Gran?" I asked when Eli returned to the car alone.

"Myrtle is going to bring Eve in her car. She'll stay the night to make sure Eve is settling in. Her flight isn't until tomorrow afternoon. I fixed things up with the hotel."

"You can call her Gran."

"Rest."

"You'd have drugged me already if you didn't have to carry me from the car."

"Don't make me caring about you sound predatory."

"I know you love me." I smiled at him.

About halfway home, Eli looked at me for a second before looking back at the road. "Can I tell you something I've told no one?"

"We're married. That kind of comes with the territory."

"I've been in love with you since we were eleven, maybe even before."

"Why didn't you say anything?"

"Would you have given me a chance?"

"If we were older than eleven. I hadn't even started noticing anyone at that age. At fifteen or sixteen, I would have jumped at the chance to have a relationship even though I was still coming to terms with my sexuality."

"What would have happened when you went to university across the country?"

"You know how I cling to people. We would have been fine and I think I would have chosen somewhere closer if I had a guy like you waiting for me." I smiled. "I hope you realise you're never getting rid of me unless you want me to leave."

"Part of the reason I married you is so you couldn't leave easily if I screwed up," Eli said.

That statement made me feel slightly uncomfortable.

I let my forehead rest against the window and watched the paddocks pass. They were filled with sugar cane or sheep and cattle with the odd orchard or collection of horses. My life would never go back to the way it was before I walked into that house, but there was a calm to how static the rest of the world was.

I pretended to take the last sedative when Eli pressed it into my hand. A week had passed since the attack and I finally felt like I had the strength to have a serious conversation with Gran.

Two hours later, I brought a full tea tray to Gran's room.

I watched Gran sip her tea. I'd been quiet for two minutes, wondering how I could ask her for a way to gain some kind of control over my life. "I want to know how to control ghosts."

She dropped her teacup. It shattered, sending warm liquid and chips of fine antique porcelain scattering across the light hardwood.

"I'll clean that up." I fell to my knees, carefully placed the pale mint ceramic pieces in a pile and wiped up the tea with my cardigan. The dark liquid stained the sandy cable knit.

"Why do you need to know?"

"It's best you pass on your knowledge while you're visiting."

"Did you really slip in the shower? Or did one of these ghosts you want to control hurt you? What's going on, Dex?"

"I walked into a house where someone had opened a dimension gate. A demon attacked me." I threw the damp cardigan across the room. "I'm defenceless. You have all these skills and you won't share them with me." I scratched at a chip in the wood grain with my fingernail. "I also had an encounter with a ghost who tried to possess me."

"Why are you going into strange houses?" Her pastel pink lips pressed together. Her blue eyes bubbled with fire as she processed what I'd said.

"Mayor Chesterfield and Mrs Gregory's idea. It's a punishment for not dancing on their strings like a good little puppet."

"Why did you come back to this town? None of this would be a worry if you never looked back."

"Is that what you had in mind when you taught me magic in the first place?"

She sighed. "When I made that decision, I was still angry about not getting the chance to practice magic officially. I used you as a 'fuck you' to the system. I'll always regret that."

"Why teach me and not Ralph?"

She gave me a long, sad look. "Ralph has no magic."

"I've had a long time to think about this, and the one thing that stuck out about my learning magic is I couldn't see the ghosts—spirits, whatever you want to call them—until you taught me how."

She paled then grabbed my teacup and downed the liquid in a couple of hurried mouthfuls.

"I thought about teaching Ralph for a long time then decided against it when I told Dorian what I was considering. I'll never forget the way he looked at me like I was some stranger who had come to hurt his family rather than the woman he loved. He didn't let me be alone with Ralph for a year."

"Why me?"

"I thought your parents were done after Ralph, and with Myrtle never having children, I thought it was over. I'd never had to give in to that dark voice in the back of my head telling me what would really make them angry."

"Who?" I said.

"Your grandfather, the Agency and the Nate Island pigs who decide what's best for us all from their golden thrones." Her mouth shut with an audible click of her teeth.

"Nate Island?"

"It's home to the magical ruling body." She hissed the final three words, and spittle landed on my face.

"And me? How does this connect to you telling me about magic against everyone's wishes?"

"Something happened. I was angry and in a dark place. You were the perfect age to learn and you'd just failed your test."

"You illegally pulled me into the magical world because you were angry?"

"When Dorian found out and realised you weren't going to forget, he let me teach you on the condition I'd never introduce you into the underground magical community."

"Why was Pop so against me learning magic?"

"It was the method, not the act of learning, he was against."

"I'm sick of family secrets. I'm going to tell Grandfather everything you did."

"The only thing they can give you is a job as an exorcist. You won't make it a year. You're a disposable object to them. You better not tell them our secret while either of us is still breathing if you know what's best for you."

"Excuse me?" Had she just threatened me? My head spun as I struggled to keep my balance and pull myself to my feet. That sounded like a threat! Surely she wouldn't threaten someone she was supposed to love.

"We'll both go to jail for illegal use of magic. You're an adult who kept using it. You can't claim innocence, Dexter."

"I was a child. I trusted you and you took advantage of me because you were angry at someone else."

"We share a great secret."

I stood with a shaky growl. "What you did to me was worse than never knowing about magic."

Her damp blue eyes suddenly focused on me. "Why do you need to know how to control spirits?" She poured more tea into my abandoned teacup.

"I think something has changed. A subtle change in the atmosphere. That's why there's so many hostile ghosts all of a sudden. I know most ghosts aren't hostile, but Dunn seems to be full of them," I said.

"I never thought I'd say this, but call the Agency. They have to have exorcists on staff," she said.

"I'm sick of being the damsel. I don't want to be a defenceless thing people have to save because I can't save myself. What if someone dies because they're trying to save me? Or because I can't save them?"

Gran stared into my eyes for a couple of minutes. She reached out and took my hand in both of hers. "What do you want to know?"

"Everything you know about our ability." I put my other hand on top of hers and squeezed them gently.

She gave me a thin smile. "If you want to learn how to use your ability, you have to follow everything I say. Can you promise me that?"

"Yes. I promise." I looked her in the eyes again and returned her smile to express the hope I felt. I also wanted her to be part of my life again. We'd once been so important to each other but had drifted apart when she moved to America to live with Aunt Myrtle and connect with Pop's American family. I wanted to mean something to her again in the aftermath of so many I cared about lying to me.

I wanted to be more visibly angry at the Lacys, Grandfather, and my brothers, but what could I do? I was dependent on them in so many ways. I still cared about them and didn't want what had happened to cause a rift between us. The only people I was close with since I'd returned to Dunn were my family and Eli's friends. All of my friends had either moved on from Dunn or built their own lives without me in them.

I had no idea how to make friends at my age without having in common a place one had to be all day. Adults older than thirty still felt like *real* grownups, untouchable, as I tried to figure out how to jump the ravine between child and adulthood. I'd scrambled for stability midair after I'd been pushed off the childhood side at high school graduation.

"You need to learn how to sink into yourself and clear your mind. I know this sounds stereotypical, but other thoughts, worries and anxieties are background noise that will interfere with your ability to communicate with ghosts," Gran said. "You need to put a barrier between them and the part of your brain that is you."

I nodded.

"I need you to learn how to meditate, like we used to when you were a kid. There's nothing better for your safety than the ability to reach that state of mind in a second."

"It felt like the ghost who tried to possess me grabbed onto the essence of my being and tried to wrench me open so she could fit inside," I said.

"You also need to be able to get yourself to safety while you have most of your mind locked away because they can still physically harm you most of the time," she said.

"She left a bruise on my arm." I ran my fingers over the spot where Nora Rowe had grabbed my arm. "Eli saw."

Gran inhaled sharply. "When Nate Island agents come for you, go with them willingly and do anything they say. Just remember my freedom, my ability to live a normal life, is lost the moment they can prove I taught you magic. The moment they can prove what I've done, they will be preparing the execution block for me."

"You don't think he'd tell. He'd realise what happened, and he'd never hurt us like that," I said.

"I've had someone put safeguards on your mind, but others aren't so lucky," Gran said.

"Safeguards?"

"How do you think they found out your grandfather was gay? He was the founder's son and never acted on it, but they pulled the thoughts and desires from his mind and used them against him."

I swallowed, unable to form a response. They would pluck the memory from Eli's mind and use it as another piece of evidence against me.

"You play the grateful and willing puppet until I say when," she said.

"When?"

"You'll know," she said.

"I want to know when you had someone place safeguards on my mind," I said.

"Enough. I need to rest." Her voice was hard and final. I knew the tone from my missteps as a child. She couldn't berate and threaten to hit me for being a naughty disrespectful little boy as an adult. What she could do was ignore me. I wouldn't get anything out of her she wasn't willing to give.

I grabbed the tea tray and loudly packed the cups back onto it. No one told me anything. I'd always be a child or a hapless mortal in their minds.

Pity I couldn't have a piece of mind-reading magic.

I left Gran's bedroom and took the tray to the kitchen to wash the cups. After I was done, I dropped the last sedative pill down the drain. I needed to be wholly aware of my environment at all times to keep myself safe. The idea of drugged drowsiness made me incredibly uncomfortable and aware of my mortality.

The fragility of my mortal body.

After almost two weeks in my bedroom, I needed to get out.

I went on a walk and found myself on Short Street in front of the diner. I felt the ghost a few meters down the street at the back of my mind. I pushed back against the intrusion with a simple 'no' and pulled open the diner's door.

When I walked into the diner and ordered a pot of Earl Grey tea, I didn't notice anyone else in the quiet building. At 2:30 in the afternoon, everyone I knew was at work.

As I opened my phone, a hand with long, neon yellow fingernails wrapped around the pole of my table number.

"Not even a smile or a wave? Am I being snubbed?"

I looked up from my phone. My cousin Kat was twisting my table number between her pale fingers. She met my eyes, smiled, then walked off with my number towards her table. I grabbed my bag and rushed after her. A laptop-tablet hybrid sat on the table beside a stack of books and loose paper. Two expensive-looking silver pens held Kat's straight but messy brown hair in a bun. A notepad was about to fall from the front pocket of her baggy emerald button-down shirt. The navy pants gave the impression she'd dressed in the dark, the colours not quite matching in the stark light of the diner. Maybe she thought they were black. "Are you still writing for that rag?"

"Yes, and it's not a rag."

"Ignore me. I'm a prick."

"I haven't had a real conversation with you since your graduation party."

"I know." I accepted my pot of tea from the waitress. "What do you want?"

"Don't be like that, Dex," Kat said.

"I'm not sure you have the right to be offended. I didn't notice you. We used to be thick as thieves. Now we live in the same town and never say more than a quick hello," I said.

"Communication comes from both ends, Dexter."

"I'm sorry."

She looked down at the blue, red and white checkered cotton tablecloth. "I'm sorry too, because I want something."

"What?"

"My boss wants an interview with your husband."

"Why?"

"It's about the town council election."

"Why would your boss want to interview Eli? Lacy Senior is the one running for the election."

Kat held up a hand to silence me. "Eli's the one running for town council. The rest of his family has no desire to. I heard they tried to push Viola into it, as she is a far more acceptable age, but she refused. None of the cousins would give it the time of day. There is the expectation they will field a candidate, which leaves Eli." She reached out to pat my hand with a smile. "Don't look so worried. He's twenty-three, no one is going to seriously vote for him."

"Has anyone mentioned how messed up this town is? Certain families expected to field council candidates. I hardly think Eli is serious about this."

If he were, he would have told me.

Wouldn't he?

Kat gave me an odd look. "Check he isn't serious before you say anything. Maybe he's looking for the best time to tell you. It's not public yet. His grandfather was the one who leaked it to the press."

This was why Lacy Senior made me promise not to run for council if I could marry Eli.

"We have a date tonight."

"He probably plans to tell you then. Try to act surprised."

"Is that the cousin advice of the year?" I said.

"Yes." She grabbed my teapot and filled her empty coffee cup. I tried not to look at the sticky, gritty coffee and milk residue that floated in her tea. How long had the cup been sitting on the table before I arrived? I slid my cup away from my hand. I was done with tea for the day.

"I heard about your accident. I'm glad to see you're okay," Kat said.

"Accident?" I said.

"The attack." She looked me straight in the eyes.

She knew the truth! She'd gone to Dunn Academy with Eli, of course she had magic.

"How many members of our family know about magic?" I said.

"The only people who don't know are your parents, Ralph and your mum's family. If someone doesn't know, it's because they're not a good fit for magic."

"Not a good fit?"

"They tested you just before you went into first grade and you got cut. Everyone who has magical parents or grandparents may take the test."

"A test I can't remember taking when I was six decided the course of my life?"

"It takes a long time to learn magic. Primary school kids are socialised with the mortals and taught basic spells in an after-school programme. We specialise in high schools like Dunn Academy. After graduation, most take apprenticeships or traineeships. There are university courses, but those are for the top ten per cent of mages or those who need mundane degrees."

"You never wanted to tell me?" I said.

Kat looked into her tea. "It's more important than ever to keep the secret. Mortals have nuclear weapons, enough power to destroy the world many times over. Magic isn't enough to keep us safe from those who fear us any more."

"There's that word again: mortal. Magic doesn't make anyone special."

"Dex." She reached out to touch me.

I pulled away from her, stood and left.

The realisation hit me as I looked at the green and yellow checked picnic blanket. We were sitting on the beach, but none of the sand had migrated onto the rug. When I asked Eli about it before, he claimed it was a sand-repellent picnic blanket Mrs Lacy Senior had seen on an infomercial.

God, I was dumb. Infomercial my arse; he was using magic to keep the sand off. I needed to go to the beach more because I obviously had no idea how sand worked. I turned my gaze from the blanket and back to eating my crumbling piece of fish.

Glad Eli couldn't see my flushed cheeks in the dull light.

"You must be hungry. You haven't said a word since you saw the food." Eli had managed to finish his fish without turning it into a mass of small, slippery pieces that wouldn't sit on a fork. He placed a heavily sauce-dipped chip in his mouth. He'd dragged it from the paper to his mouth without even a hint that the sauce might drip onto his navy polo shirt and colourful, geometric patterned board shorts. Some people managed to make messy food look elegant. Most of my public eating involved a small nasty voice in the back of my head telling me that any second I would be kicked out for a gross display of public indecency. I stopped myself from running a sticky fish- and lemon juice-covered hand through my curls. I was having a bad day if I was self-conscious of my eating around Eli. He had to be using his magic to keep the sauce on the vinegar-soaked chip. At this point, the thing shouldn't have held itself together.

To be able to use magic with such ease.

I forced myself to keep a neutral expression as the wave of jealousy flooded me.

I pinched my thigh through my cargo shorts; the pain distracted me from the anger and envy that threatened to show on my face. I was in love with him, and I was happy for him. I focused on the thought to will away the jealous spite I felt towards one of the most important people in my life.

"Dex? Are you okay?"

I looked into Eli's eyes. "What is your magic?"

"What can I do?"

"Yes."

"I guess in simple terms you'd call it Telekinesis."

"Show me."

He took a few seconds to scan the empty beach then smiled at me, his eyes almost brown in the golden hour light. "Don't eat all the chips while I'm gone."

I took a long look at the half he'd doused in vinegar and barbeque sauce.

He seemed concerned I might steal his food, but that had to be a joke.

Right?

I usually avoided kissing him until he'd had a drink when he ate like this.

I hated to imagine how it tasted going down based on the secondhand aftertaste.

I watched him go to the edge of the dunes and return with a handful of small ocean-smoothed rocks. I knew why I'd never beat him at rock skipping; he was a dirty rotten cheat. He'd likely cheated at skipping rocks right from the beginning of our rivalry as kids.

I watched him skip the rocks on the water. They were entirely under his control, the waves no obstacle, some flying meters into the air. I watched each of the stones as long as the fading light allowed.

I gave him my best sly, teasing smile. "That your only trick?"

He smiled at me. With an unnecessary flick of a finger, he brought a couple of chips over to where he stood. His lack of effort was almost disappointing, but this was Eli.

What had I expected?

A big, fancy show that would require actual effort!

Eli took a long, loud breath and walked back over to sit beside me. The smile slipped from his face. "I'm sorry I never told you about magic. I knew you were living your best life and I didn't want to complicate it."

My best life?

I wasn't sure I could ever live my best life in this town, even with Eli.

I hated working for Mayor Chesterfield and Mrs Gregory. I'd only become a librarian because I'd never been good at anything. Never unique in any way. Books were the only thing I could fall back on, and reading wasn't a special skill. I admired what librarians did, but I was more and more sure it wasn't for me with each day. I couldn't remember doing much practical work at university. Those days melded together in the back of my mind as a fuzzy mass. It was sickly distant and hard for me to feel attachment to that time, even though it had only been a couple of years.

What was wrong with me?

I sat up. The crawling feeling against my skin made me want to scratch my skin off.

"Dex, what's wrong?" Eli said.

"I don't know."

It felt like a part of me had been torn out and I just didn't notice it until now. I couldn't tell him that; he'd think I needed mental help. Did I need help?

5

It was silent when we drove into Dunn, the streets abandoned for the night. A group of people stood under the statue in the small park in the centre of town. The group of four walked out onto the road the moment we had nowhere to turn. One figure walked forward as several others moved from the buildings to block the street behind us.

Eli slowed the car to a stop ten feet from the first group and kept them illuminated with the headlights. "Let me deal with this. It's a work thing." He gave me a long look. "Don't get out of the car for any reason. No matter what you see or hear. I can take care of it."

"Should I call someone?"

"It will only make them angry." He stepped out of the car. The locks retracted the moment he closed the door.

I pulled on the passenger lock experimentally, but it wouldn't move. My shaky, sweaty fingers slipped from the grey plastic as I pulled harder. I gave up on the lock and turned to watch.

The group wore ski masks, the leader in all white and the minions wearing red. They wore carefully tailored three-piece suits, a symbol stitched with silver thread that reminded me of the Knights Templar over their left breast pockets, and a silver chain led from their shirt collars into the pocket. The most striking part of their outfits apart from the symbols were their heavy black boots, which indicated they weren't above physical activity to ensure their aim. They were obviously going for elegance, but the boots and ski masks made their outfits look borderline laughable, like a try hard character out of one of Eli's video games.

I assumed the leader was a man because of his stature. As Eli walked in front of the car, more people stepped out of the shadows and walked over to the vehicle. I pulled on the door handle and cursed when the door wouldn't budge. Hopefully what was keeping me in would keep the group slowly circling the car out.

The leader, at least six feet tall, towered over Eli, who wasn't a hair above five feet six. I felt an overwhelming urge to stand between them, but what could I do? This was clearly a magic thing; they didn't care to hide from me now they weren't breaking the law.

I took a few shaky breaths to calm myself and focus on their voices through the closed window.

"We know it was you," the leader said.

"Your illustrious organisation must be mistaken," Eli said.

"We're not." He pulled a pair of blue rubber gloves over his black leather ones as he walked over to Eli. "Do you know how long it took to make that potion?"

I couldn't see Eli's face from the car. I wondered what expression he wore. This man was clearly after something Eli had confiscated over the course of his job. I slipped my phone from my pocket into the sleeve of my cardigan, unlocked it using my fingerprint and slid it from the end of the sleeve just enough to access the slider for the brightness.

I quietly swore as the cabin lit up from the fraction of the screen revealed. I slid the brightness down to zero and looked outside the car. No one paid me any attention; all eyes were on Eli and the white-suited man.

They clearly didn't see me as a threat.

I ground my teeth in anger.

I'd show them.

I slid the phone out of my sleeve so the camera could take photos, jammed down the two buttons that took pictures and sent an SOS message.

Someone on the list would know who to call to get help.

The phone slid from my fingers and clattered to the floor when I remembered Eli's name was on that list and his phone was in his pocket. I clenched my hand into a fist to still my fingers and waited for them to notice. After about a minute, I slowly bent down and scooped up the phone, squinting at the screen. Even if it was only on vibrate, White Suit and Eli would have noticed, but they stood in the quiet street an arm's length from each other. No one said a word. The top right of my screen reflected the streetlight.

I had no reception.

The message wouldn't have gone through. Even in the middle of

Dunn, five bars were standard when outside, especially in the middle of the street.

Did they have a signal jammer?

Is that why no one was paying attention to me?

The leader looked to the car and met my eyes. He pointed straight at me then down towards the ground. I was sitting straight-backed in my seat before my mind caught up with my body, my eyes still on his. He gave me a curt nod then turned his attention back to Eli. One second, he stood calmly with his eyes fixed on Eli, and the next he punched Eli hard in the stomach.

Eli cried out in pain and doubled over.

I screamed.

The locks flicked open with a loud click that made my ears ring even above the rapid hum of my heart.

My legs refused to move when I shifted to open the door. Before Eli could recover, two of the figures grabbed his arms and dragged him to his feet.

White Suit sighed loudly and looked down at Eli. "Everyone will know that you've crossed us. What will your precious family do then?"

The next punch was aimed directly at his nose. The noise Eli's nose made as the fist connected chilled my blood. I swallowed the bile that rose in my throat and pulled the door handle. I pushed the door open, and it swung back against me.

My legs wouldn't move!

Nothing below my waist would move.

I looked around the group; my heartbeat rose. My breath quickened as I waited for one of them to wrench me from the car. I was the perfect thing to threaten Eli with. I had to get out of here. I couldn't save Eli alone, not against this many mages. There was a payphone on Short Street. If they thought I ran away scared, I could get to it and call someone.

Eli spat blood at his attacker, staining the elegantly crafted silk suit. "Cunt."

After hearing Eli speak, I didn't need to see his face to know his nose was broken. I pushed the door and leant over as far as I could, and when it clicked open, I felt a flood of relief. One of the assailants looked at me and the car door. Under the red mask, I imagined a raised eyebrow and a quizzical look on her face. She looked at me then at the park across the street, daring me to run. Her posture was relaxed, as though she was watching a small child reach for a cookie jar that was impossible for them to reach. I gave her a hard, angry look and threw myself out of the car onto the road. The sound of Eli being hit again covered the noise I made as I hit the ground.

My teeth clicked together as my chin took the brunt of the fall and smashed against the bitumen. I ignored the warm trickle of blood that ran down my chin and lifted my head. I heard an annoyed sigh from the woman next to me. She took a step towards me. "You were told to sit still and shut up. You're going back in that car."

"You're not my mother." Blood dripped from my mouth as I hissed each word.

Fuck!

In a panicked movement, I ran my tongue over each of my teeth, careful to check the stability of each one.

"Get back in the car before you hurt yourself. Our quarrel isn't with you; we have no desire to bring an innocent civilian into this." She and a man pulled me from the ground.

"Innocent civilian? Why do you care? You're criminals!"

She laughed. "Is that what your *boyfriend* told you?"

"No." Without meaning to, I looked behind the car towards the diner at the intersection of Main and Short. A fuzzy frame flickered under the dark edge of the streetlamp. My dazed mind had lost its grip on my self-imposed filter.

As I blinked to clear my eyes, the animal part of my brain refused to acknowledge what I saw. There was a reason there was no nightlife in this part of town.

We were in *her* territory.

I blinked one last time before a cold settled over my nerves like a weighted blanket. Pinned under her sway, I found it impossible to move. The realisation that I'd made a fatal mistake wormed its way into my chest. My eyes met the voids that had once been hers. What colour had they been? Under the fear, I felt a pang of sadness. When I was ten, she was a scary ghost; at twenty-three, she was a sad dead girl who had transformed into a monster. She couldn't have been older than fifteen.

Who had she been?

Did her mum and dad know what had happened to her? I went slack and stopped fighting the people who pushed me towards the car.

Blink.

She wasn't a black and white, fuzzy flicker trapped halfway between this world and the next. She was as solid as the curb she stood on. One with the world, her skin was deathly pale, and the long blonde hair that fell over her face was dirty, scraggly and matted in tight clumps. She wore a brown leather jacket, her back and one sleeve caked in mud, the other sleeve torn.

Tears formed in my eyes.

In that second, she became a person.

A reflection of a dead girl.

I was forced to look away from her as I was turned around and placed back in my seat. The woman who had ordered me back into the car used magically enhanced strength to her advantage. I hadn't even noticed when she picked me up. When I looked through the windscreen at the white-suited man, he looked straight at me, his gloves stained with what could only be Eli's blood. He pointed at his still lips. *"Done screwing around, honey? I can paralyse more of your body to stop you from embarrassing yourself further."* I heard his voice in my head. It sent a chill down my spine.

Could he read my thoughts?

All his cronies laughed, but the noise faded as I watched Eli's crumpled form; he couldn't stand by himself anymore.

What were they going to do to me after they were done with Eli?

I carefully watched White Suit. Had they heard what he'd said to me? There was no way he could focus on what he was doing, project his thoughts to so many people and read mine all at once.

He pulled a wooden object shaped similarly to a police baton from its strap on his back and used the tip to lift Eli's chin. He examined him as he admired his handiwork. "Not so pretty anymore. One last chance to tell me where your little cronies took the potion you stole."

"I'd rather die than be a snitch."

White Suit looked up at me again. *"He's not worth your tears, sweetheart. If you knew what he's capable of, you wouldn't be marring those pretty eyes with tears for him."*

I felt my skin crawl under the intensity of his gaze, his voice as solid in my head as my own thoughts. *"You're going to close your eyes and put some music on. Volume as loud as you can without it hurting, and make sure you keep those eyes closed as tight as you can until someone touches your shoulder."*

They were going to kill Eli!

I wasn't going to let them.

I was the only one who could save him. The moment he looked away from me, I quietly opened the glove box and took a paper takeout menu from it.

The blank back was perfect for what I was about to do.

When I noticed his attention moving back to me, I slid the menu under my leg. I knew one spell that might help. I needed to distract them and get that prick to let go of my legs. *"I'm not doing anything until you have headphones in and those pretty chocolate eyes closed tight."*

I let out a shaky breath and pulled my headphones from my pocket.

I jammed them into my ears as hard as I could and closed my eyes. I did as he said and turned my music up as high as I could.

I needed a sigil to have the best control over the ghost. I slowly slid the menu from under my leg and kept it from sight.

I dripped my bloody spit onto the blank back and drew a sigil.

I cleared my mind and I drew in all the inner strength I had.

I sent my thoughts through the poorly patched hole Nora Rowe had used in the back of my mind. *Noise. Please. Make noise. Hurt them. Make them bleed.*

I knew this was going to hurt Eli's ears, but I had no choice.

The lights in the street all blew with a collective shatter. I opened my eyes; the group had looked away from the car for the assailant. With any luck, they didn't have someone who could stop her or warn them. I closed my eyes, poured my will into the sigil I used to communicate with her again and mentally screamed at her.

The loud, high-pitched noise she made shattered all the windows and lights in the street.

The street was covered with a layer of glass.

I pushed past the pain and dizziness, ears ringing, to force myself to move. I flung open the door and fell straight to the bitumen.

Again.

My head spun. I closed my eyes tight and took a couple of deep breaths.

They couldn't recover before I did.

The feeling in my legs started to return. I ignored the pins and needles and the glass that dug into my skin to stumble over to Eli. I grabbed him and managed to get him to walk after he realised it was me. His eardrums were burst like the others. I forced back a wave of nausea when I looked at his face and threw him into the passenger seat. I slid over the bonnet of the car to distance myself from White Suit.

He looked at me with a dazed expression while holding his bleeding ears. I broke from his gaze before he tried anything and dove into the car.

I sped out of town towards a gravel back road I knew would take me to the Lacy's land.

I took several turns at a hair-raising speed, almost losing control twice.

Five minutes later, I was on the right road.

I ripped the headphones from my ears and one was coated in blood. Origin of dizziness revealed; fuck, I hoped someone could fix that. I called Eli's sister Viola using the car Bluetooth, knowing she'd be one of the few people who'd pick up. She was also the only person I trusted to have unconditional sympathy for Eli. I'd move Heaven and Earth for my little brother, and I knew she would do the same. The things the prick had said about Eli tangled in my mind and spun themselves into a knot of worry. If he was right, or thought he was, I needed to be careful with my next move. I wasn't stupid. I knew I couldn't take Eli to the clinic where I'd recovered. If the accusations about Eli were true, the doors would be left unlocked for White Suit and his ilk. If Eli did what he was accused of, he had a reason.

I knew he had a reason.

I had to trust him.

I also knew I'd be too much of a coward to ask him.

"What the fuck, Dexter? We just got all your texts," Viola said. "Where's Eli? Are you okay?"

I could only hear out of one ear.

"Someone attacked us. They've hurt Eli," I said.

"Who attacked you?"

"I don't know, some criminal group. White and red suits with a silver symbol like the Knights Templar."

"Don't go to the clinic," she snapped.

"What?" I was startled by the harshness of her voice.

Jesus Christ! I forced myself to swallow my growl of anger and frustration. I tightened my grip on the steering wheel to ease my rage.

"Come home and I'll drive where we need to go. Mum can start healing him on the way."

"I'm heading there now."

"I'll wake them." She hung up. If Eli's mother could heal him then she was his best hope.

Viola looked ready to yank me from the car until she saw the blood on my face. "Get him in the back and hop in the passenger seat." I helped Eli's parents move him to lie on the back seat, his head in Cynthia's lap and feet on his father's. The moment they were settled, Cynthia used her magic on Eli with one hand in Burton's, the other hovering over Eli's battered body.

"Stop gawking and come on," Viola said.

We left the rest of the family to follow in another car.

Hopefully, the group wouldn't ambush us.

Could they know what our next move would be? We turned north onto the main road and she hit the gas.

Forget those fuckers, the cops were going to pull us over first.

I was tense until we reached a gate, where we were asked for our IDs.

Viola flung her wallet in the guard's face and told him why we were here. We were escorted to a two-storey red brick building like a typical aged country hospital. We watched as a bed was wheeled out for Eli. He was taken behind a sealed door with his parents in tow. A stony-faced nurse held up her hand to stop Viola and me from coming in then fled after Eli.

"But I'm his next of kin." The words spilt from my lips in shock, and the look on Viola's face made me want to pack them straight back in my mouth. I knew Eli's parents were the best choice to be with him, but I hated being left behind to wonder. I needed to know he'd be okay. Would he hate me for not doing something sooner?

No… but his family might.

They seemed to like me as a person, but I constantly felt like I had to prove myself good enough to be his partner. Sometimes I felt like they'd placed me in the "consort" box, as though I only existed to occupy Eli.

Because I wouldn't give him children.

"You might get a serve over moving him if Dr Tims is on duty," Viola said.

"What else was I supposed to do?" I said.

"Ignore the prick. You did the right thing." Viola pulled herself tighter into her plum-coloured silk wrap to shield against the cold night air.

"Where are we?"

"Morse Bay."

"The holiday village?"

"Alchemist community."

"Alchemist?"

"Another group of magic users. Do you really think Nate Island has full control over magic? The people who attacked you won't come here." She walked over to me, grabbed my face and looked at my chin then my ear. She ran a finger through the drying line of blood leading into it. "Let's get that ear seen to. Mason would never forgive me if I left you damaged."

"What about Eli?"

"They won't have anything new to tell us while you're in with the doctor."

After Viola helped me with the doctor, she led me into a quiet hall with a hot drink vending machine. "Are you sure about who those people were?" she said.

"Yes. It happened on Main Street; I could see them clear enough," I said.

"Main Street? They attacked you in the middle of town?"

"I guess they disabled the CCTV first. I avoided any cameras on my way out of town."

The damage my solution caused was going to be all over the news; no one needed to know it was me.

"What did they want?"

"They wanted a potion. They think Eli stole it from them. The leader paralysed my legs while he beat the shit out of Eli. He told me to put some music on and close my eyes. I thought they were going to kill him."

"They wouldn't be that stupid. As long as he can produce an heir, he's too valuable to kill. They likely didn't want you to see him moved to a second location. Never let someone take you to a second location unless they have a strong motive not to kill you. If you let someone take you to a second location, you're dead."

"Why are you telling me that?" I forced myself to keep a calm expression and meet her eyes.

She'd scared me ever since we were kids, both accidentally and on purpose. "Men don't think about their vulnerability enough," she said.

"If what you said about Eli was true, why are you so scared of them? It's just some work thing, isn't it?"

I wasn't an equal to her; she was only ever going to see me as her friend's kid brother or Eli's pleasure thing, or worse, her shitty ex-boyfriend's favourite brother.

"Why did they just let you go?" She narrowed her eyes at me.

"They wanted to give him a chance to give the potion back," I said.

She sat on the floor beside the machine. "I knew he was into some stupid shit, but I didn't think it was this bad."

"What's going on?"

"I knew for sure when he didn't want to tell you about the community after the wedding. He wanted to hold you at arm's length to keep you safe."

"A fat lot of good that did. I was on the other side of a hospital curtain two weeks ago."

"They were only bold enough to approach you like that because you know."

"The guy in charge threatened Eli's life if he doesn't hand the potion back," I said. "He thinks Eli's life is equivalent to a potion."

"To him." She clenched her fist so hard her perfectly manicured nails broke her skin. "That fucker's lucky they wear masks. Whoever's under there, if I get the chance, I won't hesitate to show him how much Eli's life is worth to me."

"That's why I called you. I knew you'd help me without heaping on parental disappointment. Part of me wanted to call my brother, but I knew he wouldn't have the same concern for Eli."

"I know you love Mason despite everything, but I need you to promise me something."

"Anything."

"Don't tell Mason about this or anything regarding Eli and this group in the future."

"Who are they? I need to know to ensure I don't let anything accidentally slip."

"It's complicated political shit," she said.

"We've got some time and I'm good at listening." I got us both a cup of strong black coffee from the vending machine. I'd need a bucket of it to pull through to tomorrow when I was due back at work. I knew no one could know Eli was hurt. I wanted to know more and at least it'd keep her from asking what I'd done to escape. She needed to see me as more than the little boy who used to trail after her, Mason and Ralph when Eli got too intense.

"We practice magic under the administration of a place called Nate Island. Any magic user who calls themselves a mage and lives in communities near mages is required to follow the rules they set or find themselves branded a criminal. Places like the Agency are tasked with helping ensure the members of their communities follow the rules. They decide who learns magic, who knows about magic and what magic is taught or allowed to be used," she said.

"Some people with magic aren't allowed to use it because they say so?" I said.

"There's this deep dark secret no one likes to mention because it might make them feel just a little less special." She paused then whispered her next words. "Anyone can learn magic."

"Anyone?" Gran's anger made a sick kind of sense. Without her father teaching her magic, her life path would have been entirely different.

Would I exist without her and Pop connecting over magic? Not in a universe where they were strangers. Would I have survived the demon attack if she had listened to Pop and refused to teach me magic? I would have walked into that house without any knowledge of the creature inside.

"It's hard, but anyone can learn. The test that prevented you learning magic looks for people who have the aptitude, skills and personalities found in the greatest mages."

"It's a test for six-year-olds."

"I know. There's a lot of flaws in the system, which is why so many people are unhappy with it."

"And you think Eli is one of those people."

"Yes. I think he's part of a group acting against the authority of Nate Island."

"Where do the people who attacked us come in?"

"They are a secret society, a militant group dedicated to preserving the power and administration of Nate Island. Hell, they like the idea of the Knights Templar so much they mimic them."

"What does Nate Island get out of maintaining power over places like Dunn?"

"Power. Like all good vassals, we have to pay tribute. The founders of Nate Island had an extreme hard-on for feudalism. I'm surprised they were so revolutionary when it came to magic."

"Revolutionary?" I said.

"They created a whole new system. Everyone in Europe practised general and varied alchemy until the Enlightenment Era. Then it became chic to specialise in only two or three types of magic. The ideal alchemist of the Old World had a vast knowledge of magic. Some of today's mages can't even protect themselves if they choose to specialise in non-combative magic."

"I guess it's not good for Eli to be part of a rebel group."

She gave me a stony look. She shared Eli's eyes, and it was utterly unnerving to look into them. He'd never looked at me like that. "It's fucked. The whole family is fucked if they have enough evidence against him. I can't believe he was stupid enough to let slip who he was."

"What do we do?"

"I don't know."

"Is Mason part of this? Why did you mention him?"

"I don't know one hundred per cent. It's a secret society, but he is from a good family, and with his personality, job and skill set, he'd be a perfect recruit. Lewis and Ned would be ideal too."

"I can't imagine Ned joining a group like that." The idea of the youngest of my three brothers being capable of that made me angry. How could she suggest that of her own?

"You haven't seen him at work or heard his opinions on magic. Your brother is a grown man. I know he was still a teenager when you left. There's a big difference between thirteen and nineteen. He and Lewis aren't the little boys that exist in your head anymore," Viola said.

If only she'd extend that mentality to me and saw me as a whole human, something other than Ralph's worshipper.

"What do we do?" I asked.

"Pretend nothing happened. If they had the evidence to bring official charges, they wouldn't be lurking in the shadows. They're fanatics Nate

Island uses to do their dirty work. How were you hurt if you were in the car?"

"I tried to get out and hurt myself," I said. "Like I said, the leader paralysed my legs, but Eli's magic kept me locked in the car."

"Just don't let Eli pull you into his shit. You have an idealist view of the world and the people in it. An attitude like that will only get you killed."

"Idealist?"

"You only see the good in people until it's too late. I'd love to see the world the way you do, but I can't. I can't even see my brothers that way. I truly believe Eli would sacrifice anyone to save himself, me and you included." She blinked her tears back. "If it gets to that point, don't let him win."

"Don't talk like that."

"He's my brother. I've seen the absolute best and worst of him. It takes decades for people like you to see the worst in their partners. Siblings and parents have a front-row seat to the shit show. People are a contradictory mess; the sooner you learn to be wary of people's motives, the longer you'll live."

She said that as though I hadn't known him my entire life.

Had I really known him?

I'd never been told about the most important thing in his life, then there was this.

"Eli would never leave me in danger," I said.

"Don't get any ideas about learning magic. It will only get you killed. You're too ignorant for our world. Keep the fuck out, or you'll be dead within a year. No one will hesitate to kill you. You're hardly more valuable alive than dead." She stood up and downed the rest of her coffee. "Get some rest in the waiting room."

Before I could say anything else, she walked off.

I walked in the opposite direction to find a place to be alone.

I entered the first waiting room. I found myself in the same room as Lewis and Eli's grandparents. They turned to look at me but didn't say a word as I sat down across from them.

Hostility between his family and me over this was the last thing I needed.

I threw my coffee away, pulled my legs up onto the lounge and rested my face against my knees.

Why had I come back to this town?

Shit like this was the reason I'd walked away in the first place.

I couldn't deal with the political baggage that came with magic.

All these people claimed to love me, yet I had no one to hold me and tell me it was going to be okay.

Was it going to be okay?

I screamed into my knee, using the limb and fabric to silence the sound and block out the world.

I knew they could hear, but I didn't care.

6

After a long, sleepless night, I went home to have a quick shower. It was my first day of work since my accident and Eli had used his only moments of coherency since the accident to tell me to go to work. Once Cynthia noticed he was awake, she gave him a potion that put him back to sleep.

Main Street was the busiest I'd ever seen it on a Thursday morning as I pulled into my spot behind the town hall. The middle of town was barricaded, which meant the situation had become official. It didn't matter that the Agency's law enforcement department weren't *real* cops.

If they wanted to arrest Eli or me, they could and no one would stop them.

Arrest me.

I'd committed a crime.

Hurt people.

Maybe even killed someone.

Every person who was there the night before had people who cared about them.

I wasn't wearing a mask when it happened.

They would investigate and realise it was me.

Gran's family had a history of mediumship.

She had basically said they knew about her but didn't have enough evidence to execute her.

This was the smoking gun they needed.

She'd been so careful all these years and now I'd ruined that.

She had made a mistake when she decided to teach me magic.

My hands were numb as I opened my car door. I was fucked and needed protection from Grandfather. I needed to plead for him to help Gran. I needed him to understand he had to save her for me, even though they didn't like each other. The cause of that rift I'd noticed between them had become obvious.

There had to be some limits on Agency power if they hadn't done anything about Gran's illegal magic use. I hoped that Grandfather had the power to push those limits to protect both me and Gran.

I walked down the street around the yellow barricade that surrounded Centre Park and part of Main Street. People milled about, pretending not to gawk at the spectacle. I heard whispers about the whole town centre being blocked off until six o'clock as I walked towards Short Street.

The ghostly girl's place on the curb was unnaturally cold and empty as I passed on the opposite side of the street. I froze and half-turned to look at the place where she would typically be. Had an exorcist exorcised her without a second thought as to why she might have been there?

Ghosts were an impression, a fracture of the person left in reality when someone died a violent death. A creature made of pure magic. I'd used the last remnants of her existence on earth for selfish reasons, and I felt guilty.

I stepped backwards and straight into someone walking behind me. I heard glass break after I felt them crash into me, the air knocked from their lungs.

I spun around to face them. "I'm so sorry."

The person I'd crashed into bent down to pick up his phone. A bag that had clearly been on his shoulder was on the ground beside him.

Had something in there broken?

He was a tall, dark-haired man on the younger side of thirty. His dark brown, wavy hair was cut into careful layers that ended just above his shoulders; a pair of large tortoiseshell glasses framed his moss-green eyes. His dark lashes were so long and thick it almost looked like he was wearing eyeliner. He wore an unbuttoned knee-length lab coat over his green three-piece suit. Unlike most of the Agency workers, his suit wasn't plain but was covered in a shimmery black pattern. It reminded me of Victorian-era wallpaper or drapery. While the suit brought out his eyes, the design clashed horribly with his glasses.

He held his hand out to me, a panicked look forming on his delicate facial features. The angles of his face struck a perfect balance between sharp and soft. "It's okay. I was reading while walking. Mum told me it was a bad habit and ebooks on my phone haven't helped." He smiled and withdrew his hand before I could shake it. Had I noticed his hand twitch, or was it my imagination?

I noticed a crack in his phone screen when I looked down at his brown leather-gloved hands. He was clearly an Agency forensic worker and what I was about to do was stupid given my connection to the crime. I needed to worm information out of him to know how screwed I was.

"I could buy breakfast to make it up to you. I was just heading there." I pointed to the diner just up the street. "I shouldn't have been walking backwards."

"A shared moment of stupidity. Mr...?"

"Dexter. Don't even think about mistering me. I don't know how things work in America, but here people tend to use each other's first names."

"I'm from Canada." He gave me a warm smile. "I'm Cory."

"Well, Cory from Canada. How about I show you the fine food of Dunn?"

"Lead the way." He picked up his bag and followed me.

We sat across from each other in a booth as we ate our first plates filled with food, the coffee freshly placed on the table.

Mine a flat white and his an iced coffee with whipped cream and ice cream.

"Were you reading anything interesting when you crashed into me?" I stirred some sugar into my coffee. An embarrassing amount ended up on the tablecloth when I opened the packet, but he had the courtesy to pretend not to notice.

"Just rereading *Frankenstein*." He poured maple syrup onto his small stack of pancakes, pile of bacon and scrambled eggs. A literal sea of it filled the empty space on his plate. In an almost artistic movement, he stopped as it reached the edge of his plate.

I noticed a flush on his pale cheeks: guilty pleasure reading, then. I'd lied before about what I was reading when someone who clearly wouldn't understand asked. Even when I was reading average books, it was awkward when someone who hadn't read a book since high school asked what I was reading. Finding someone offline who liked odd speculative fiction books was akin to discovering unicorns were real. I didn't say anything about his blatant lie; for all I knew, he could have been reading the most mainstream smut book I could name. I'd already made things awkward by breaking his phone and forensics kit.

"*Frankenstein* wasn't as good as I thought it'd be," I said after I swallowed a mouthful of coffee.

He raised an eyebrow as though that wasn't what he expected. It almost felt like a genuinely unguarded moment. Then his features relaxed as he focused on carefully cutting his mushy pancakes. "I liked it."

"You're allowed to," I said.

"Tell me what you didn't like about it." He nodded at the name tag on my shirt. "From your professional perspective."

Why had I thought this was smart? I had no idea how to ask what had happened to the ghost without him becoming suspicious.

Cory's eyes snapped to my coffee cup as he watched me finish the last of it. "I'm sorry for what I'm about to do and hope that one day you can forgive me."

I almost dropped the cup as I pulled it away from my mouth and threw it down on the table.

I tried to stand up.

My vision blurred as my brain went blank; my thoughts broke apart and floated off into the universe. When I landed back in my body, I'd managed to sit back in the chair.

He slowly took his glasses off and used a cloth from his jacket pocket to carefully clean them.

"Is this magic, or did you put something in my drink?" I said.

"You did something very stupid last night," he said.

"What do you want with me?"

"Let's go for a drive," Cory said. "I am your friend, and nothing is wrong. You want to go with me."

The command melted away any resistance I felt towards him and the situation. I let him wrap an arm around my shoulder and help me stand. He kept a very tight arm around my body as he walked me from the diner. I felt helpless under the gaze of several people I knew who didn't even notice. I tried to get the owner's attention as we passed her, but my cry for help wouldn't leave my mouth.

My body felt light, my connection to my limbs distant as every attempt to trip myself or stop walking was met with Cory carefully guiding my body where he wanted me to go.

He'd done this before. Used this trick to get someone to come with him.

He was parked down the street at a park that people didn't visit much due to its proximity to the better parks on Main Street. It was a four-car carpark, small dingy toilet block and patch of grass. No one was around to notice us even if I could scream for help. He opened his back door and pushed me into the back seat, where I lay in a heap.

"You'll be all right. We're not going far." Cory tucked my legs in and slammed the door shut.

Five minutes later, he pulled me from the car, and I got my first look at the parking lot we'd pulled up in. It was a private concrete area outside a large building I'd seen before at the local history museum. It was a massive structure built from sandstone brick with a brown tiled roof. The

Lacy-Thornton Hotel was the reason Dunn had been built. I'd heard it had been turned into private office space.

With a sick feeling, I knew where I was.

This was the Agency headquarters.

Hidden in plain sight on the hill that the town had been built around. No one looked at us twice as Cory led me into the building a hand on my shoulder. I hoped I'd see someone who knew me, but the only people we passed were strangers or people I vaguely knew because I'd seen them around town a few times. While there was at most three degrees of separation between everyone in Dunn, it was still large enough not everyone knew each other, especially generations who didn't grow up together. I was sure I knew these people's kids if they were in their early twenties. We'd have at least gone to primary school together.

We took an elevator to the second floor and walked down a long winding hall that reminded me of a hotel corridor before Cory pulled me to a stop in front of a large double wooden door.

"If you tell me you're doing this for my own good…" I said.

"I'll be seeing you," Cory said.

"No, you won't."

Cory sighed then knocked on the door in a pattern. He waited a few seconds then opened the door and pushed me in.

The door closed behind me before I could react.

"Drink your tea."

All the fight left me when I turned around to face the person who sat behind the desk. I knew who it was the moment I heard the voice.

Grandfather sat behind a massive desk made of a polished dark red wood in the centre of the bookshelf-lined office. I walked over to the desk, grabbed the dainty royal albert teacup and downed the milky tea in one long gulp. I slid into the chair in front of the desk as the cloudiness drained from my mind. When did Cory have the chance to slip a potion in my coffee? I thought back to the diner, but I couldn't remember a single moment where I was distracted enough. But it could have been any time he wanted because I hadn't been expecting to be spiked at the diner in the middle of the breakfast rush.

We'd been in a place where I felt safe and in control of the situation.

Grandfather cleared his throat, forcing me to meet his eyes, and sighed. "Evelyn has been a thorn in my side for fifty-two years. Do you know why people didn't like the Gerstle family practising Death Magic? Because it was forbidden until the eighties unless practiced by officially sanctioned mages like Archibald Gerstle. His son and granddaughter didn't pass their tests. The magical community was strongly superstitious and heavily religious until recently." He tapped his desk with a finger.

"It's not illegal for those outside of the mage community to learn magic, but they are not supposed to live in our communities. Your gran broke that rule when she moved to Dunn with that alchemist boy toy of hers."

I pooled my fear into anger. "I don't understand what you're saying. Are you telling me Gran has magic t—" The words died in my mouth when I saw the look on his face. His features hardened.

He pointed his finger at me. "I'm not fucking stupid, Dexter. No one is falling for this fucking crap any more. I turned a blind eye for too long to avoid getting you and her in trouble and it almost got you killed. No fucking more. I'm putting a leash on your neck and separating you from her influence. I should've done it the moment I first suspected. I just wanted one of my grandkids to live a normal, safe life without the danger of magic constantly bearing down on them."

"Forced to be normal. How is that fair?" I said.

"Fair? You really are a stupid child. Life isn't fair! Look at what happened to the kids in that house," he said.

"You will start your exorcist apprenticeship this afternoon."

"Exorcist training? I'm a librarian."

"Not any longer."

"Are you saying I have no choice in this?"

"Not unless you want to be arrested for illegal practice of a controlled magic."

"Why exorcist training?"

"What do you think people who focus on the mediumship branch of Death Magic do, fluff around and play nice with ghosts? Someone needs to teach you control. Death Magic is a dangerous and carefully controlled magic. Practitioners are only trained according to demand."

It wasn't supposed to happen like this! I was supposed to be the one in control of the situation and plan for when this encounter happened. I remembered Gran stating I needed to go with them and play along.

She knew this was going to happen sooner rather than later.

"Go with them when they grab you" wasn't an appropriate warning.

"After that display last night, you're lucky Cory grabbed you before anyone else did," Grandfather said.

"He's your agent?" I said.

"Yes."

"I have no choice?"

"How daft are you? They still have enough evidence to get you as an accomplice for summoning that demon and murdering those kids. You have no choice unless you want to be arrested for murder."

"Murder?"

"They were high school kids. Even between the six of them, they couldn't have summoned that demon. Someone will need to take the fall for what happened to them," he said.

"I don't have the skill to do something like that. I thought we were close. I thought you loved me. Do you honestly believe I'd be capable of something like that?" I forced myself to hold back my tears.

"I'm thinking about how it looks from the outside. Someone with a key to that house did have the ability to summon that creature, and you contaminated the crime scene. The owner swears up and down that you were the only person with a key, an illegal Death Magic user. There was no magic used to get in. It had to be someone with a key. The forensics team have the main suspect pegged as a man older than thirty, and the prosecution will be looking to connect the two of you."

"I wasn't exactly thinking about crime scene contamination when I was running for my life."

"I'm sorry. This is less a punishment and more a realisation that I can't keep you safe by distancing you from magic. I have five years at the most before they force retirement on me. Entrenching you in this organisation is the best way to keep you safe. No matter what the future holds, I love you. I'm doing this to keep you safe. I need you to remember that."

I blinked away the tears in my eyes before I looked up at him.

"I feel like I've dropped some of the strings I was holding and you've paid the price," he said.

"Okay," I said.

"Okay?"

"I'll do whatever you want me to. Just lead the way."

"The team you will be assigned to is currently on paid leave. Their apprentice was killed in the line of duty."

I nodded.

"I'm going to have a Death Mage from another department teach you the basics. It will be a good transition from your chosen career," he said.

"It's going to be hard to let that go," I said.

"I know they socialise you to think one job will be the end-all, but life often doesn't work out like that. You're only twenty-three, a great age to train in a new field."

"Do I have to start today?"

He took a long sip of his own tea. "It will keep you out of trouble. I can't trust you to live with Evelyn or have unsupervised contact with her."

Before I knew what I was doing, I punched the desk. "Sometimes I think you're just jealous of the relationship Gran and I have."

67

"You need to stay away from her, or she'll have to be arrested for the crimes she committed in training you. It was part of the deal I made with the other board members. Do you really think I'd do all this on my own volition? I'd be arrested too. If you cut unsupervised contact with Evelyn and are found innocent, you have a long career ahead of you working for this agency."

"I have to look after her, there's no one else," I said.

"Mason and Ariella are to look after her," he said.

"But Ariella's pregnant again."

"Her young children can share a room."

"Have you asked them?"

"The move is happening as we speak. You can only talk to her from now on if Mason or his wife are there. Understand?"

I felt sick and closed my eyes to block the wave of dizziness that rushed over me. I'd been set up. "I understand."

"You can't tell anyone, especially Evelyn, about the deal we've made here."

"Can I tell Eli? We've made a promise not to keep any secrets from each other any more."

"And I can see that you're doing incredibly well at that. How is he going to respond when he finds out that you can do magic and never told him?"

I was done.

I forced myself to stand. "I need the toilet.

I managed to hold back the tears until I closed the door. I walked down the hall, looked at the ground and blocked out everyone I passed until I found a bathroom.

I walked into the bathroom, stood at the sink and looked into the mirror; my eyes were red and wet. It was obvious I'd been crying. Fuck, I was such a whingey little coward. I knew it was okay for men to cry, but fuck. I cried at every little thing that went wrong in my life.

What was wrong with me? But this wasn't a small thing.

I brought my fist down on top of the sink as hard as I could. I hissed as it throbbed with pain. When Eli found out about this, it would be the end of our marriage. There was no way he'd forgive this after all the promises of no secrets and how hurt I'd been over the things he'd kept from me.

Why had I done it in the first place?

I clearly wasn't emotionally mature enough for marriage. I said yes when he asked me after only eight months of dating because I didn't want to lose him. Ready to bare all to Eli and live with his family for the rest of my life. I was still trying to pull myself together. How could

I healthily enter a permanent relationship commitment if I didn't even know who I was? Eli hadn't been in love with me for thirteen years; he'd been in love with an idealised version of me that didn't exist.

Freely being able to use my magic to help people was a dark little fantasy that had hooked itself in the back of my mind. I wasn't sure I could deal with the negative consequences.

I stopped short of punching the mirror.

I let my hand rest against its cold surface as I watched the tears roll down my cheeks.

This wasn't a small secret; my marriage was over when Eli found out about my magic. No one would ever love me like that again. Eli had been my last chance. I'd spend the rest of my life a lonely unwanted prisoner of this town.

Gran was going to hate me when she found out what had happened. There was no going back and repairing our relationship; no matter what I said, she'd think I betrayed her trust.

I splashed a double-cuffed handful of cold water over my face, not caring about the water that soaked the front of my shirt. When it didn't stop the tears, I locked myself in the back stall and curled up on the closed seat. Soaking into the embrace of imagined privacy, I turned into a hyperventilating, weeping mess, the worst things I'd heard or thought about myself invading my head for another attempt at a hostile takeover.

There was a light knocking on the stall door. "Dex? Is that you? I was told you were here talking to your grandfather."

The profound realisation it was Eli made it worse, and my breath quickened to the point I loudly gasped for air between sobs. Any semblance of rational thought left my brain along with the oxygen it needed to function.

Before I knew what was happening, the lock on the door had flicked open and Eli took me in his arms. I let him hold me one last time as my body was racked with a new wave of sobs that almost spread my breakfast all over both of us.

Eli held me close, kissed my forehead and ran a hand through my hair. "What did he do to you?"

"I love you." It started with those three words and became a mantra. I couldn't stop repeating them more intensely as the sobs subsided.

Eli put a finger against my lips. "What did he say to you?" He turned my head so he could look into my eyes. "You need to tell me what he did so I can fix it."

I took a couple of ragged breaths. "This isn't something you can fix."

"No, it isn't."

My heart sank, and I started crying again.

Eli pulled me against him and kissed my forehead; this time he let his lips rest against my skin. "I'm not angry at you."

I had no idea how long we sat there. Eli had relocked the door when he heard someone come in just after I'd managed to stop the panic attack. Christ knows what anyone else using the bathroom thought we were doing in the stall together.

Eli put his phone back in his pocket after sending someone a quick text. "You know you can tell me anything?"

"Gran trained me in Death Magic, and now they're forcing me to work for them as an exorcist."

"Them?"

"He called it the board."

Eli stiffened, his body almost uncomfortable under me. "I'm sorry."

"Sorry?" I said.

"I didn't know it was going to be like this."

"He said that you definitely wouldn't want to stay married to me after you found out about me knowing magic."

Eli let out a long, shaky breath. "I'm only letting this go out of respect for your relationship with him. I know you're close to him. Today is going to be a long day."

I looked at him, truly looked at him. If I'd known he was interested in me when we were eighteen, I could have saved myself so much pain. It was easy to be raw and open with someone I'd known my entire life, easy to love him.

"I want you to take me to the person who will train me," I said. "I don't want to see Grandfather again today."

Eli nodded. "You stay here for a minute while I tell Edwin to call ahead."

7

I was surprised when Eli pressed the button for B1: A when we walked into the elevator.

Were there offices in the basement, or was he showing me something else?

The hall we walked into was dark.

As Eli left the elevator, the motion lights flicked on with an electric buzz. The walls were lined with a dark wood panel and the floors of worn, chipped lino had seen better days before I was even born. A directory and public toilet outside the elevator betrayed the level's once-prosperous status. The floor was listed as B1: A "Living Magicks: Non-Flora/Fauna."

I could hear soft folksy pop music as we passed the quiet offices. They had pinned open the wooden double doors at the end of the hall and the room itself was an ample office space turned common room. Several people were in the room, and most were talking in a single group while they downed coffee or tea. The workday hadn't started for this department. The instant we crossed the threshold, the other people in the room turned to look at us in unison.

"Morning," I said. The smell of their coffee already had me craving another cup. After several mumbled greetings, they all went back to their previous activities.

"Please leave him with me, Elijah," Cory walked in from behind Eli and me to stand in front of us.

"What is *he* doing here?" I pointed at Cory.

Eli frowned at me. "Apparently Cory is going through mentor

training. Normally he would just observe, but one of his specialisations is Death Magic, so he will take a more active role in your training," Eli said. "He's the person I was told to bring you to."

I knew then why he had been assigned to the Short Street incident. Send a Death Mage to investigate a ghost attack.

"I'm primarily a Blood and Medical Mage," Cory said. "But I do dabble in Death Magic."

"What's up with the cloak and dagger stuff anyhow?" I said.

"This is where they hide those with problematic magic," Cory said.

"'Problematic Magicks' doesn't have the same ring to it as 'Living Magicks: Non-Flora/Fauna,'" Eli said.

"It sounded less suspicious back when this department was a grey zone from a legal perspective." Cory clicked his tongue. "Almost every mage working here primarily practices once-illegal magic."

"Explaining the prime office space," Eli said.

"Do you know why you're here?" Cory said.

"Do you know why I'm here?" I raised an eyebrow and looked Cory in the eyes.

"I've been given a dossier." Cory pinned Eli with his eyes. "Please leave us, Mr Lacy. Your husband is a big boy and can handle himself."

Eli gave me a pat on the shoulder and walked out of the room without looking back.

"You have potential if rumour is to be believed," Cory said.

"Rumour?" I said.

"The ghost on Short Street. Ring any bells? The only reason we had to exorcise her was because you riled her up," Cory said.

"They told you what I did?" I said.

"Dexter. Let me give you an idea of how things work here. A few people on the investigation team for that incident will have been victims of your petty trick," Cory said.

"Trick! The fucker in charge would have killed Eli. What was I supposed to do?"

"The only reason you're not in more trouble is because the only damage you caused was a little temporary hearing damage."

"And because that group isn't one hundred per cent legitimate," I said.

"You seem to know a lot about the group who attacked your husband for an outsider. Who told you about them?" Cory said.

"Someone after the incident. I was told they're fanatics who do Nate Island's dirty work and they are allied with the Agency."

"They can be a little extreme."

"A little?" I hope my eyebrow raise looked elegant.

"They do exemplary work. You just haven't had the chance to see it."

"My gran thinks Nate Island brainwashes the people here, and you're all part of a cult." I said.

"How about you get to know the magical world before jumping to that conclusion? Spend a few years with us while we're teaching you magic instead of locking your abilities and erasing your memory. If you don't like it here, you can join the alchemists. Given your maternal grandfather's reputation, I'm sure they'd be glad to have you," Cory said.

"What do you mean by 'lock my powers'?" I said.

"It's what will happen if this arrangement doesn't work out. Mason wanted to take you on out of brotherly duty, but this is the only department you can work in."

"So if I fail here?"

"Bye-bye magic." He gave me a sickly amused grin. "Not that you'll know."

"What do you do down here?" I asked.

"We get orders from upstairs. My mentor and I do forensics, but it's a small town, so we aren't kept too busy. We sometimes protect th—"

"You're not detectives?"

"God, no. What gave you the idea that everyone working here is a detective? You will train as our third exorcist," Cory said. "If you like solving mysteries, you're in luck. You will need to confirm the ghost or demon is a threat. It's considered a waste of resources to exorcise something that isn't a thr—"

"Can you just backtrack for a minute? Did you just say 'demon'?' I'm expected to banish demons?" I said.

"It's part of the job description of an exorcist. We class ghosts or spirits as demons." Cory sighed and took his glasses off to rub the bridge of his nose between two fingers. "Did your maternal grandparents tell you what demons are?"

"Creatures from alternative universes and Earthbound magic creatures."

"Or creatures created by magic. Ghosts are, as far as we can tell, one of the few creatures humans create using pure magic."

"There's no chance they're the souls of the dead?" I said.

"There's no such thing as the soul. What would be the point?" Cory said.

"The point?" I asked.

"In both the theological and evolutionary theories, the soul thing would be a waste of time and energy."

"People use their dying moments to create pure magical creatures imprinted with their consciousness?" I said.

"I can imagine that people who experience violent or sudden deaths don't want to die. Have you been told about the other common ghost?"

"There's another?"

"There are entire fields of magic based on using only thought to power a desired outcome. The small energy used to focus on the thought builds because magical energy is absorbed by the surrounding environment." Cory paused and looked at me, wanting me to put the pieces together.

I closed my eyes for a few seconds as I thought. When I opened my eyes, I met his. "Ghosts can be created through the thoughts of living people. Haunted houses, the ones with stories. Tell the same story enough. Many people thinking about the same ghost can create one. Does that mean some ghosts aren't imprints of actual people?"

"Yes. A lot of urban legends spawn monsters that are ghosts, though some urban legends are inspired by people who witnessed demons."

"How are they living creatures? Wouldn't they be magical constructs?" I said.

"I don't know enough about them to answer those questions. The physiology of ghosts crosses from Death Magic to Eldritch Magic or Demonology. All I know is some ghosts are similar enough to some creatures from the void, and it's hard to tell the difference." Cory looked at me for an uncomfortable amount of time. "You showed real promise controlling that ghost. Do you know how many people could do that without proper training?"

"No."

"Few. Death Magic is a hard magic for people to learn," Cory said.

"Why are you assuming that I wasn't trained properly?" I said.

"You would have used a tactic that didn't risk damaging you and your husband's hearing."

"I put my headphones in first."

He gave me a thin smile. "How did that work?"

"I burst one eardrum and got hearing damage in the other ear from the volume of the music."

He pulled a thick string-bound manila folder from the leather satchel slung over his body. "I have your training programme."

I noticed my name on the top righthand corner of the folder. "Officially?"

Cory tapped the folder. "Created in collaboration with your future mentor, the board and the local magical university in Beckham. It had to be personalised due to the assumed knowledge in the official program."

"Let's get started, then." God, I sounded artificial. Did he know I was playing him too?

I looked into his wide green eyes. Magnified by the glasses, they gave him an almost owl-like appearance. They almost seemed to have a genuine spark of curiosity in them.

"Great." Cory stood up. "I just need to get my outside gloves."

"Outside gloves?" The words were out of my mouth before I could stop them.

He looked at me, confused, as though I asked an obvious question. "You don't know?"

"No." I narrowed my eyes.

He pushed his glasses back up his nose. "Blood Magic is best done with fresh blood. It's considered a waste of time and magic to heal the wounds the blood comes from."

"Oh." I shivered; nausea formed in the pit of my stomach as the realisation sunk in.

"You'd know all about using the tools available." He turned and walked off before I could respond.

What had they told him?

Cory waved a hand towards the door. "After you."

I nodded and walked into the hall before him.

My heart leapt into my throat when Cory pulled his car to a stop outside Nora Rowe's house.

Time unwound and suddenly I was three weeks back, fighting for my life against her ghost. I'd been so sure of myself back then, even though I'd barely escaped.

Had that only been less than a month ago?

I felt like an entirely unfamiliar person.

I jumped from my thoughts when Cory opened his door. "Are you coming?"

I slowly looked at him. "Yes."

"Great. Let's clean up your mess."

I followed him from the car. "I hardly think it's my mess."

"You didn't report a hostile ghost."

"I… I…"

"I what? Didn't want anyone to know your precious little secret? It wasn't much of a secret, Lacy. Evelyn Patton isn't as sly as she thinks she is. In fact, she's a rather fine example of what can happen if you're not careful with magic."

"Excuse me?" I said.

"The accident that left her visually impaired and paralysed below

75

her waist. I found her medical records from that little alchemist hospital when I researched you," Cory said.

"You just happened to find her medical records?"

"Yes."

I stopped and he turned to face me.

We were halfway up the path in the middle of the day.

Our fraction of the world absent from human activity.

For a few seconds, it felt like we were the only people in the world.

A thought snapped from my subconsciousness: *You'd know all about using the tools available.* There was blood in the spit I'd used to draw that sigil.

I'd used both Blood and Death Magic.

The fucker would have known. I pointed a finger at him. "You're one of those Templar fuckers who attacked Eli and me."

He swallowed but said nothing, his attention fixed on me.

"Did you think I wouldn't be able to figure it out? At least give me some credit."

"They warned us about you in the mission brief and I wanted to see what you could do." He let out a loud breath and looked down at the sidewalk. "When I saw what you could do, I realised they'd made a mistake when you were rejected for training. The test is necessary to limit the number of mages, but it causes some people to fall through the cracks. I went to our boss with a report on your skills."

"You decided that I'd make a good exorcist while you were bleeding out from burst eardrums?"

"It only took me a few seconds to heal myself. If you're actually as innocent as you claim, you show great promise."

"And if not?"

He smiled and met my eyes. "Every rose has its thorns and they can be easily snipped."

"Tell that white suit fucker I'll rip his throat out if he ever punches my husband again," I said.

He chuckled, another smile forming on his face. "That's quite a threat."

"No matter how long I take, I will become strong enough to kill him."

"If he ever touches your husband again." He chuckled almost mockingly.

"Yes."

"You've got some balls, Dexter Lacy. I'll give you that."

"Give me that!" I placed a hand on my hip with a smirk. I'd never found it this easy to talk with someone I didn't know.

"It's something you can take advantage of. Honestly, you will never contend with the best mages at the Agency. If you keep at it for as long as you're physically able, you will be better than the vast amount of magic users."

"I get that, but if your little boss comes after us again, I will make it my personal mission to end him. He'd be at least forty to have that position. I'll just wait until he's old or win over his trust."

He gave me a forced smile that didn't reach his eyes. "I'm not passing that on because I value my life." The tone of his voice made me realise he was taking the piss. He thought my threat was a joke; that smile was him trying not to laugh. "You can laugh all you want."

"Enough chit-chat. It's time for your first lesson." He turned on his heel and faced the door. He stopped where I'd fallen on the concrete. He sunk to his knees, licked a small white piece of paper he pulled from his pocket and pressed it to the path. The side that touched the concrete came back dark red as though it was soaked in blood.

"I think that's mine."

"Yes. I saw." He carefully placed the paper in a small zip lock evidence bag.

"What do you mean you saw?" I gave him a hard look. Had they been watching me longer than I thought?

"It's 2018, Lacy. Household security cameras are everywhere." He slowly glanced over at the house across the street without turning his head. "They have a doorbell camera and you signed out the keys to Nora Rowe's house."

I'd hidden all evidence that I'd been in Rowe's house. I knew they had caught me, but I still wanted to know how they knew about the keys. "You know that? How?"

"When you use correction tape on something, make sure what you wrote doesn't leave an impression on the page underneath it."

I felt the ground drop from under me as I swallowed my pride. I'd been foiled by something a five-year-old could've discovered. "She's dangerous. She tried to possess me."

He walked back over to me and stood behind me. He placed a single, leather-gloved finger on my temple. "Close your eyes and focus on my voice."

I closed my eyes.

"You need to forget everything you think you know about magic."

"Everything I think I know?"

"Ninety per cent of what you think you know is wrong."

"Stop fucking with me." I spun around and faced him. "Why should I listen to you? A guy who's part of a militant cult?"

"If you want to leave that house alive, you must listen to everything I say while we are in there." He placed his hands on my shoulders and started guiding me towards the house.

"I can't do this," I said.

"You have no choice. If you can't handle this task, then how are you fit to work for us?" He patted my shoulders before he let go. "They promised you protection. There are worse things than the ghost in this house or that demon that almost killed you. Some people would gladly hurt you to get revenge on your family. To have protection from them, you need to work for the Agency."

"The reality isn't that easy."

"Does the next Rowe family member who walks in that house deserve to be possessed? Do they deserve to die because you're scared?"

"No."

"It is our duty to protect people. Now she has learnt how to possess people, anyone who walks into this house is a target."

"I know." I looked at the ground for a minute before I looked back at him. "If you really value my safety, you tell me the truth about magic. Any question I ask. Everyone I've spoken to has given me their own version of bullshit that contradicts what everyone else has to say. I want actual answers."

"In exchange, you'll do anything I ask," he said.

I met his eyes with a determined glance. "Anything."

He sat down on the dead lawn and looked up at me. "Okay. Shoot."

I looked down at him, my mouth agape. No one had ever given me their time like that. Paid their end of the bargain before mine. I guess this was a long-term bargain and it wouldn't hurt him to give a little. I wondered just how far he'd go to get me into that house.

"You said you have questions," he said.

I realised I was staring at him. "Can anyone learn magic?"

"With the correct instruction. Should just anyone be able to learn magic is the ultimate question."

"My grandparents seem fixated on the idea that magic ability is genetic."

"Until genetic testing was widespread, that was the belief. Modern science hasn't found a magic gene." He gave me a thin smile. "A lot of the older folks like to cling to the idea that we're special. That them learning magic wasn't happenstance, and something destined them for it no matter what."

"No one cared to notice that anyone could learn magic?" I said.

"You're rather attached to this idea. Think about how more people can read now than ever before. To learn magic to its highest level, one would have to know how to read and write, preferably in a second language for their spell casting. It can get a bit messy casting spells in one's everyday language. They would also need to have access to a skilled instructor and a safe environment. The European witch hunts weren't just political. They caught plenty of weaker magic users in the net."

"Political."

"Most of the accusations were about stealing possessions, getting rid of people who weren't liked or intelligent women intimidating weak men by existing. Weak, careless magic users did nothing but confirm the mindset of those who passively sat by and let it happen. The average citizen needed to believe witches were the devil's minions. They couldn't feel guilty about sending a lynch mob to Aunt Mary's house if she was evil."

"Are you saying I should just shut up and be grateful?"

"You're lucky enough to have the ability to learn magic and ask these questions."

"Grandfather kept a huge part of his and my brothers' lives from me because he wanted me to be normal. They kept me from fully knowing them," I said.

"You can never truly know another person, Lacy," Cory said.

"So I've been told. Call me Dexter, please. It still feels weird to hear Lacy."

"It's professional for me to use your surname."

"You're sitting cross-legged on the dead grass like a kindergarten kid at lunchtime. How is anything about this professional?"

He laughed. "You are…" He shook his head with a smile.

"Don't laugh at me," I said.

"You jump from empathic to judgemental with barely a breath between. It's actually difficult to keep up." He picked a piece of dead grass off his suit. "One minute you're teary-eyed about the plight of orphans and the next you're sneering at the poor for daring to exist."

"Be serious."

"I am. You need to decide who you are." He looked me in the eye again. "Are you an honourable person who can afford to be empathetic, or are you a judgemental snob?"

"I don't know. God." I looked away from him, red-faced. I could feel tears of embarrassment building behind my eyes as I tried to taper my anger. I'd never felt so exposed in my entire life.

"The best armour against possession is a sense of self. The confidence of a powerful personality." He stood and turned towards the house. "If you want to be alive in a year, it's a skill you need to learn.

Everyone who works here has gone through shit. Let's do our job and prevent other people from going through shit."

"You see yourself as some kind of hero?"

"I see myself as corrupted. Who better to prevent others from going through similar tragedies?"

"I have one more question before we head in there."

He pulled his hand back from the door handle. "Okay."

"Was our first meeting a setup?"

"Yes."

"What exactly is it I'm accused of?" I said.

"That's two questions."

"Just tell me." My stomach dropped when I saw him stiffen at the tone of my voice. He turned to face me, right hand in his pants pocket, a hard look on his face. "There's an illegal Death Mage named Nox. He's caught up in some proper dark shit. He recently got an Agency board member's kid killed. They describe him as very similar to you, both magic- and appearance-wise."

"Why the fuck would people think that?"

"Many of the sceptics believed it when you married Elijah Lacy. They assume you rekindled your relationship with him through his side work."

"There's no way Eli would be involved in that kind of shit. Take it back," I said.

"Excuse me?" Cory said.

"You heard me. Take it the fuck back." I pointed the finger at him. "God, people are stupid. Fucking fucks. I've known Eli since before I could even walk. What was I supposed to say when a handsome man asked me out? Me! No? Get stuffed. Eli was my last chance. My only chance. Take what you said back. Murdered kids? He'd never do that kind of shit. Why is it so hard to believe that a guy like Eli might like a guy like me? I'm no—"

Cory clicked his fingers, and I started coughing. He waited until the coughing fit had subsided to speak. "Do you do that often? Is it something I should plan around?"

"Mother fucking cun—"

He did it again, sending me into another coughing fit that almost had me on my hands and knees. "The foul language isn't cute, Dexter Lacy. Neither are the angry rants. You're a man in your twenties, not a teenager. If I hear one more crazed rant or another F this or C that out of you while you're working with me, I'll dump your sorry arse. Understand?"

"Cute? What the hell is that supposed to mean?"

"You want people to think you're attractive? Consider your words before opening your mouth," Cory said.

"Excuse me?" I said.

"You heard me. No one likes that kind of language. I'm sick of hearing it. You're attractive until you open your mouth."

I found myself unable to respond.

"With the right spell and knowledge of the human body, you can sense the signs that someone's attracted to you," he said.

"You use magic to make people attracted to you?" I said.

"No. If I want something from someone, I use magic to sense what actions arouse the person I'm talking to. If you're even reasonably attractive, you can use it to your advantage when working with people. It's a subtle manipulation." He crossed his arms. "It's no secret that attractive people have an advantage in life. You can make yourself the most attractive person in the room to whoever you need to manipulate to get what you want," Cory said.

"Is that what you've been doing to me?" I said.

"I saw an opening and took advantage of your natural attraction to me. When I first saw you, I thought it'd be easy to play the weird pushover blinded by his cock. Then you had to open your mouth."

I bit my tongue to stop the word "cunt" from leaving my mouth.

"If you're really who you claim to be, then you'll let me help you learn this job. Do you understand?"

I let out a long, tired breath. "Yes."

"Have a drink out of that fancy water bottle of yours. We're exorcising this ghost now. I'd like to get to the bakery in Oak Breeze before they run out of chicken curry pies."

I nodded and walked back to the car to have a minute to relax while I drank some water. This arsehole would be a lot harder to deal with than I first thought.

When I joined him on the stairs, Cory had opened the front pocket of his satchel. The pocket unrolled with the pull of a silk ribbon to reveal a long row of smaller round pockets. It almost touched the ground and held hundreds of writing implements, from cheap pens and expensive art markers to chalk or oil pastels. He pulled a pristine piece of chalk from a pocket halfway down his thigh and handed it to me. "It's far from the best tool to draw a ghost trap, but it's the easiest for a novice mage to use. Please be careful; that's a stick of what's considered the best chalk in existence, and the company is no longer in operation. There'll be duels to death between mages and mathematicians over the last piece."

"Got it."

He pulled a notepad and small pencil from the front pocket of his suit jacket. He drew a circle with a rounded pattern in the middle that was a cross between a cartoon flower and a pentagram. "I want you to draw this. Ideally on a piece of clean, hard floor."

I carefully studied the simple sigil after he handed it to me. "There's no clean floor in there."

"What we're about to do isn't ideal, but it's a safer choice." Cory handed me an A4 piece of black cardstock. "You may as well copy it out here. Draw another exactly the same on the palm of your hand but leave a slight gap that can be closed in a single stroke. Damage either one with your sweaty fingers and we die."

He gave me a look so serious I laughed.

"We die? I'm pretty sure it's your job to make sure that doesn't happen." I felt like a kid doing arts and crafts. I carefully copied the sigil, drawing it in the same order Cory had. When I finished, he nodded at the door handle and I opened the door.

He pointed to my hand. "Remember not to smudge that." He had a small, green, metal torch in his bag. When he shone it into the house, there was no sign of Nora Rowe.

"It's almost been a month. How do you know someone hasn't been in here?"

"This place is made of asbestos prefab. We had it declared condemned and placed magical locks on the entrances. The only people with permission to be here are us."

"Every house in this part of town is built solely from asbestos and lead paint. Sixty per cent of the houses in Dunn should be condemned," I said. "This place is a dump, toxic waste included. Everyone raised here probably has permanent brain damage."

"Please focus," Cory said.

"Why go to the effort of placing magical locks on the house but not remove the ghost?"

"You have to clean up your own mess." Cory's torch flickered for a few seconds then went out. He clicked his tongue and shook the torch until it flickered back to life. The temperature in the room had decreased rapidly in the few seconds of darkness. "Sorry, it does that. I need to buy a new one."

"You need to buy a new one? Seriously!" I said.

"It's not high on my to-do list."

I looked at him and mouthed, "She's here."

He stepped closer to me, stood on my foot, and gave me a sharp look. "Let's check the other rooms to make sure we have all those books.

Mrs Gregory is rather mad at you for running out of here like a scared baby the other day. You know ghosts aren't real, right?"

Scared baby? The prick was purposely trying to provoke me. I smiled at him and carefully checked the sigil to make sure I hadn't smudged the chalk. The card stock was already damp where I held it between my sweaty fingers.

I closed my eyes for a few seconds and took a deep breath.

I could do this.

I had to do this.

I met his eyes and he looked at the ground for a few seconds. After he looked up, I carefully dropped the card on the ground, thankful it landed face-up.

We waited and pretended to have a mundane conversation as Nora Rowe slowly came towards us. Positioned against a door, a wall, and the end of the hallway, there was only one way for her to approach. When she reached the sigil, I finished the chalk copy on my palm and closed my eyes. Nora didn't belong in this world; she had to go. She had to vanish.

Had to leave.

My ears popped.

Cory tapped my shoulder and I opened my eyes.

She was gone.

"Maybe I can make something of you."

I was careful to give him back the sweaty chalk in one piece. The whole "be careful" thing felt like a threat, and I didn't want to see what would happen if I wasn't. "It worked?"

"It's not always going to be easy. Be sure the person was mortal before you use that tactic. It wouldn't have worked if she knew what a sigil was."

"How does a mortal leave a ghost?"

"Like I said, everyone's capable of magic. Most of the time, they're created through sheer determination. Base-level magic is created mainly through thought; the last of their energy powers it. The desire or need to stay here. The last thing they want in this world is not to die."

"It sounds sad when you put it like that," I said.

"It is," Cory said.

"That felt too easy."

"Don't get too big for your boots. It wouldn't have been that easy if you were alone."

I rolled my eyes. "I know that from experience."

We walked out of the house and back to Cory's car. "I feel like that was a setup."

He turned to look at me. "I made it easy for you."

"Easy for me?"

"I placed some runes in the hall."

"Runes?"

"They're on the walls."

I snatched the torch from his hand and marched back into the house. The walls were covered in letters—runes. They were hard to see; he'd written them in a marker almost identical to the colour of the paint. I sensed him behind me as I shone the torch around the space. "Why?"

"You need to learn the process one step at a time. I wanted you to focus on banishing her and learning a basic sigil."

"What are they?" I said.

"A spell. They're letters. It's an ancient magical language. Ancient Roman alchemists used this spell language." He pulled a small spray bottle from the bag and sprayed a thin layer of mist over the walls. He carefully used a microfiber cloth to remove the marks. "Death Magic is my third magic and my focus is on Necromancy. We will hit a wall eventually. Hopefully not before I pass you on to the people who are supposed to be training you."

"You could teach me some Necromancy," I said.

"No," he replied. "I'd be skinned alive if I did that."

"Everyone specialises in two or three types of magic, right?"

"Almost always two, but I don't get out much."

"Unless you're taking part in compulsory cult activities."

He laughed.

"I want to learn Potion Craft. I used to watch Pop make potions; I find it fascinating," I said.

"You need focus on learning one type of magic at a time," Cory said.

We drove half an hour to Oak Breeze, a small coastal town ten minutes north of the secluded beach where Eli and I had our date. It was daunting to think that was only last night.

I joined Cory, who sat at a bird-shit-stained wooden picnic table in the beachside park. Development on this part of the coast was almost to the sand. I looked out at the ocean as I forced myself to sit down at the table. "Don't you have a spell or something to clean this?"

"A slightly dirty table will not kill you, Dexter." Cory bit into his curry chicken pie.

I started eating mine. "These are good."

"I know," Cory said.

"But not an hour round trip out of our way good. There are three bakeries in Dunn alone."

"I know. I live there too."

"You do?"

"Yes." The moment the pie was gone, he turned his attention to the cupcake he'd bought. It was simple with pastel pink icing and rainbow hundreds and thousands.

I'd always wondered who bought those things.

My grandmother would call it a patty cake.

He met my gaze. "Please stop judging my food."

I laughed. "I can't help it. It's *cute*. It looks like something Mummy would bake last minute for her daughter's fairy birthday party. Not a grown man's midday snack."

"One, I'm not a man, and two, who cares about how the food looks? The taste is all that matters. Is your masculinity so fragile that someone eating a cute cake beside you makes you uncomfortable? I think this reflects more on you than me."

"This is just another test," I said.

He smiled then ate it icing first like a toddler. "You aren't the only transmasculine person in Dunn. My pronouns are he/him or they/them. So you haven't been misgendering me this whole time."

"Why are we really here?" I said.

"You need a grimoire and your own supplies."

"A grimoire?"

"Every mage has at least one book to store their spells. Usually they buy or make one at each life stage. Elijah would have gotten one as a marriage gift."

"Make it? I don't have to make it, do I?"

"No. They're most effective when handmade by the user, but most people don't have the time or desire to learn the skill."

"As much as I love books, I can't say I've ever wanted to hand bind one," I said.

"There are different levels to it from binding pages to making the paper," Cory said. "It's really fascinating. The best Spell Crafters weave spells into the pages and make incredible works of art. I'll show you sometime. There's a collection at the Agency."

"A collection of grimoires?"

"Donations from dead employees and tomes they've brought from academic institutions. Though Beckham University has the best collection outside of Nate Island if they're to be believed."

"Is this a magic town?"

"Yes."

"How many magic towns are there?"

"Four affiliated with Nate Island. Dunn, Beckham, Oak Breeze and Indigo. Dunn was the original Nate Island settlement," Cory said.

"Can I get one of the suits you lot run around in? They seem suspiciously versatile," I said.

"We can stop at the tailor shop."

"Is that why people need permission to live here?"

"Yes."

"So it's like Morse Bay?" I said.

"Morse Bay is an alchemist town. How do you know about that, anyhow?" Cory said.

"Eli and I were taken there to fix your boss' handiwork."

"From what I recall, any damage done to you was self-inflicted."

"Your motherfucker of a boss tried to kill my husband."

"How many times do I have to go over this? They tasked us with abducting him for questioning. Killing a Lacy would be more trouble than it's worth."

"What exactly do you think Eli has done?"

"What do I think Elijah Lacy has done? It's an extensive list," Cory said. "He has this thing, you see, where he runs around in a cream and silver domino mask and matching 1700s dandy-inspired silk suit like a tacky fifties comic book villain and commits crime."

"Because you're one to judge," I said.

"I'm not a criminal," Cory said.

I took a sip of my energy drink. "Of course not."

"What was that? I can't hear you when you talk into your drink." Cory carefully used hand sanitiser and a paper napkin to clean the cake crumbs from his fingers. "It sounded like you would like to keep beating that dead horse. I get it. My boss is your new nemesis."

"Today wasn't quite how I imagined it, okay?" I said.

"Surprisingly enough, people are multidimensional and have lives that don't revolve around you." He pulled a thermos from his bag and poured some pink, floral-scented tea leaves into it. "Would you rather be running for your life from a demon? I'll tell my favourite demons that you want to get off."

"You're not the sassy smart arse you think you are."

"I know. I'm a total loser. I try very hard to be weird because I want to be seen as interesting."

"I want to know who she is," I said.

"Who?" He seemed startled by the change of topic.

"The ghost on the corner of Short and Main Street." I frowned at him. "Did she ever try to hijack your mind?"

"Yes. It was quite annoying, like a mosquito buzzing around my ear."

"Why wasn't she considered a greater threat?"

"Because we don't have the time and resources to take care of every issue. She was only a threat to the five Death or Life Mages who live in Dunn."

"You said you were practically languishing in boredom like a Victorian heroine," I said.

"I can only do the jobs my bosses assign to me. If I try to play hero outside of work and someone gets hurt, that's on me."

I looked down at his cup of tea. "Are you going to share?"

"I thought pink tea would be too feminine for your masculine sensibilities." He took a long sip from his handpainted clay cup. I didn't understand how he carried the thing around without breaking it and its matching saucer.

Magic.

It was always magic.

I had to remember it existed; most people who would want to hurt me from now on would have no trouble remembering.

I placed my empty water bottle beside his thermos.

He sighed and poured some tea into my bottle.

8

After Cory left me at my car, I drove home for dinner before returning to collect my things from my desk at the library. I didn't want to see Mrs Gregory's smug face. When I was a child, she laughed at me when I said I was going to be a librarian. I wasn't going to give her the satisfaction of looking into my eyes now that she had won. She'd never wanted me employed in the first place.

It was dark when I walked from the hall towards Herald Park to put my bags in the car. I shook by the time I reached the edge of Herald Park. A small wooden footbridge over the river, hidden from view, would take me to the parking lot at the back of the town hall. The light from the parking lot faded with each step.

I was alone in the dark park. With every step I took, I expected to come face-to-face with a knife-wielding assailant.

I inserted the key in the lock and let myself in. I closed the door so quickly I almost shut it on my pants leg. I'd still be welcome, right? I knew now there had to be magic guarding the place.

Fifteen minutes later I wrapped my arms tighter around the two boxes that held my things as I walked from the safety of the asphalt of the town hall staff parking lot and onto the short gravel path that ran between the hall and the bridge over the creek between the hall and park.

"Lovely night for a stroll in the creepy park."

I screamed and almost fell over the bridge's knee-high railing. The only thing that saved me was a firm grip on my arm.

I spun around and hit the guy who spoke to me with my key-armed hand. For a sick second, I thought he would let me fall into the river below when the end of my keys hit his arm and his grip loosened. When I took in the red of his suit, I tried to pull myself free and jump into the river.

"We need to talk about what you just did." He dragged me from the bridge to a spot on the bank and spun me around to face him.

"Addicts shoot up here and meet with their dealers. I hardly think it's the place." I met his eyes. "How about another day?"

"You know, most of that bullshit is just to keep kids in at night. You can't tell me that's why you're so scared."

"What the fuck are you doing here?"

"I deplore a pretty mouth being used in such a crude way."

"Oh, for shitting gods fuck." I took a step back and almost fell backwards down the bank. He grabbed the front of my shirt to keep me from falling. After I recovered my footing, I pointed a finger at him. "You are the most annoying arsehole I've ever met, Cory Corvin."

He put a finger to my mouth and pointed to his red ski mask. "Shhh. It's supposed to be a secret."

"What do you want from me?"

"To make sure you're not an evil Death Mage named Nox."

"I just needed to get some stuff from my old place of employment."

"By walking through a park you're terrified of?"

"Just leave me be. This has nothing to do with Nox."

"Hang on." He flicked a device and turned back to me.

"What was that?" I tried to get a better look at the object as he slipped it back up his sleeve.

"At least four other groups are watching you. It gives us some privacy," he said. "It looks suspicious, a decent boy like you coming to a place like this."

"Four other groups? They'll see you."

"We're still in a blind spot."

"You were talking before."

"There's an enchantment on my mask that only allows someone to hear me if I want them to. I also used a Teleportation Mage to teleport to this spot so no one would see me." He focused on me. "I can't help but think you keep changing the topic."

"You said you'd answer any question. I want you to tell me who is following me."

"If you tell me what I want to know."

I nodded.

"I'm here because I'm on a team following your hubby and his extracurricular activities. We followed him as he tracked you down. He must have wondered where you were."

"How did he find me?"

"I don't know. You might want to get that checked out."

"Eli wouldn't believe the rumours about me." I heard my voice shake.

"You don't sound so sure about that."

"Who else?"

"The head detective on the case investigating the claims you're Nox and the head of the team looking into the demon that almost killed you. Plus their backup," he said. "The Templar group in charge of the Nox investigation. Last group? No idea. I know they aren't from our side."

"This is mental." I waved my hand towards the park where I assumed they were. "Don't you lot have anything better to do?"

"Not really. Dunn's rather sleepy."

"Well, I know what I'm getting you for Christmas."

"What?" he said.

"A TV," I said.

"Ha ha."

I knew I'd won when I saw his lips twitch as he tried to hold back a smile.

He clicked his fingers and pointed towards me. "Tell me something useful or I'll have to arrest you."

"I was there when they broke into that basement," I said. These people were investigating the same case, which would irritate Dominguez and maybe get her off my back. "Nox and a mage in green that made portals. Called himself Dark Matter."

He nodded.

"I was honestly just down there slowly working and slacking off," I said.

When I turned back to look at him, he was gone and I was standing in the cold park alone. I felt a little safer with all the eyes I knew were on me as I walked back to my car.

When I arrived at work the next day, Cory took me to an empty office on the floor I'd been led to the day before. The office held only a desk, a rusty filing cabinet, three battered chairs and a yellowed computer with a CRT monitor. A printer, furniture catalogue and a pile of textbooks were on my desk. Taped on the front of the furniture catalogue was a note from Grandfather: *Pick something nice and get studying.* Below the sentence was a schedule for classes that didn't start until July. They had pressed the restart button on the life I'd barely begun.

I ducked under the desk and hooked the power board into the wall. After a long couple of seconds, an image flickered to life on the screen. Though the office looked clean, it was clear no one had worked there for a long time. In the top desk drawer, I found a dusty desk phone, ceramic coaster and a pen holder filled with long-dried pens. One pen was a freebie for presenters at the 2003 Beckham Job Fair. The login screen in front of me was for a version of Linux. The last account signed into the computer was ccorvin.

Cory had set up the printer.

I logged into the computer and opened my email.

The email from Cory was comprised of a single wink emoji and several attached forms relevant to writing a report about the exorcism of Nora Rowe.

Forms that had to be handwritten.

The directions document clarified that only printed forms filled with the worker's own hand would be accepted. Beside my mouse was a fresh packet of pens.

I threw the furniture catalogue in the bin. The last thing I needed right now was my colleagues seeing me get new furniture.

There was a knock at the open door and I turned to glance at it.

"Nice office."

I looked up at the sound of a woman's voice. I had expected Cory, Grandfather or maybe Mason. The colour drained from my face as Dominguez and her partner Hawking walked in.

What did these people want now?

She sat down across from me and placed an open file on the desk between us. "I'd like you to work with me. I believe you are a smart but inexperienced man with friends in prominent places. You have a bright future if you can move past the criminal element that you have found yourself embroiled with."

"Criminal element?" I had to force myself not to hiss the words. Gran wasn't a criminal element; she just wanted to live a peaceful life practising magic on her own terms.

Surely they couldn't honestly suspect me of being Nox.

"We know you've been illegally trained in Death Magic. You should tell us who opened that portal and let the thing that killed those kids into our reality." Of course they knew. I wasn't here for the fun of it. They had caught me out.

Grandfather had caught me out.

What was she trying to prove? I grabbed the wrist about to turn the page and looked into her wide hazel eyes. "I have no idea who opened that portal. It was like that when I got there."

She made a *tsk* sound and yanked herself away from my grip. "You have balls, I'll give you that." Her voice was just as mocking as Cory's, only the humour had been replaced with hostility. "You might just survive your future career if you choose the right path. The only reason we are giving you a chance is because you can't be expected to know any better."

"There's one thing I need you to look into as a woman of the law. Have I ever shown a propensity to do the crime you're accusing me of? It's not a crime to know something I shouldn't. That's why I was offered this job. You can't prove I aided in or committed any crime regarding that house because I didn't. I was a victim, the same as those kids. In the wrong place at the wrong time. Only I had a number I could call for help. Why would I stick around and not just flee if I knew who opened that door?" I said.

"The sharks are circling and you need an out," Hawking said.

Dominguez slowly glanced around the room. "The lame-duck act won't work with me; I've dealt with people worse than you."

"Has anyone ever told you that you sound like a TV stereotype?" I said.

"What's more stereotypical than a black-clad, masked Death Mage named Nox?"

These people honestly ran around in masks like discount supervillains from the Comics Code era? If I weren't being accused of multiple accounts of murder, I'd laugh. If it hadn't resulted in the shit being bashed out of Eli, it would be funny.

"Nothing to say?" she said.

I heard a chain jingle as she ran a hand along the handcuffs attached to her belt. She'd adjusted her unbuttoned tan blazer so I could see them. As I looked away from her hand, she met my gaze.

"There's nothing I could say to you."

"Why did you leave the clinic without being formally discharged? Did you know I was coming to question you?" Dominguez asked.

"I felt suffocated and alone. Ask anyone, I run away when things get stressful," I said. It was not the desired personality trait of a master criminal.

"What were you doing in Dunn Town Hall last night?"

"Cleaned out my desk without being forced to look at Mrs Gregory's smug face."

"I'll find out what it really was."

"Go for it," I said.

Dominguez stood. "It is a crime in the magical world to know something you shouldn't. We have used knowledge of magic as a justifiable reason to have some unconnected mortals executed. If you refused to work with us, we could have taken you by force. Ask your grandfather about his deadline."

"Just knowing about magic is a crime?" I said.

"Yes. If you were an unconnected mortal, the person who told you would be executed and if your memory couldn't be wiped, you'd join them. Remember that before you let your traitorous tongue waggle. Tell someone you shouldn't about magic, and we put you to *sleep* forever. You'd get a public trial first, but that's usually just a formality designed to allow everyone to see you for the person you really are." She left the office without looking back at me. Her lapdog gave me a smug glare before he tailed her into the hall.

I threw the pen I was holding across the room. I'd had enough of this bullshit. After giving her plenty of time to leave, I stood up, left the office and headed for the cafeteria.

After I grabbed my lunch, I noticed Eli sat alone with a distant look on his face as he looked through the wide glass window. It faced the ocean, though we were too far away to see it. I could almost imagine what it looked like. Maybe I could see a speck of blue in the distance. I blinked my eyes again and it was gone. From the hill the building stood on, I could see the entire valley that held Dunn. The houses and livelihoods of over nine thousand people took up an oddly small amount of space.

I walked over to Eli, who didn't notice me until I sat down. His eyes were a kaleidoscope of colour in the early afternoon light. The way they managed to be three colours at once had always taken my breath away. In the afternoon light, the golden-brown was the most predominant colour in them. Today, something in his gaze made my heart ache. Part of me wanted to find the person who'd done this to him and punch them in the face.

I smiled at him. "Hey."

"Hey." He smiled back. It was a small, forced, 'I'm unhappy but I smiled because I love you' smile.

I placed my hand on his and met his eyes. I hadn't talked to him at all the night before; I'd been asleep when he got home, and he was awake and gone before my alarm. "Are you okay?"

"I had another talk with my suited friends last night."

"What?"

"It's okay. They were a little nicer. Daddy was off somewhere else."

"Daddy?"

"The white-suited prick who broke my freaking nose."

"Oh," I said. "What happened?"

"They want me to spy on you and they'll forget about the potion they claim I stole."

"Spy on me?" I bit my tongue before I could tell him I was dancing to Cory's whims. Cory, who was taking directions from our white-suited *friend*. "What are we going to do?"

"I'll spend every night with you until they get bored. A creative way to keep me out of trouble too. When that Nox prick strikes while I'm watching over you, the surveillance teams will have no choice but to admit that you aren't some kid-murdering psychopath."

"Do they even know if that demon thing was actually Nox's fault?" I said.

Eli shrugged.

"Did you know?" I said.

"About what?"

"The Nox thing?"

"That they were accusing you officially? Not until last night," Eli said.

"How did you know?" I said.

"Someone I thought I could call a friend told me."

"A friend?"

"It doesn't matter. I'm just a stupid fool everyone is trying to use in their political games."

"Don't talk like that."

"It's true."

I pinched my leg under the table. Why was I so stupid? Cory wasn't looking out for my best interests. It was the whole playing-into-that-attraction thing again. He'd flat-out stated he was manipulating my needy arse. He knew I wouldn't cheat on Eli, but he also knew I was desperate for a friend. The only people I hung out with were Eli, June and our families. A bubbly, pretty, nerdy friend who liked books and tea was the perfect match for me. Someone I'd be desperate to hang out with; an approachable mentor figure a few years older.

I needed to know what Cory knew. A thought overcame me. I could log in to his computer and look at his emails and find out what he knew about both Eli and me.

I walked to the end of the hall where Cory's office and the morgue stood. I carefully pushed open the door and let myself in.

Thankfully, I was faced with a pastel yellow hall rather than someone dissecting a body. I took a deep breath to still my beating heart. I walked down the hall and followed the sign that pointed to Cory Corvin's office.

If they got a warrant and looked through my and Eli's things, they might find enough to incriminate Eli for his own crimes. Access to our house meant access to accidentally looking through Eli's stuff. My loyalty to Eli came first, even if it made me look more guilty. I couldn't let the Agency use me to take him down.

I smiled as I walked down the hall.

I wanted to piss Cory off.

His disinterest in me meant he wouldn't come looking for me in my office. He had pushed those forms onto my plate to get rid of me for the day. While that fucker was distracting me, the rest of his gang had been terrorising Eli and his boss had been off doing God knows what. How was I supposed to prove my innocence if they never gave me the chance? Every time I crafted an excellent defence of my actions, the Templars, detectives like Andrea Dominguez or someone else pulled the rug out from under me and levelled a new accusation.

How the fuck did they expect me to trust them?

Even Cory had pretended to believe me so he could be the one who unmasked the evil Death Mage. I guess he wanted bonus points with his boss.

Could their primary intention for going after Eli be getting to me? Was that potion thing a trap?

Had I played right into their plan when I revealed my powers?

The way Cory had acted at Nora Rowe's house when I got angry, he was ready to fight for his life. He saw me as a potential threat. Did he believe I was bluffing about the extent of my abilities?

That the way I used the Short Street ghost was a distraction so they'd think I was powerless? Cory's words slipped back into my mind: *'If I want something from someone, I use magic to sense what actions arouse the person I'm talking to. If you're even reasonably attractive, you can use it to your advantage when working with people. It's a subtle manipulation.'* I couldn't pull off Cory's brand of masculine leaning femme fatale, but if he wanted to believe I was playing him, I would use the idiot's gambit. I was willing to play the gullible idiot and sacrifice my reputation to get out of this in one piece.

I walked into Cory's empty office and closed the door behind me. I went straight to the top drawer of his desk. If I was right about the person he was, he'd have his unnecessarily complicated password written somewhere. Even if he'd memorised it, there'd be a forgotten notebook, Post-it or slip of paper with it. I carefully looked at every piece of paper in his desk drawers. The contents made little sense; most of it was spells, information about cases I didn't know about and medical jargon. Notebooks filled with information I didn't have the knowledge to fully understand.

I touched a thick, softcover A5 book at the bottom of the drawer and instantly pulled my hand away as pain shot up my arm. A spell had burnt the tips of my fingers. The pain and bright redness of the digits made me second-guess trying to touch the thing again.

I wondered where the nearest sink was, then realised the only sinks would be in the morgue.

I wiped the tears from my eyes with my sleeve.

I'd have to push through the pain.

The leatherbound book was obviously a grimoire. The leather was a dark mauve, and it was held closed with a long braided piece of tan suede. The edges of the pages were painted with a metallic black colour that reminded me of the suit he'd worn the day before.

The longer I looked at the book, the harder it was to pull my eyes and thoughts from it.

It was really the most beautiful book I'd ever seen.

I reached out to touch the book; the part of my mind that knew something was wrong had lost the battle with my curiosity.

What was wrong with me?

I forced my shaky arm back to my side, my burnt fingers still outstretched towards the book. I could feel a headache slowly building in the back of my head, my eyes dry from staring at the book.

My heart pumped so erratically I could feel each beat throughout my body.

"Didn't anyone teach you manners?" Cory grabbed my shoulders and turned me away from the book.

I felt my face turn red as I was forced to look in his eyes.

He pulled his glove off and dunked his thumb in a small pot of black ink from his satchel. He placed the soaked thumb onto the middle of my forehead, drawing a simple sigil as he said a few quiet words. He gripped my chin firmly to stop me from looking back at the book.

The urge to look at the grimoire slowly faded as he held me. I was captivated by the way his nails dug into my skin.

A weight I didn't even notice had been wrenched from my mind.

He let go of me.

The headache slipped away as I looked at the grey carpet, unable to face him.

What the hell?

My nose was assaulted with the potent smell of the alcohol wipes he carefully used to clean the ink from my forehead.

Sometimes he looked at me like he'd lost me behind an unbreakable glass wall.

It unnerved me more than it should have. The cynical part of my mind reasoned it had something to do with what I'd forgotten, the gaps in my memory.

He was both familiar and unfamiliar.

Maybe that was why I had a hard time trusting him.

When would we have had the chance to meet before?

"What made you think it was a wise idea to go through a mage's things?" Cory said.

"I don't know."

"I think you do." He looked down at me through his glasses; his arms crossed over his chest.

"I came to visit you," I said.

"And you just developed an overwhelming urge to go through my desk?" Cory pushed his glasses down slightly and massaged the bridge of his nose. "You honestly think there wouldn't be security measures in a magic user's desk? What the hell is wrong with you?"

"I don't know."

"Glad we've established that because I don't know what's wrong with you either. What unhinged idea have you come up with this time?"

"Unhinged? You're the two-timing arsehole who's working for the people trying to get my husband to spy on me."

"He told you?" Cory said.

"Yeah. He told me," I said. "Were you there when they abducted him?"

"I was making a deal with you while they talked to him."

"I just wanted proof that you honestly don't think I'm Nox before I trust you."

He waved a hand towards his desk. "How does this get you that?"

"I was angry."

He looked down at me for a long time. I could almost see the thoughts rushing behind his emerald eyes.

"I'll talk to my boss and get the others to back off Elijah."

I nodded. "Let's go have some tea then. Lead the way." I waved my arm towards the door.

His eyes widened as he saw my fingers.

I looked down at my hand. "I'd forgotten about that. The pain went away when you cast that spell on me."

"Let me fix it before it causes permanent damage. I should have realised you would have touched it." He walked over to the sage filing cabinet behind his dark mahogany desk and pulled a large first-aid bag from the top of it.

9

Cory tapped his fingers on the layer of plastic protecting the diner's tablecloths. He hadn't said a word to me since we left the office. He sat across the table from me and stared me down over his sugary flat white, a sour look on his face.

I looked him in the eyes. "I know you want to say something, so you might as well say it."

A bitter laugh escaped his mouth. "I wish I wasn't being dragged into your orbit again."

He spoke the words so quietly I wasn't sure I heard correctly.

He clicked his tongue, took a deep breath and looked down into his milk froth-covered drink. "I hate how you have no respect for other people's boundaries and think your problems are more important than everyone else's."

"Excuse me," I said. "But you don't even know me."

"Ed owes me so much for this shit." Cory poked the table so hard the perfectly manicured but bare nail of his right index finger broke.

"What does my grandfather have to do with this?"

He stared at me with hard eyes until I broke eye contact and took a long sip of my black tea.

"Someone needs to be honest with you about your behaviour, but shaping you into the person I want you to be makes me feel dirty," Cory said.

"Why do you even think that's your job?"

"They made me your mentor because everyone else is too scared of you to work with you," Cory said. "And it's my office you broke into."

"I just wanted to know what you knew about the Agency spying on me."

Cory placed a finger over his lips. "That's not something you should talk about here."

I looked around the diner that had been caught somewhere between the golden age of the fifties and the late nineties. The family who owned it only ran it because they felt obligated to the community. I wasn't sure how they made money with a ten-dollar all-you-can-eat buffet breakfast in this day and age.

Was this place bugged, or was it the workers who were spies?

Could they make money selling information to the Agency?

The diner had been here since the town had the power to only allow those with magic and their families to live in town limits.

"You want me to respect your boundaries?" I poured more tea from the lilac pot into my cup.

"What were you trying to do in my office?"

"Log in to your emails."

"You were searching through my desk for what? A piece of paper with my password written on it? Christ's sake, Dexter, this isn't one of your books. People don't leave clues out for little rats to find."

"Little rat! We're practically the same height."

Cory rolled his eyes and downed the last of his coffee. "Pity they couldn't have given me several more shots of coffee. I need them to deal with you."

"Pleasant as always, Mr Corvin," I said.

"It's Doctor Corvin, and you're not so pleasant to deal with either. I wasn't the one rifling through your office and acting like a spoilt brat after being caught." Cory stood up and grabbed his jacket from where he had placed it over the back of the chair. He looked down at me through his glasses and threw a ten-dollar note at me like I was a two-bit whore. "The change better end up in the tip jar."

"I don't need your money," I said.

"There's no way I'm letting you pay for my coffee." Cory threw his jacket over his elbow and stormed from the diner without another word.

Hawking sat down in the seat Cory had vacated with a smile on his face. Strands from his greased, dark auburn brown hair had started to slip from their hold and sit messily against his pale sweaty forehead. "Even your babysitter doesn't want to deal with you, Lacy."

I looked down into the tea at my reflection and ignored him. I only looked up slightly when I heard the chair across from me make a bone-scraping creak. He was sitting in the chair so it only stood on its two back legs. The aluminium legs strained under the weight of a man who was average in height but had a thick build with sculpted muscle.

He leant back in the chair and smirked. His undone black blazer flowed around him like a cape. "He is right, you know. You are a spoilt brat."

My hands shook with anger as I poured the last of my tea into my cup, the spout of the teapot clinking against the porcelain so loudly it cut through the quiet chatter of the diner's other patrons. For a few seconds, it felt like everyone was looking at us. Staring me down in one of my safe places, a place I always knew I could come and feel comfortable. That sense of security had slowly slipped from me since the clouded glass between me and the magic world had been broken. My life spiralled more and more out of control as I picked each piece of glass from my eyes.

"What do you want from me?" I said.

"For you to answer for your crimes," Hawking said.

"Pretty cliché for a cop," I said. "Do you practice that line in front of the mirror?"

He grabbed his metal straw and took a long, hard sip of the green juice he'd brought with him. A small, dark part of me hoped he would chip a tooth with the way he ground his teeth. "You act like you're all for the average person, but you're still a pig," I said.

"You act like I had a choice," he said. "Families like yours pick the life path for the rest of us while their own children get away with some of the sickest shit imaginable."

I paused as I reached to grab the money Cory had left on the table. "What is that supposed to mean?"

He picked up the paper remains of one of Cory's sugar packets to play with it. "Did you break yourself, or did someone else break you?"

"Break me?" I said.

He pointed to his right temple and raised a surprisingly well-groomed eyebrow.

"Stop it. Just tell me what everyone is keeping from me." I snapped my mouth shut when I realised how loud I'd said that.

"I'm not going to be held to that responsibility." He spoke in a low, measured voice. "If upper command is wrong about you or taking me for a fool, I'm not going to be responsible for what you'll do when you find out."

"Ten corrupt cops and one good cop is eleven corrupt cops," I said.

He sighed. "Read that on the Internet?"

"I've had enough of this."

"All you have to do is tell me what you know, and I'll probably be able to leave you alone. Dominguez and I both," Hawking said.

"But not the Templars," I said.

"You did something to piss off someone higher than your grandfather and his friends who coddle you," Hawking said. "And don't look at me like that. I moved to Beckham for high school, I honestly only knew you by reputation until I was assigned this case."

"So you don't really know me," I snapped.

"I know people like you, and that's enough." The legs of his seat hit the lino floor with a surprising loud crack as he decided to sit like an adult and not the six-year-old class clown who hadn't yet had the chair legs kicked out from under him by a bully.

For a few seconds he looked shocked, as though I'd caused his chair to right itself. His pale, sparsely freckled face started to turn red as he looked at me open-mouthed and hard-eyed, his teeth bared halfway between a shock and a snarl.

Wait, had someone done that?

A man walked up behind Hawking and placed a hand on the chair. "For you to have the integrity you claim, Hawking, you'd have more respect for other people's possessions."

The sandy-haired man was in his early to mid-thirties but had an almost timeless appearance and looked like sex on legs. He wore a pair of tight light grey slacks and a black dress shirt with a high neck covered by a simple grey blazer. It was far too hot for the outfit with the diner's heating, but I couldn't see a single trace of perspiration on him. He had an atmosphere around him that drew me to him even though a voice of reason in the back of my mind told me not to relax around him.

"Thornton." Hawking clenched his teeth so tightly I almost didn't understand what he'd said.

"If it's such a tragedy you're a cop, why are you playing one off-duty? Go back to your family. Your mummy is getting worried," Thornton said.

I looked over at the table Hawking had been sitting at. It held five people: one young man looked close to his age, a middle-aged couple, an older woman and a teenaged girl. All shared his dark auburn brown hair, pale blue eyes and various versions of his strong but stocky build.

He'd come to hassle me while he was having dinner with his family. What the fuck? Bowling for Soup was right when they sang "High School Never Ends." I felt like I was sixteen again and my mum had asked if some arsehole from school who'd come to bother me was my friend.

Hawking's mum looked over at my table with a worried look on her face as though I currently had her baby boy pinned down on the table as I used a butter knife to dissect him.

Not a bad idea to entertain.

The man who'd walked up to the table, Siegfried Thornton, the head of the almost-extinct Thornton family, gave me a revolted look like I was dog shit he'd stood in.

Had he just heard my thoughts?

I'd heard of the man and the Thornton family. I'd been told to stay away from them because they were social pariahs. Even though they were a founding family, they were to be avoided. Now Siegfried himself had approached me in public where everyone could see. I looked at both men across from me, sighed and stood up. I didn't need this heat, and I didn't need to sit here and take whatever they wanted to hassle me with. Getting more information out of Hawking wasn't worth it.

I stuffed Cory's note in the tip jar at the counter and paid with my card. I walked from the diner without looking back at my table.

When I walked into the parking lot, I remembered Cory had driven his car and left me here. I didn't stop in case Thornton decided to walk out of the diner after me. I pulled my jacket on and started to walk towards home at an angle that would obscure me from anyone who walked out of the diner. It was still light and the five kilometres wasn't far to walk on a nice, clear evening.

On the edge of the town's business district was a small rundown stationary store. It was in the first emporium built in the town, the original general store. I turned from the main path and up the worn wooden stairs onto the veranda, also made of a worn grey wood. The shop was painted with a blueish grey green that would have been made using arsenic when the building first opened. I assumed it had been repainted since then, but the faded paint looked almost old enough to have lead in it.

The two large shop windows held a collection of the type of fine writing instruments and papers that littered the desks of the old families and the new money that had entered town with the expensive housing estate they were building on the north edge of town. I bought a spiral bound notebook, plastic folder and pack of simple blue plastic pens.

I left the path along the main road and walked into the state forest at the edge of town limits. It was late, but I needed to make my next move somewhere private. Cory was right about the diner having too many eyes and ears. Once I was past the tree line, I ran until I reached the first fork in the paths. I took the longest one, which ran back towards town for a kilometre. No one following me would expect me to go this way.

My light brown wingtip shoes sank into the mud as I wound my way through the bush I'd grown up in. Even though the Lacy and Arkwright houses were on different sides of town, they both backed onto this state forest.

I closed my eyes and breathed in the cool air of a mid-autumn afternoon. The birds and insects that littered the bush were a choir that propelled my walk. I knew this place well enough not to fall off a cliff if it got dark before I started home. Thinking of the Lacy's house as home was still odd.

The scent of the eucalyptus trees on the cool breeze refreshed me as mud caked on the bottom of the useless shoes I'd been made to wear to look professional. The only artificial sounds out here were my breaths, the sound of my hard leather satchel as it hit my side and the scrunch of the plastic bag I held.

As a kid, I'd been terrified of being alone—any place where I couldn't hear another human or another human couldn't hear me if I screamed. I had been so fearful of ghosts, cannibal witches in the woods and fae that I could barely function. As an adult, I revelled in the freedom of my own private world.

The Echo was a small valley at the end of a river with a waterfall and a pool. Only a handful of the locals from the old families knew about it.

It was a three-kilometre hike, two of them downhill from the Lacy's house. Once I reached the small clearing, I sat on my usual large, smooth rock, ripped open the pack of pens and placed the notebook on my lap. I had to investigate who was framing me and discover what everyone was hiding from me. If even Hawking wouldn't tell me, it had to be bad.

Did it have something to do with the gaps in my memory?

It was a little silly to be writing my thoughts down, but I had to have my thoughts in order before I asked Eli and Kat to help.

I was sick of being a passive observer to my own doom. I needed a good case to get Eli to let the truth slip. Someone had got to him and told him that telling me the truth would hurt me. I needed him to understand it wouldn't.

The only people working in the Agency's interest had to be the Templars and Detective Dominguez. Maybe Hawking could be convinced to help me if he was the unwilling passenger of the Agency and Nate Island's agenda he claimed to be.

I tapped at the paper, leaving a spot of blue ink. Cory had promised to tell me the truth, but his connection to me and how he seemed to know me was something he danced around.

I could bring both to my cause against the Agency if Cory was one of Grandfather's loyalists like he seemed to be.

If Cory was with Grandfather, there was no way he'd truly believe in the Templar's mission.

All this left the big question: why was the Agency trying to frame me for Nox's crimes? Were they doing all this to get to Gran? Was I an easy way to make her seem like a danger to the public? So, they could point to the dangerous criminal she taught magic to.

This wasn't about me at all. I was just a pawn in a bigger game between Gran, Grandfather, the Morse Bay alchemists and Nate Island.

I sealed the pens and notebook in the airtight plastic folder I'd found and buried it in the sand under a rock a good distance from the one I favoured.

As I lay back on my rock to watch the light vanish from the sky and the first stars appear, I responded to a text from Eli.

10

I was always fascinated by how quickly the light fled at dusk. As though one could close their eyes for a minute to steady themselves, and the process of sunset to darkness would be complete. It was dark by the time Eli reached me; the moon hadn't yet crested the edge of the valley I lay in.

I saw the light from the strong electric lantern he held before I heard him on the rough track up the hill behind me.

He sighed as he sat down in the river sand in front of me. His eyes were almost brown in the dim light and went straight to my mud-caked shoes.

"I guess we've both had a long day." Eli curled his knees around himself so he could rest his chin on them.

"Cory took me to the diner for afternoon tea to reprimand me, then got all pissy and left me there without a car," I said.

Eli ran his fingers through his hair, closed his eyes and muttered something that sounded like "heaven help me." His head snapped up, and he forced me to meet his eyes. "What did you do?"

"Tried to hack into his emails." I pulled at a lose string on the end of my black blazer sleeve.

"Why?"

"I wanted to know what information he has on me," I said. "It's obvious he has been tasked to spy on me."

Eli nodded.

"Cory needs to trust me to believe I'm innocent and I ruined that."

"Let Cory believe you fall for his crap. Play the naïve fool blinded by his attraction, and it'll play on his heartstrings a little. He's a honey pot. The goal is to make you spill your guts to him. I say we give as good as we get."

"I don't know how to play sexy," I said. "And he's already using my attraction to him to his advantage."

"Sexy to a guy like that is a submissive bloke who finds him attractive. I've seen the way he looks at your arse, he's queer and attracted to you. Just act desperate for him."

"He knows I'm loyal to you."

"I'll make hints I don't mind sharing. It's not cheating if you have permission."

I gave him a confused look; he didn't mean what I thought he meant. Did he? "Don't mind sharing what?"

"Your arse. As long as I get a slice of Cory's."

"Is there something I should know?"

"If you ever get the overwhelming urge to spread your legs for him or anyone else, invite me along," Eli said. "If he tries anything and you're comfortable with it, play along."

"Elijah, this is serious."

"I know." He looked me in the eyes, a firm expression on his face.

"I'll think about it," I said.

"How about we spend the night here and have a break from other people?" Eli said.

"That could be nice, if we didn't have to go back home first," I said.

"Don't worry, I brought supplies." Eli jumped up, a wide smile on his face as he went to collect the camping supplies he'd hidden behind a tree at the start of the path. They included a double sleeping bag; a cooler filled with food, water and a six pack of cold beers and a small tent.

I peeled my shoes and socks off then threw them onto the sand.

"I need a swim." He stripped the rest of his clothes off and waded into the water. After a minute under the water, he slid into a back float with a loud sigh. It wasn't worth reminding him we had a pool back at the house; he was as transfixed by this place as I was.

"I don't know how you can stare at this water and not want to hop in," Eli said.

"Coming." I stripped down to my boxers and swum out to him. The chill of the cold water clawed its way under my skin to numb my limbs.

"Boxers? Who do you think is going to see you?" Eli said.

"You never know," I said.

"As it's only you and me here, do you think you could forego the coverage just this once?"

"I just don't like the idea of swimming naked in a public place."

"It's weird. The only person within ten kilometres of you is me and I've seen you naked plenty of times."

"You never know who could come along."

"Then they'll get a show. You're naïve if you think they aren't expecting it. I'm pretty sure you're the only person to have ever worn swimmers here." Eli smiled, sure of himself, and stepped back far enough to lose his footing and slip under the water. His next words had been about to leave his open mouth. I laughed as he resurfaced, coughing and spluttering. As he recovered, his eyes landed on me. The look of sure determination returned to his face. Before I could take a step towards the bank, he tackled me and pushed me under the water.

As we ate dinner, I stared at Eli, wondering how I would bring up the idea of asking Kat for information. She worked for the newspaper, so she'd have some of the information I needed.

"You okay?" Eli took a swig of his beer.

"I was thinking I could see what Kat knows about the Nox thing," I said.

Eli raised an eyebrow.

"The Agency must feed the newspaper information, right?"

"I guess." Eli looked away from me.

"I sent Cory a text on the way home and asked him to meet me at Kat's house tomorrow," I said. "I think if I'm open with him, he'll believe I'm innocent."

"You want me to come with you?" Eli dug his nails into the grass under us.

"Yes."

It was a long time before he looked up and answered me with a nod.

Cory was already waiting when we pulled up in front of Kat's house. He got out of his car and leaned in our passenger window when I wound it down.

"Morning," Eli greeted from the driver's seat with a smirk.

"Hey," Cory responded. He looked over his shoulder out of the corner of his eye. "Thank God, you finally made it. The curtain twitchers were about ready to call the cops."

I glanced at the window of the house behind him without making it obvious. "That's Mrs Gregory's house. She probably thinks she owns the street. Just ignore it."

"Really?" Cory said.

"Yes. I cleaned her gutters a few times."

Both Cory and Eli started laughing despite the early hour.

"What's so funny?"

"I can't imagine you'd be the type to do yardwork," Cory said.

"He's not, which is what makes it so bizarre." Somehow Eli had stopped laughing long enough to speak.

"I knew you two would gang up on me." I pulled on the car door handle, and Cory stood aside to let me out. I didn't turn back to check on the two people behind me who giggled like schoolgirls as I crossed the road to Kat's.

Kat looked at me like I'd grown a second head when she opened her front door to me. She wore an ankle-length floral nightgown more suited to a woman three times her age under a knee-length, obscenely fluffy, pink dressing gown. Her dark hair was so messy it had a massive knot on one side. She squinted as the light from the morning shone in her eyes.

She looked me up and down before sighing loudly, "morning, Kat, glad to see you at 8:30 on this bright and sunny day." She gave me a thin smile after she finished speaking.

I swallowed my guilt as I realised I'd woken her up. I looked down into her eyes. "I have an offer."

"Give me ten minutes to kick the boy toy out the back door and get dressed. He shouldn't stay overnight, but he's lazy." She shut the door in my face.

I opened a book up on my phone and started to read. It took the arseholes behind me three minutes to recover enough to walk to the door.

I still didn't know why the concept of me doing yardwork was so funny. At least they were getting along and not trying to tear each other's throats out like I feared when Eli suggested he come. How could Eli act so collected around someone who could have broken his nose?

They knew each other.

The thought caused me to become hyperaware of them as they made their way towards me.

They knew each other as Cory and Eli.

They wouldn't be this comfortable around each other otherwise.

Kat let us in ten minutes later, giving Cory a slight look of confusion. She wore grey jeans and a light green baggy tee shirt with her wet hair pulled back in a messy bun. She led us to the kitchen and started making her breakfast as we took seats around the table.

"Kat, this is Cory. He's working with us," I said.

"Not that I don't appreciate the visit, Dexter, but it's Saturday morning. What's this offer?"

"Eli has agreed to do that interview about the campaign if you help us with some research."

"Okay," Kat said.

"I'm being framed for a crime."

"Shouldn't the cops be involved in this?" Kat asked. "Who's framing you?"

"The Agency is blaming him for a crime he didn't commit," Cory replied.

"There's a woman who does the fact-checking for the local papers. Apparently, she inherited a vast collection of information that's been collected by her family for generations," Kat said. "Who all did the same job she does."

"That's the kind of super-weird shit I'm looking for," I said.

"Weird shit! You're worried about weird shit?" Kat said. "You just said you're being framed for a crime."

"They need to realise I'm too boring and weak to be Nox."

"Step back a bit. Who thinks you're Nox?" Kat said.

"Law enforcement and the creepy Templar fuckers," I said.

Cory gave me a sharp look.

"She works for an official magical newspaper, she knows about the little cult," I said. "I think everyone does."

"I know what a freaking dangerous cult the Nate Island Templars are. God, Dexter, I know you being Nox is laughable, but you need to take this a little more seriously. Where the hell would they get the idea that you're Nox, anyhow?"

"Nox and another guy called Dark Matter stole from a stash of magical artefacts, and I was the last known person in the area," I said.

"How do you know about that?" Kat said.

"I was in the basement when they broke in."

Cory sighed and ran a hand through his long dark hair before he stood up and walked over to the hall that led to the rest of Kat's house. "I need to find a room to scream in."

"You'll get used to it." She washed up her breakfast dishes. "Two doors down on the right."

"Where did he go?" I said.

Eli rolled his eyes and gave me that 'are you clueless' look.

"The bathroom, dumb arse. God, you're so dense," Kat said. "Can we trust him?"

"Yes," I said.

Kat nodded.

"I told June," Eli said.

"Excuse me?" I looked up at him.

"She's my best friend, I tell her everything," Eli added. "She wanted to know why I cancelled our plans today."

"You can't just go around telling everyone."

"You just told her." Eli waved his hand at Kat as Cory quietly walked back into the room.

"Okay, kids. I have a plan." Kat sat back down at the table. "One of you has to pay Aubrey Quinn with a favour in return for the information, because I'm not going to."

"A favour?" I said.

"She's from an old Beckham family. She doesn't need money if you want something from her; the only bargaining power is a favour," Kat said.

Both Eli and Cory looked at me, and Kat shook her head. "It has to be someone with the power to give something worth her time."

"I will," Cory said.

"What is it you do, exactly?" Kat asked.

"I'm the forensic pathology resident and assistant mortician for the Dunn Agency," Cory said.

"She'll want you in her pocket as payment for supplying the information."

"There has to be some other way," Eli said. "Are you sure we can't just write her a cheque?"

"I'll call her." Kat picked up her phone from the bench. "What was your name again?"

"Cory Corvin."

"Okay." Kat smiled and left the room.

"I thought we could investigate all day," I said.

As I was bidding Kat farewell, I felt her stick something in my back jean pocket; I finished hugging her goodbye like nothing had happened and left with Eli.

As soon as we got home, I locked myself in the bathroom and pulled the small slip of paper from my pocket. It contained a simple, straight-to-the-point message: *'ditch the Baggage and meet me on Cheshire Road.'* I smiled as I mushed the note into tiny pieces and pushed it down the drain. I knew the perfect way to ditch Eli; he hated chlorine in his hair. If we went swimming, he'd have to take a shower afterwards. I had to know what Kat's grand idea was.

11

I waited until Eli had his hair soaped up in the shower before I closed the bathroom door and yelled that I was going for a walk. The moment I was out of sight of the house, I sent Kat a text as I walked through the garden. Once I crossed into the national park next to the Lacy land, it was a ten-minute walk to the back road she wanted to meet me on.

"What is all this about?" I said as I hopped in her car.

"I needed to ditch your nannies."

"So we could what?"

"Investigate on our own. Neither of them seemed keen to do Aubrey a favour, so we'll go to the Thornton House. We'll find more information in that house than Aubrey could give us. Siegfried Thornton is a professional blackmailer."

"Are you telling me we're breaking into a house?"

"We're not going to take anything."

"Cory and Eli wouldn't be up for this."

"I know."

"Are you sure there's no one there?"

"I'm pretty sure Siegfried Thornton is out of town."

"Pretty sure?"

"I know someone who is really interested in sinking that ship, and I asked before I slipped that paper in your pocket."

"That sounds slightly unhinged, but I'm willing to take your word for it. Is that who you spoke to?"

"Yes. I'll contact Aubrey if we can't get the information we need here."

"Okay." I looked out the window. "If Eli and Cory find out about this, they'll skin us alive."

"You just said you went for a walk, right?"

"Yes."

"That's all he needs to know," Kat said.

"I guess. I promised there would be no more lies."

She gripped the steering wheel tighter as we made our way closer to Thornton House.

Thornton House was on the southern outskirts of Dunn on a hidden road fifteen kilometres outside of town limits. Thornton House was the third-oldest building in the area. It was also known as the Castle. It looked like one to anyone who hadn't seen an actual castle. It was a massive five-storey sandstone mansion. The house had been built in the mid-1800s when the area around Dunn belonged to seven wealthy landowners: the Arkwright, Lacy, Chesterfield, Thornton, Dalton, Carson and Dominguez families.

I could feel the energy radiating from it halfway down the unnecessarily long gravel driveway. I wasn't sure if I should enter a place like this at all. The Lacy and Arkwright houses were old, but they didn't have the bloody history of Thornton House.

Several people had been murdered in the home since the first bloodbath within its walls in 1887. The entire Thornton family in residence at the time, including their several children, had been brutally murdered; the oldest child was just seventeen. The only surviving member of the family was the eldest son, twenty-one-year-old Devin, who had been away at university. There were rumours about Devin's involvement in the event, but there was no proof. Almost everyone who'd lived in the house on and off since 1887 had suffered an untimely death. I'd even heard rumours about a cult that hated the Thornton family and wanted to drive them from town.

About a minute after the buzzing had built in the back of my brain, I felt nauseous. I knew what was coming when I felt the heart palpitations and shortness of breath. I forced Kat to stop the car and stood on the side of the road, hands on my knees, while my head spun as I took panicked breaths.

Back in the car, I kept my mind fixed on the number of stones on the first floor of the house.

"Are you okay?" Kat touched my shoulder with a concerned look creasing her features.

"I just need a minute." I rested my face in my hands to block out the light as I tried to calm down my brain. A lot of ghosts were in this house, but Jesus, I needed to get a grip.

I sat in my seat for a good ten minutes sipping at my water bottle before I felt well enough to walk into the house. I looked in the car mirror before I walked away from it. My tee shirt was noticeably soaked in sweat, and my face had paled. I ran a finger over the black bags under my eyes. I'd convinced myself that only I could see them, but now I knew everyone else could too. I gave my reflection a thin smile.

Kat had parked the car behind a line of bushes out of sight of the distant main road. Even if someone came down the lengthy drive, they wouldn't see the vehicle. We were on a back road only locals used. If someone saw her car, they'd assume it was Siegfried Thornton's.

Kat and I snuck around the back of the house.

My stomach dropped as she stepped on the first step of the back veranda.

"Follow everything I do and you'll be fine. My main magical ability is Retrocognition," she said.

"Retrocognition?" I said.

She shook her head. "Sometimes I forget that you're new to this. I can see the past. I'll know where any protection spells or traps have been placed. Just don't go anywhere unless I tell you it's safe."

"I trust you." I followed her into the house, hoping we wouldn't encounter any of the ghostly inhabitants I could feel behind its walls.

It wasn't long before we found their creepy portrait hall and I came face-to-face with a life-sized portrait of a child Siegfried and his family. Besides his parents, the painting had two other occupants: two baby girls who looked like twins. They had to be his sisters. I knew his parents were dead, but where were they? Did they live in this house? They couldn't be any older than me. Siegfried was about the same age as my older brothers. If he was around ten in the painting, that placed his sisters in their early twenties. Had they moved back here with him after their parents died? Even with the property prices here, I barely knew anyone my age who lived on their own unless they worked for the Agency or in an office in Beckham or Tallow. Lower property prices didn't matter to locals when wages reflected the lower cost of living.

Kat had only mentioned Siegfried when discussing the house. The Thornton family's wealth didn't mean Siegfried lived alone; it was normal for the offspring of founding families to live in their ancestral homes until marriage.

I wanted to bring up the possibility of someone else being in the house, but I also didn't want to look like a fool when Kat told me they didn't live here anymore. She might treat me like I was an idiot for not knowing the current status of the Thornton family. Siegfried's grandparents moved from town when his father was a kid. The house had been notoriously empty until Siegfried had moved in when I was in my early teens.

"I think we look in any room that looks like an office first."

"I'm not looking forward to going to the attic."

"You and me both. Don't touch the sets of armour."

"You have to be joking." I looked at the shiny silver suits of armour. They looked like stereotypical props from a tacky medieval or horror film: the possessed, hollow knights that followed the heroes through the haunted mansion.

"Hard metal objects with deadly weapons. They're perfect to cast an animation charm on."

I forced myself to take a shaky step forwards. "Okay."

"I'll tell you if anything is unsafe."

I nodded. I wouldn't investigate anything on my own; I refused to be the idiot who set off some kind of trap.

We found an office on the third floor that had clearly served that purpose for decades. Every receipt from their business, which I learnt was object enchantment, had been carefully catalogued in an adjoining room. Kat said it was safe as long as I didn't step on the threshold when leaving the room. *Take one big step when I enter or leave the room.* I repeated the thought inside my mind as I looked around the room. Kat had gone to find his personal office, hoping to gain an advantage with her extra freedom to move around.

I was flicking through the second draw of the filing cabinet when I heard a gasp.

A wide-eyed young man stood in the doorway and looked straight at me.

Fuck.

The piece of honey covered toast he held fell from his shaky, pale fingers and onto the polished light wood floor. The toast fell right onto the line that marked the threshold between the two rooms. The messy-haired man's eyes went even wider as he looked down and took in where the toast sat.

"This isn't what it looks like." I walked towards him and waved my arms in a placating gesture, forcing his blue eyes to meet mine.

As I got closer, I realised how strongly his facial features resembled Siegfried's. This had to be one of his siblings. One of the siblings from the painting? This man was young but definitely not a teenager.

"My friend and I just need some information," I said, my voice sounding panicked as the slow realisation that he'd set off an alarm or trap set in. I had to convince him to contact Siegfried and tell him everything was fine. They had to have ways to contact each other. There had to be the off-chance this man would accidentally set off a trap or alarm.

My mind went blank as his eyes captured mine in a hard stare.

A slow feeling of anticipation had built in my chest since the toast had been dropped on the threshold and I felt like I was waiting for someone important to arrive. I knew I had to get out, but I had no idea how to get out without setting off a trap.

Siegfried's brother blinked and broke eye contact with me. He ducked down, grabbed the piece of toast then ran off.

Fuck, I needed him to contact his brother to tell him not to come and that it was all a big misunderstanding. I froze halfway through taking a step.

Could the alarm have activated new traps?

I was startled from my thoughts by the sound of a magical portal opening. I heard him thank someone and then footsteps head towards the room I was in.

"What are you doing in my house, Dexter Arkwright?" Siegfried clicked his fingers and it felt like the air had been let back into the room. His voice was calm and measured with a savage edge that cut into me.

I took a few gasping breaths before I could speak. "I wasn't going to take anything, I promise." I backed into the full-length window behind me. The impact caused the entire row of glass windows to vibrate. Could they break and leave me dead on the concrete below?

He hummed, raised an eyebrow and bent down to pick up one of the pages I'd thrown. His sickly sweet smile thinned slightly as he took in what he was reading. I had no idea what page he'd picked up, but he'd know what it was. He carefully picked up the folder and tucked the pages back into it, ensuring he had every piece of paper before he turned back to me. "Did you find what you were looking for?"

"No," I responded before my mind could catch up with my mouth. The word sounded twisted, like it had been forcefully wrenched from my mouth.

Kat!

He was using magic on me and he would ask me something that would make me give away Kat.

I tried to speak and distract him, but no words would leave my mouth.

Siegfried met my eyes. "You shouldn't speak unless spoken to."

He bent his finger, and I nodded.

"Good boy," Siegfried said. My body was fixed in place against the window and I was unable to move my weight from it. I felt the aged wood and glass slowly bend from the strain. My eyelids slipped closed, and I pushed against the call of sleep.

"Unfortunately, by coming here you've forced my hand. I need to use you to send a message."

I felt tears rolling down my cheeks.

"There's no need for that." He used his thumb to wipe the line of tears from my right cheek. "You won't disappoint me, I promise."

My thoughts were getting muddier as I stood there. My eyes closed again. I extended the mental net I used to seek out ghosts. I found myself only able to sense as far as the edge of the room.

"Don't try that." He moved closer to me and grabbed my jaw hard, forcing it open. He poured the contents of a small bottle down my throat. He forced my mouth closed and blocked my nose until I swallowed the bitter concoction he'd forced into my mouth. Siegfried let go of my neck and let me hit the floor.

My mind spun the exact way it did when I drank.

The ghosts were gone.

My magic was gone.

I moved my eyes to meet his and hoped they portrayed my anger.

I needed anger, even though I was terrified.

"The original Nox vulnerable and under my power. I feel giddy." He had an enormous smile on his face. His eyes sparkled as he bounced around the room. He chuckled and ran a finger down my cheek. "Our mutual friend will regret what he did to me when I send him your corpse."

Original Nox? What was he talking about?

This unhinged psycho planned to kill me!

Fuck that!

He lifted my drooping head up by tucking one finger under my chin. "You won't remember why I hate you. It's easier if you don't. It will be easier to make you submit to my will. How rough I get before I kill you will be your brother's fault."

I felt spittle land on my face as he yelled.

"Everyone's been wondering if you really went through with it. I know you wouldn't have been idiotic enough to break into my house if you still had your wits about you. Does it damage a person's brain as much as they claim?"

"Did what?" My voice shook as I pushed past the barrier. I sensed everyone was still keeping a secret from me and I needed to know what it was.

"When I hurt you, it will be his fault he made me angry."

"You can't."

"Because you're married to a Lacy? Pretty sure the old man will be glad to have you out of the picture. Given your *nature,* I'm sure he's convinced he can pair Elijah with someone he can get pregnant with the right incentive."

I didn't respond and stared at the ground. I didn't bother trying not to think of Kat; he was already in my head and knew about her. I could only hope that she got away while he was occupied. I didn't want to think about what he would do to her.

"I'm not going to do anything to your little friend. I don't get my own hands dirty unless I have to," Siegfried said.

It took everything I had not to vomit when I realised where he was going.

He wanted me to do it.

Siegfried pulled a large hunting knife from his jacket pocket and waved it in front of my face. "You will take this and deal with your friend."

"I'm not a murderer."

"Not you. That's your problem and why you're no longer Nox. They had to find another way for you to support the cause. You refused to do the dirty work they wanted and you were removed."

I met his hard eyes. "I won't hurt her."

"The new guy has made an incredible amount of progress. While you refused to kill anyone, he seems to get off on it. Too bad he uses your name and looks so much like you. Precious Ralphie really outdid himself this time."

Ralph!

He was talking about Ralph.

My Ralph.

"My brother's not a cold-blooded killer. You're a lying snake." I waved the end of the knife towards him.

He slapped me across the face. "You really are an arrogant little fucker."

I tossed my head back, coughed up some phlegm and spat in his face.

His mouth hung open for a second before it settled into a hard line as he ground his teeth together in anger. He slowly wiped his face with the back of his sleeve. He slapped me again, open-palmed and hard enough for me to bite my tongue. He placed his hands around my throat and squeezed as he pushed me up against the wall. He ground his body into mine. "If you didn't have a job to do, I'd make you regret that. Use it to escort her off my land."

Did he or didn't he want me to kill her?

Was this some kind of test?

I just stared at him. After he let me go, I fell to the floor, my legs jelly.

Sobs racked my body.

His fingers wormed their way into my hair. He grabbed the back of my head and pulled me from the floor.

"Do I have to do everything myself?" He placed the knife back in my hand.

I felt something wet run from my nose into my mouth; it tasted metallic.

"You're weak. Make yourself useful. I need a drink." He ran a hand through his hair.

"No." I forced my hand to open and let the knife clatter to the floor. If he wanted me to kill her, he couldn't do it himself. If he couldn't kill her, maybe he didn't actually have it in him to kill me.

"Pick it up," he said.

I lost all strength in my knees and sank to the floor. My hand shot out and grabbed the knife. I clenched it so tightly that my hand hurt as I looked up at him.

Siegfried laughed above me. "You still think you will escape and live a carefree life? No one knows you're here. No one is coming to save you." He grabbed my hair and pulled me to my feet again. "Now stop making my floor dirty."

I looked him in the eyes. "Have you ever killed someone before?"

He let me go.

I slid to the ground, my legs numb.

He stared down at me in horror and stepped back from me like he'd been burnt. The spell that had controlled my body and clouded my mind faded. I looked up to see him running his hands through his hair. When I met his eyes, he said, "Fuck."

"What the fuck, Sig!" The brother ran into the room and put himself between us. "What was that?"

"You should be careful. The next person who wants to use you as a tool in their revenge won't stop. Hell, the next person will probably just kill you without thinking about it." He threw me a white monogrammed handkerchief.

I caught it without thinking.

"It's clean," Siegfried said.

I carefully looked at it as I brought it up to my nose. I could only hope the blood stained it beyond repair. It might make him think before he assaulted the next person. "Are you okay?"

He waved an arm at me. "No. The brother of the lunatic who killed my partner broke into my house. What part of this is okay?"

I didn't know how to respond.

"You broke into my freaking house." He looked at me like I was the one in the wrong.

Was I the one in the wrong?

"What do you mean?" I said.

"Mean?" Siegfried said.

"What makes you think Ralph killed your partner?"

"He made sure I knew it was him." He pushed his brother to the side so he could reach me, grabbed my chin, rubbed his fingers in the blood still leaking from my nose then threw me hard against the floor.

"Let us leave," Kat said from the doorway; she must have followed his brother.

The brother screamed, scrambled backwards on the floor and crashed into the wall as she pulled a gun from her pocket.

Where the hell had she found a gun?

Could she actually aim?

What did she think we'd do if she actually shot him?

What if she shot me? Or the brother?

"Or you'll what? Shoot?" Siegfried took a step towards her. "Breaking into my house and threatening me with a gun, it's not a good look."

"I will shoot you," Kat declared.

I saw a drop of blood drip from his closed fist, his fingers moving against his palm.

I tried to warn Kat, but he drew his foot back and kicked me in the stomach.

Seconds after he opened his hand, he revealed a sigil and opened his mouth.

I couldn't look away and stared into Kat's panicked eyes. The ringing in my ears drowned out the sound of his voice as he spoke the words of the spell. I regretted every year of distance that had grown between Kat and me. I desperately craved the close friendship we could have still had.

Nothing happened.

Both Siegfried and Kat stared at each other in shock. Then I realised Siegfried was physically frozen. I took a few seconds to realise who had cast the spell on him: his own brother.

I heard the floor creak as the brother got to his feet beside me. He waved his hand towards Siegfried. "Enough. I've had it. We will behave like civilised people and talk this out."

The laugh that escaped my throat sounded deranged, but once I started, I couldn't stop. I rolled on my back, still laughing as blood ran down the back of my throat.

I was hesitant to drink the tea but too scared to look rude. I took a sip of the orange-flavoured tea as Kat dipped a piece of shortbread in her black coffee. We were in a redwood-panelled and -floored room that looked like it belonged in a 70's cabin in the woods rather than the grand sandstone mansion we sat in. We sat in front of a grey stone fireplace on two dark moss green Victorian chaise lounges, which faced each other with an ornate coffee table the same wood as the panelling, like every piece of wood trim on the furniture in the room. It sat between us with the tea set carefully arranged by an actual housekeeper, who'd quietly slid into the room with a golden tea trolly.

Why in the hell had Kat thought this house would be empty? I leant my head back and banged it lightly against the wood frame of the chair to ground myself in the room.

Why had I listened to her?

Siegfried and his brother, Wyatt, sat across from Kat and I. Wyatt was a very short man with wild, thick hair the same sandy colour as his brother. It was puffy and about chin-length, and it looked like he'd been running his hands through it without care for how harried it made him look. It conflicted with his carefully crafted facial hair, a thick handlebar moustache which had the same slightly red hue as his freckles. Wyatt carefully traced Kat and I with his blue eyes, enlarged by black-framed glasses. It felt as though he was carefully cataloguing every aspect of us, mentally and physically.

It made him creepier than Siegfried.

"Why did you break into my house?" Siegfried said.

"I want to know why the Agency is framing me for Nox's crimes," I said.

"Because you used to be Nox. Then you drove into town about eighteen months ago acting as though you'd been in Perth since graduating high school in 2012," Siegfried said.

"I have a degree."

"You did it by distance." I hadn't even thought to look at the details for my degree. I'd only had to show Mrs Gregory and the town council's human resources department my diploma to get my job.

"If the Agency is framing you, then it was them who messed with your pretty little head. If they really, honestly think you're still Nox, then it was someone else," Siegfried said.

"I feel like there's an 'or' you aren't telling me," I said.

"Or you're faking the memory alteration."

"I don't want to believe the current Nox is who you think it is," I said.

"A person working under that persona killed my partner and made sure I knew," Siegfried said. "I know who I think it is, but the one thing that doesn't make sense is them using it as a threat for me to stop *information gathering* entirely."

I'd heard rumours about Siegfried collecting secrets and blackmailing people. Now I knew how he did it: Mind or Emotion Magic.

"Do you really think it was my brother?" I said.

"The evidence that it was him doesn't match the motivation." Siegfried looked tired, physically defeated.

I looked at Wyatt. "I'm sorry I scared you."

"It's okay." Wyatt gave me a thin smile. "Do you want to know who fucked with your memories?"

"Excuse me?" I gave the younger man my full attention for the first time.

He twisted his pale fingers together, his perfectly square nails shot with a thin line of dark plum nail polish at the top of each nail. "I specialise in Mind Magic. I work for the Agency as a memory consultant. I only look at memories, but if someone officially working for Nate Island altered your memory, I'd know them. Maybe even pick up remnants of their magical signature."

"You work for them? Fucking with people's memories?" I said.

"Don't look at me like that." Wyatt pointed to his chest. "I'm twenty-two. I wasn't surgically altering your memory at barely twenty years old."

I sighed, my anger dying down slightly. I shouldn't blame Wyatt when he was likely groomed into the position he had now. Maybe even forced into it, given his older brother's hobby of blackmail.

"You can find that information out?" I said.

"I can try and ask. It won't happen overnight if things are as dangerous as you and my brother claim," Wyatt said. "This is some dangerous, high-security shit."

"Either the Agency did it or my gran and Ralph wiped my memory to use me as a sleeper agent," I said. "I'm sorry, Siegfried. It has to be my brother and Gran. Why would the Agency erase my memory then forcibly recruit me, anyhow?"

"Because they couldn't entirely get rid of every memory you experienced for years and only hide certain things. Or they wanted to remove any risk you had of betraying them. Start with a blank slate," Siegfried said. "They're afraid you saw something that triggered a hidden memory."

"Nora Rowe's ghost," I said. "They knew I was attacked by her because the neighbour has a home security camera."

"I don't know anything about Ralph that he would kill over,"

Siegfried said. "It was made to look like an accident; the Agency wouldn't investigate, but whoever did it made sure I knew it was a murder and the message behind it."

I drank the last mouthful of the now-lukewarm tea and turned to Kat. "I need to talk to Ralph."

"What? No, I'm not going anywhere near him," Kat said.

"*I* need to talk to him," I said.

I'd vanished so far into my head as I thought about my next move, I almost missed the sound the door made when it flew from its hinges and crashed into the opposite wall.

Eli and Cory stood on the other side of the door. I'd never seen either of them that angry.

"Try to touch either of them or stop us from leaving and we'll kill you." Cory fixed his gaze on Siegfried.

Eli used his magic to take the knife from its place on the coffee table and bring the tip to rest against the back of Siegfried's neck.

Siegfried looked down at me out of the corner of his eye.

I stood up and nodded at the brothers.

Cory met my eyes then glanced at the door. I grabbed Kat's hand, forcing her from her shock, and pulled her down the stairs and out of the house.

Neither Cory nor Eli said a word as Eli grabbed my hand from Kat and led me to his car.

Cory took Kat in hers.

Eli's knuckles were white against the steering wheel as he drove from the house, his face set in a hard expression. I pulled down the sunshade and examined my nose in the mirror. It didn't look like he'd broken it. I pulled a small packet of pocket tissues from the glove box and used them to wipe the dried blood from my nose.

Eli stopped at the rest area outside one of the national parks. Cory pulled in behind us.

"What the hell was that?" Eli said.

"I don't know." I sat down on the bench and looked at the dirt under my feet.

"How the hell did the two of you survive childhood together?" Cory said.

"It was my idea." Kat walked back over to us. "Please don't be angry at him."

"I'm angry at both of you," Eli said.

Kat looked terrified as she took a step back from him.

"What made you think it was a marvellous idea to break into that nosy creep's house?" Eli said.

"We needed information for the case," Kat said.

The look Cory and Eli gave her stated that was the wrong thing to say.

"This 'playing detective' thing stops now," Eli said. "Leave it to the professionals."

"The *professionals* don't care." I pointed a finger at him. "They want either Ralph or me to be the fall guy."

Eli gave me a dirty look.

I stood up. "The hell are you angry at me for?"

"You and Kat shouldn't have been in that house," Eli said.

"Goodbye." I walked away from them.

"Where do you think you're going?" Eli caught up with me.

"Away from you." I had to clench my fists to stop myself from grabbing the fucker and shaking some sense into him.

How was any of this my fault? "Don't follow me if you know what's good for you," I said.

He stopped walking and stared at me, his hazel eyes wet with tears.

I regretted what I'd said the moment the words left my mouth, but I didn't care to correct it even though I sounded like a monster. Maybe I was a monster and didn't remember.

He wasn't sorry for the nasty thing he said to me.

I kept walking, glad I couldn't hear him following me anymore after I walked into the bush. Once I broke the line of sight, I started to run.

It had been one of the longest days of my life and I wasn't sure where I found the energy.

I punched a tree when I stopped to catch my breath. "Fuck you!" I screamed at the top of my lungs. No one was around to hear me. I collapsed to my knees in tears, thankful no one would see me break down.

I wiped the blood from my torn, bruised knuckles on my jeans and walked again.

I came to a halt as I reached the edge of the highway. My shoe soles scraped against the sharp edge of the asphalt road and snapped me from the distant place I'd been inside my head.

I looked at the cars speeding past me on the highway with a sense of regret.

Why in God's name had I run away like that?

I had a vague idea of where I was, somewhere on the highway between Dunn and Tallow, but it would be a long, hot walk home. Even though it was late autumn, it was an unseasonably warm day and I was on the side of a hot road under the early afternoon sun.

I pulled my phone from my pocket and did what would have been unthinkable a couple of hours earlier: called Ralph. I was shocked when he picked up the phone when it had almost rung out.

"Dex."

I could hear the annoyance in his voice, as though he was sick of me trying to contact him.

I held the phone tighter in my hand as sweat slid into my eyes. "I know someone fucked with my memory."

"Where are you?"

"I'll send you my location," I said.

I waited until I reached a rest area where he could pull off before I sent Ralph a text with my location. I sat under a tree and waited for him.

When he pulled up the car, the first thing he gave me was a cold bottle of water. "I thought you might need this."

"Thanks." I took the bottle, broke the seal and drank half of it in a couple of minutes as I enjoyed the cold air of the car's air con. "This heat wave was unexpected."

"I guess you don't watch the weather report." Ralph spoke without looking from the road as he pulled back onto the highway.

"Wow," I said.

"Sorry." Ralph bit his lip, as though he felt guilty about the way he'd just talked to me.

I nodded.

"Is he taking care of you?" Ralph asked.

"You mean Eli? Yes." I was a little shocked he asked the question. "I'm just being a fuck-up."

"You're the fuck-up when you're the one who is walking alongside the highway in the middle of a hot day?"

"We had a fight and instead of talking it over like a normal person, I ran away."

Ralph tapped the steering wheel. "I don't have much advice about your relationship because I'm no good at that sort of thing either."

"Why did you steal that book?" I said.

"Straight to the chase, I see."

"I'm being blamed for it."

"I know," Ralph said. "Someone I'm working with wanted a spell from that book without the owner knowing."

"Gran?"

"No, actually. Someone else I owe a favour."

"Was it you and Gran who changed my memory? Set me up to be a sleeper agent?" I said.

Ralph pulled into the parking lot of a lookout and turned to face me. "We'd never do that to you."

"But someone did."

"I know." Ralph hit the top of the steering wheel with an open hand. "Gran thought it was best you were able to forget, to move on from the life we'd dragged you into. After someone hurt you like that and her accident, I guess the danger sunk in for her."

"Everyone lied to me. Gaslit me." A bitter laugh escaped my throat. "So I could live a normal life?"

"Even knowing about magic without permission from Nate Island is enough to warrant execution. That's how magic is kept secret. Most people don't want to doom themselves and someone they care about to death."

"I can still see ghosts without trying."

"Messing with someone's memory magically is a cluster fuck," Ralph said. "And useless. Unless the person knows you very well, it's almost impossible to erase an extensive number of memories. Most Mind Mages read or control simple thoughts and alter memories before they can become long-term."

"Is this why it's hard for everyone to believe what happened to me?" I said.

"Yes," Ralph said. "Someone very gifted in mental magic would have been given a list of key memories to remove by someone who knows you well."

Which is why Ralph and Gran were likely suspects for those who believed me. I followed him from the car to the empty viewing area. I took a long sip of the water he had given me.

"I regret listening to Gran about keeping quiet. I think Elijah regrets listening to Grandfather. If he cares about you the way he claims he does. He couldn't stay away from you."

"Do you know what I do about the Agency agents investigating me?" I said.

"Keep ignoring them. They're doing all this to get to me and Gran," Ralph said.

"They're using me to get to you?" I said.

"I'm the current Nox," Ralph said.

I nodded.

"We shouldn't be seen together. They already had enough to use against you," Ralph said. "I'll take the back way and drop you off at the edge of that state forest that runs by the Lacys' land."

"You won't tell me anything more."

"No."

"Siegfried thinks you killed his partner," I said.

"I promise I didn't." Ralph's dark eyes met mine. His short, wavy hair blew in the cold breeze that had formed to precede the dark clouds on the eastern horizon.

"I believe you," I said.

"The thing you need to do is play along with the Agency for both you and Gran's safety. Can you do this for me, Dex? For us?"

"Yes."

Ralph reached into his jeans pocket. He pulled a tiny bottle and small index card from it. The small bottle held only around a quarter of a teaspoon of liquid. I knew it was a potion from hours watching Pop make them as a kid.

One of Pop's potions.

My heart beat a little faster as I noticed his handwriting on the index card.

"This is a teleportation potion. Only use it if you are in danger, it will take you somewhere safe." Ralph handed me the bottle and card. "Burn the card after memorising the instructions."

"I promise." I placed the items into my pocket.

"Pop used to sow the bottles into his clothing," Ralph said. "Maybe it's something to think about in case someone searches you."

I had to force myself to look at him as I nodded, unable to trust myself to speak. I could do everything else he asked but didn't know if I'd burn the card. Not sure I could bring myself to destroy one of the limited pieces of Pop left in the world.

He smiled and relaxed his entire body against the light aqua railing as he stared down at the town we both loved in our own way. The home to those we loved and wanted to protect.

12

When I walked through the waist-high cast iron back gate, I noticed all the lights downstairs were on and I could hear people from the patio as I walked onto it.

I looked down at my watch and saw the date. I'd forgotten about the monthly family dinner the Lacys held. Tonight was the second one my family had been invited to.

I took a couple of slow breaths and opened the glass door that led into the hall beside the large formal dining room.

Everyone in the dining room turned to look at me as I walked in. I noticed Eli had invited Cory and Kat.

As I stood in the doorway, I noticed Eli's parents' concerned glances at the bruises on my neck. Cynthia kept looking at my face and I knew she was looking at my nose. I hoped I didn't have a bruise; I should have snuck off to the bathroom before I walked in.

I felt a deeper level of concern in the attention they were both paying me. A wave of sadness washed over me, a craving for parental affection.

It was something I'd never really had with my own distant parents. Sometimes I felt like they'd only had kids because that was what they were supposed to do. After a few more seconds of standing in the doorway, I ran up the stairs to my bedroom.

I ripped my shirt off and looked in the mirror. Siegfried had left bold hand-shaped bruises against my neck.

Surely Eli, Kat and Cory would have seen them.

I'd been wearing a V-neck tee shirt.

Why the hell had they let me run off into the bush alone after what had happened to me?

I let the tears that had built in my eyes fall.

I sunk to the floor, curled into a ball against the wall and leant my head against my knees.

Part of me wanted someone to come and check on me, but as time crept on, I realised I was alone. The illusion that I wasn't alone had been fractured in that abandoned house the moment those yellow eyes met mine.

The demon had shown me just how distant I was from everyone in my life. They'd needed someone to keep the secret from to feel special.

I lay on the cold tiles, let the sadness and anger wash over me and sank into the feeling.

Someone shook me as they said my name. I opened my eyes and looked at Eli, who was kneeling beside me on the bathroom floor, a look of utter panic and fear on his face. I sat on the bathroom floor. "What do you want?"

"You were having a panic attack." His eyes were fixed on the marks around my neck. "How about you lay down on the bed?"

"No." I turned my gaze to the tiles again. I didn't want to stay here, but I wasn't about to lay on the bed because he told me to, the guy clearly angry at me for getting assaulted. Annoyed that I was dumb enough to break into someone's house.

"I get that you're angry at me, but I'm worried about you. I invited Cory over to check on you... I didn't think you wanted my parents to do it."

"Why did you let me run off then?"

Eli flinched. He moved back from me and removed his fingers from me as though he'd been burnt. "I was angry."

"Some freak assaulted me and you let me run off into the bush alone because you were angry?"

"I was angry that you and Kat would do something that stupid. I wasn't thinking clearly," he said. "I didn't want to restrain you and force you to stay somewhere you didn't want to be. I wasn't angry you got hurt."

"I wasn't thinking clearly. I had no way to get home!"

"I tried to find you."

"Through tracking software, which you likely installed on my phone?" I sat up and looked him straight in the eyes.

"What am I supposed to do? That demon could have killed you and vanished the other night. If I didn't do it, Cory and I would have never found you and Kat. You'd probably be dead. What were you thinking?"

"I couldn't let her go in there alone."

He ran his fingers through his hair and looked away from me. "Fuck. You need to tell me what's happening with you, Dexter, so I can fix it."

"I've told you what's happening." I carefully reached out and wrapped my pinkie finger around his. I squeezed it before I slipped my hand into his. "You're the centre of my plan. I need you at the centre of my plan. I promise you, the most exciting thing happening in my life right now is this investigation and those false accusations. I'm not running around at night committing crimes. I'd tell you if I was."

"Please let Cory check you over," Eli said.

I nodded and allowed him to lead me into the bedroom where Cory, Kat and June sat on the end of the bed. Neither June nor Kat left when Cory examined me, both not wanting to be left out of anything. It was awkward to be stripped down to my boxer briefs while Cory basically felt me up in front of my cousin and June, who I'd once had a crush on for years. Almost asking June to be my date for the year six formal was a secret I'd take to the grave. If June and Eli discovered I'd had a crush on her, it would become another in-joke between them and I'd never live it down. The fact I'd had sex dreams about everyone in the room, apart from Kat, made the whole situation even more awkward.

Cory was careful as he checked my injuries and relieved the pain on my face and neck.

"Eli and Kat told me what happened," June said.

"Are you going to ask me what I was thinking too? As though I could have let Kat run off into some stranger's house by herself?" I asked.

"This is all my fault. I was cocky and thought we could get in and out safely," Kat said.

I clenched my teeth hard to stop an angry statement of agreement from leaving my mouth. Why hadn't she considered Siegfried's siblings? Even though I didn't know Wyatt and his sister, she would have gone to the same high school as them.

"He really could have hurt you, Dex," Kat said. "I shouldn't have left you alone. You don't have the experience to defend yourself."

"I'm sick of people treating me like a kid or a helpless idiot. Do you know how many people have told me I won't last a year in this world? They aren't trying to warn me, they're just being smug to warm their own egos. They'd be happy to be proven right, to see an Arkwright or Lacy fall. Too bad they picked the most stubborn fucker imaginable to mess with."

"You'll be okay." Eli touched my shoulder. "I'll make sure of it."

"What are we going to do now?" Kat said.

"Find out who is committing violence under Nox's name," I said.

"Even if someone related to us did it?" Kat said.

"Yes," I said. "I talked to Ralph."

"What?" Kat's voice was as hard as her face.

I brought them up to date on the information I'd been told by Siegfried, Wyatt and Ralph.

"Someone is coming," Cory whispered.

"How can you tell?" I said.

"Close your eyes and focus on the part of you that you use to sense ghosts. Imagine it's a net and mentally roll it in a ball, understand how it works, examine it. How it feels and how your mind and body respond to it."

I closed my eyes and the tone of voice he used relaxed me instantly. As I listened to his words, I followed his instructions and gathered that part of me that sensed other worldly creatures.

I wrapped it into a ball; I imagined it inside my chest, a similar place to where I felt strong emotions.

I could pull the awareness closer or extend it to sense more of my surroundings. I automatically extended it when I was outside of the house but kept it close when I felt safe.

It was an instinct I could control, even though it had been subconscious until this point.

"You have an internal reserve of energy that can be used for magic. It's typically only used for smaller spells or as a last resort. The goal of practising magic the way we do is to use energy outside of ourselves."

I took slow, steadying breaths as I spun the mental net around like a ball then extended it out then in carefully. I focused on imagining it as an object rather than what I could feel with it. A net was a perfect metaphor.

"As a Death Mage, you can use that part of yourself to sense the presence of any living creature. Practise the exercise I just taught you for a month and we can move onto the next step."

"For God's sake." The disappointment washed away my concentration.

"She's almost here." Cory spoke quieter than he'd breathed seconds before and I strained to hear him even though we were a hair's length apart.

There was a knock at the door. "Dex? Can I come in and speak to you? I want to know that you're okay."

I looked at Eli wide-eyed; it was Cynthia. He slowly glanced towards the door and mouthed, "Respond."

"I was just about to go to sleep. I feel a little unwell," I said.

"Barton and I saw the bruises on your neck, please let me in," Cynthia pleaded.

Eli, who was on my opposite side, pressed his lips against my ear and whispered, "Recording device."

When I looked at him, I saw the hurt and anger on his face as he looked at the door. His breath was shaky as he focused on giving the door the death glare meant for his mother.

"One minute while I find my robe." I'd become so comfortable around the others and distracted talking about the plan, I'd forgotten I was wearing nothing other than my boxer briefs.

Why the hell hadn't anyone mentioned it?

The others looked at each other then followed Eli into the bathroom as I grabbed my navy robe from the back of the bedroom door and threw it on.

I opened the door with a large, forced smile.

"I thought we could have a conversation." Cynthia sat down and gave me what was supposed to be a reassuring smile.

I was just as angry as Eli about the recording device.

Grandfather or Lacy Senior had noticed the bruises. This situation stunk of their over-controlling involvement.

They knew I wouldn't talk to them.

Cynthia and I were supposed to be close because she was expected to mould me into the perfect Lacy wife, as Mrs Lacy had done for her. It didn't matter that I was a man; I still had my place now I'd married into the Lacy family.

"What do you mean about a bruise?" I asked.

She sat on the bed and grabbed my hands, her eyes almost identical to Eli's drifting to my neck. "I just want to make sure you're okay."

I'm fine apart from suffering from my *stupidity*.

"I'm better than ever," I said.

"If you're involved in anything that could have hurt you, I'd like to know. I want to help you fix it," Cynthia said. "I promise you can be honest with me. If there's anything that you're involved with that has put you in danger, I want to make it better. For both your and Eli's sakes."

I looked her hard in the eyes. "I know how you value honesty above all else."

Her smile shook slightly as she took two shaky breaths and broke eye contact with me. "I want to know my son made the right choice when he picked you." Her tone was harsher than she'd ever used with me.

I took a second to glance at the bathroom door, as though they could tell me what to say through it.

I looked back at Cynthia and realised she'd noticed. She glared at me. "Is there someone here?"

"No."

"There is in the bathroom. Have you been up here with someone?"

I had no idea who she expected based on the tone of her voice, but I was surprised she hadn't expected it to be Eli and the others.

Who the hell else could it be?

"Show yourself."

"There's no one there. I was just looking at the door," I said.

"Show yourself, I want to know who's in my house," she said.

Shouldn't she know?

Had Cory masked their presence?

She had to know what Eli felt like. A Healing Mage would be able to sense people too.

Eli threw the door open and stormed out.

The noise it made when it crashed against the wall caused everyone in the room but the mother and son who squared off against each other to jump several feet.

Eli stood in front of Cynthia, arms crossed. "Take a chill pill, Mother. I hate to break it to you, but this isn't even your house."

"Elijah Charles Lacy. There is a proper way to use a door," Cynthia said. "And that's not it."

"You treat me like a child, I may as well act like one," Eli said.

The others sheepishly followed Eli out of the bathroom but kept their distance near the door.

I didn't want to be overly close to Cynthia and Eli, either.

They were thick as thieves ninety per cent of the time, and the other ten per cent they were ready to rip each other's heads off. I almost booked it the first time I heard them argue when we were teenagers, but I'd already put six months into my relationship by that point.

Maybe all the arguments I'd witnessed between them as a kid had left me numb to the situation.

"Recording a private conversation with my husband. What the fuck is wrong with you?" Eli snapped his fingers and the pen in her silk blouse pocket sizzled. She threw the pen and gave Eli a hard look as she ground her foot on it to put out the small flames it had caused. Grandfather and Lacy Senior burst into the bedroom.

As a kid, I loved showing people my bedroom, hoping they'd ask about something I was interested in.

Now, not so much.

It made me feel exposed in a sick, skin-clawing way. I didn't like when older people saw a side of me they wouldn't understand. A truth they wouldn't accept. A rejection that would take another chip from my heart or my mental reserve. There wasn't anything like that in the bedroom, but them being in here still made me feel that way.

I let my head rest in my palms and ran my fingers through the curls to massage my skull.

This was the last thing I needed right now.

Did everyone know about the whole 'accused of being Nox' thing?

Had they all been listening to the device?

Were they working on their own or with the detectives?

"You kids are rather cosy up here," Grandfather said.

I almost gagged. The tone he used made it sound like we'd been having an orgy. Eli and June were cousins, and so were Kat and I.

"I didn't know it was a crime to spend time with my friends, or for them to check on me," I said.

I looked up and met his narrowed eyes.

He sighed and walked out of the room; Lacy Senior followed. Eli looked at his mother as though he dared her to say something. She picked up the pen and left, closing the door behind her.

"What the hell was that?" I waved my hands about as I looked at the others for answers.

"Someone's got to her," Eli remarked. "I wondered why you'd seen so little of Detective Dominguez lately."

"I'm not Nox," I said.

The others slowly nodded, wide-eyed.

They seriously didn't think I was a murderer.

Did they?

I forced myself to focus on my breathing and pushed back the anxious thoughts at the back of my mind.

I just wanted all of this to be over.

I'd had enough of this day.

My head pounded again, the headache Cory had eased returning with full force.

"I want to go to sleep. Could everyone other than Eli please leave?"

"Goodnight." Kat was the first to walk out, the others said goodnight and followed her from the room.

13

Cory walked into my office without knocking and placed a pile of red cardboard boxes on my desk. After a careful look in the boxes, and I realised they contained filled manila folders. "The higher-ups have decided that you'll learn by doing."

"Doing what?"

"Cleaning out the inventory." Cory opened the top box.

"These are?"

"Cases given to your department. Mostly demons and manifestations a collection of people created with their very own brain boxes. I grabbed the easy ones because neither of us are fully trained to handle this."

"You mean urban legends people thought into existence?"

"Yes," Cory said. "Once someone works with you as your mentor, this is what you'll mainly do for the Agency."

"You think I'm weird for investigating the Nox thing."

"I don't think you're weird, I work in the Special Basement, but people outside of the department might have different opinions."

"Special Basement?"

He shook his head. "If you heard the things they say about us upstairs."

"What is 'Special Basement' supposed to mean?"

"The Special Basement where they hide all the weirdos, and that's to put it nicely. Many people still don't like the magic we practice down here," Cory said.

"What kind of magic do the people in this department have?"

"Blood Magic, Life Magic, Electricity Magic, mind-altering. We specialise in using magic that can alter the body and mind, living or dead. You'll learn to specialise in Death and Eldritch Magic plus Demonology and Monsterology to become the best exorcist you possibly can."

"And your bosses thought it would be a superb idea to settle me with that? I thought the idea was to make me less weird," I said.

"There was a trainee who was killed two weeks ago," Cory said.

"They move fast."

"You're a blank slate who's willing to learn and we need to give their mentor time before she is ready to come back to work."

"We're taking over their caseload?"

"Yes." Cory looked down at his watch. "We have someone to meet at the diner."

"You've already organised work on a case?" I pointed to the red manila folder he held.

"Yes."

I tapped the side of the bottom box. "Are all these *safe* cases?"

"Yes. You're a trainee apprentice." He pointed to the same box I touched. "You'll do red, orange and yellow cases with supervision for the first three years."

"Trainee apprentice?"

"You're in a four-year program."

The realisation washed over me like a sick wave. I'd be close to thirty before I was fully trained.

How was I supposed to catch up with my peers?

"This case was marked as a priority," Cory said.

"Anywhere else, red would be the danger colour."

"The colour levels are based on the visible light spectrum. They taught you the shorthand on how to remember those colours, right?"

"Roy G. Biv," I said. "Red, orange, yellow, green, blue, indigo and violet. I know the education system here isn't the best, but it's not that bad."

"Seven clearance levels. Red is the lowest and violet is the highest. The highest clearance level a mage would dare take on alone is green, and even that's considered a last resort. If you do a situational assessment and the level is higher than you're capable of handling, evacuate everyone and call for backup."

"An assessment?"

"I have a guide." He handed me a thick spiral bound book with information about the colour code system and how to conduct a safety assessment. "You'll be tested on that. You'll need to know how to do everything expected of a trainee apprentice in one year, or you fail."

"What happens if I fail?" I said.

"Normally you get kicked out. You? I think they'd put you on trial for illegal knowledge of magic."

"Excuse me?"

"You heard me." Cory held the door open for me to walk through and gave me a smile. "Remember to do your homework."

He'd left casually as though he hadn't just told me I was almost certain to be executed if I didn't play along and try hard enough.

It wasn't as though I didn't know, but hearing it from him made it worse.

Cory hadn't let me look in the folder, so I went into the diner clueless about what I would walk into.

We sat down across from a middle-aged man with dark circles under his wide eyes. He dressed in a long-sleeved flannel shirt, worn jeans and muddy boots, so I assumed he was a farmer.

"Marco Bailey?" Cory said.

"That's me." Marco shook both our hands.

"You reported that your sister-in-law is in possession of a forbidden creature," Cory said.

Marco Bailey's hands shook as he moved his short, white coffee cup towards his mouth. "My sister-in-law was the type of woman who always wanted kids, but she didn't meet my brother until it was too late. I honestly always thought she was the most educated and capable person I've ever met. We worked in a similar field of magic and I always admired her." Marco took a few shaky breaths. "I guess my image of her was ruined when she introduced me to that thing."

"Thing?" I questioned.

Cory gave me a sharp look that said, 'sit still and shut up.'

"I thought she was smarter than that. She says she can control it, but I'm worried. I promised Herb I'd take care of her," Marco replied.

"Are you in love with your sister-in-law, Mr Bailey?" Cory said.

"God, no. I've never really been interested in romance, sex, marriage, anything like that. She's twenty years older and someone I respected. Her work was the reason I went into magical biology." He let out a bitter chuckle. "They say never meet your heroes, and mine became my sister-in-law. I still had that naïve admiration for her until she introduced me to my new *nephew*."

"What is the nature of your newly acquired relative?" Cory said.

"It's not human. I was always told to report things like this."

"I will need a description."

"It looks like a child. When she first started talking about it, I thought she'd went off the deep end. The way she was talking, it was like she'd kept a child she found as though it was a stray dog. I paid them a visit, and that's when I was introduced to Thomas."

"It's intelligent enough to respond to the name Thomas?" Cory said.

"Yes. She called him Thomas but told me to call him Tom to his face," Marco said. "He likes Tom better."

"I need a description so I can identify the creature. I don't want to hear how wrong you think it is."

"It looks like a ten- or eleven-year-old boy. Like any other kid, apart from the black eyes, pale skin and sense of dread."

Cory looked up from the notepad. "Do you think it's an actual child?"

"An actual child?" Marco frowned.

"A baby demon." Cory tapped the end of his pen on the paper.

"That makes a difference?" I said.

"All the difference in the world. Many creatures mimic humans, especially women and children, but there are also baby demons who don't know any better and even mean no harm." Cory turned his attention to me. "Not every demon is dangerous. It started as a universal term to describe anything that doesn't naturally belong to this world."

"Including aliens?" I said.

"Anything not native to this planet or universe is a demon. The term was invented by people to describe the unknown creatures they encountered, not to describe a literal religious evil come to life. Is there a reality out there somewhere with a heaven and hell like described in the Christian Bible? Maybe, but not here. None of these creatures are pure evil or good."

I knew he explained for my benefit rather than Marco's.

"If that thing clinging to my sister is what I think it is, it's got nothing good planned for her." Marco had a stern look on his face. "I'm in no way equipped to deal with this."

"It's a creature that needs to eat," Cory said.

"Her fucking life energy." Marco dropped his cup and grabbed the front of Cory's suit across the table. He drew his other fist back, a ferocious look on his red face.

I ducked behind Cory and shoved both of my hands over his face to block Marco. "I know he's an arsehole, but we're only trying to help. Please don't hit him. We're the only people available to help your sister."

Marco's raised fist shook for a minute before he let it drop. When he let go, he shoved Cory so hard I was almost knocked off my feet as I caught him. Cory, as collected as ever, clicked his tongue and pulled a small cloth from his bag. He pulled the glasses I'd covered in fingerprints from his face and cleaned them without looking at either of us. He stood without another word after he placed the thick plastic tortoiseshell frames back on his face and walked from the diner.

"Thank you for your time, sir." I gave Marco a stiff smile and hurried after Cory.

Cory was strapped into the driver's seat by the time I reached the car. How had he moved so fast? "I hate dealing with the *public*."

He said "public" like it was a dirty word.

He sighed and looked at me. "I'm getting sick of this act."

"What act?"

"Make me truly believe you went through with it."

"With what?"

"I shouldn't still be falling for this. If you did it, you're not as smart as I thought you were. All you've done is make yourself vulnerable. Catering to their demands wasn't the way out."

"Is this about that Nox thing? You still think I willingly had my memories erased, or worse, that I'm pretending. You don't trust my brother and Gran at all, do you?"

"I still can't wrap my head around the idea that you went through with it, but sometimes I really truly believe you did." Cory looked out the window. "You found my weak point and really dug in, but you already know that."

"What aren't you telling me?" I said. He didn't know I knew about the memory thing. I wanted to hear it from his own mouth.

"I no longer care enough about you to tell you. Ask your precious husband, because he really took advantage if this isn't all an act." Cory swapped out his glasses for gold aviator sunglasses and started the car. "It doesn't matter, even if you really went through with it. You're stuck in this rat trap like everyone else."

"I don't know what you want from me." I spoke so quietly I could hardly hear myself.

For a second before he slid the sunglasses all the way up his nose, his eyes looked wet.

"You can't just press a reset button on your life," Cory said.

My head spun and I grabbed the side of my chair to steady myself. I was sure something had been done to me, but Cory's words caused doubt to claw its way back into my mind.

What if a past version of me had agreed to the memory alteration?

"Put your fucking seat belt on," Cory hissed through gritted teeth as he pulled onto the road. "I don't want to get fined."

Dr Oliva Bailey ran a small farm stay half an hour west of Dunn. Her two-storey stone, wood and glass house overlooked a vast valley next to the largest lake in the area. I'd heard the house was impressive, but seeing it took my breath away. It was a modern marvel of architecture and held stark contrast to most of the other mansions in the area, which had been built during the nineteenth century.

I looked at Cory for the first time since the start of the drive. His face was still hard as he glanced up at the house.

I forced myself to speak. "What exactly are we dealing with?"

He looked at me with his wide green eyes, his light brown skin a few shades paler than usual, mouth fixed in a thin line. I could have got lost in his eyes if his physical expression didn't fix me to the present. "A black-eyed child."

"What's that?" I said.

"A demon. I already explained this to you."

"I want to know what it could do to us. Is it an actual baby monster, or is it just pretending to be a human child?"

"It's a child. They avoid humans unless they need to feed and don't live with them. The adults are indistinguishable from normal humans unless they're feeding." Cory pulled the thin red folder from the documents compartment beside my feet. "Some of their abandoned children don't know any better."

"Don't know any better?"

"They're scared and alone. Left vulnerable to the elements. They'll feed on the life force of the humans who take them in and not mean to. They have at or near human intelligence from birth."

"Can it choose not to feed on Dr Bailey?"

"No. It needs human life force, energy, to survive." Cory looked away for a second, then fixed his eyes on mine. "We need to rehome it."

I nodded.

"We need to convince Dr Bailey to give it up willingly. We can't take her in a fight and if it looks like the situation might head that way, we need to hope she lets us leave. She has over two lifetimes' worth of experience on us. We can't beat her in a fight."

"They'd never find us, would they?" I suddenly felt the isolation of the property press in on me.

"They'd never find enough evidence. She'd make it look like we'd run off together," Cory said.

"Is that what you'd do if you had to kill someone in our position?" I asked.

"Yes. If she suspects for a second that we have any sexual attraction towards each other, she will use that to her advantage if things go south."

"If she doesn't kill us." I wouldn't deny I was attracted to Cory, he would've read me the moment we met. Noticed the way I looked at him, the way my body reacted.

"Yes." Cory left the car. He was halfway across the lawn in the time it took me to blink.

I scrambled out of the car after him. I caught my foot on the door lip and almost tripped as I exited. He looked back at me, the worry on his face for a split second turning into an eye roll.

How much of my feelings could he sense?

The flush that spread over my face was scolding hot.

He knew I was attracted to him and the exact buttons to press if need be.

He'd know the moment something aroused or upset me.

A woman I assumed was Dr Bailey opened the door seconds before Cory's outstretched knuckles tapped on the glass. She pointed her thumb at the video doorbell attached to the right door frame. "You look a little young to be offended by modern technology."

I looked at the camera slot of the doorbell. How much surveillance did she have?

Had she heard our conversation before?

I knew it was naïve to assume she couldn't have with the right spell.

What kind of biological magic did she practice? I imagined my decaying corpse being devoured by flesh-eating scavengers under her control. They'd never find enough *evidence*.

"Is my doorbell really that offensive?"

I looked up at Bailey. She and Cory were looking at me like I'd grown a second head. Cory was inside the door; I'd gone cross-eyed staring at her front porch. Bailey looked ready to slam the door in my face any second. She raised an eyebrow at me and smiled. The eye contact she made sent a simple message. She knew I feared her, so she assumed I wasn't a threat. She moved to close the door and I ran inside before it shut. I felt the door brush against the back of my body as I moved into the house. I couldn't leave Cory alone.

Bailey was a tall woman in her mid-sixties. She had neat, short brown hair with an undercut. She wore a baggy, yellow silk button-down shirt and denim knee-length shorts. She led us to a modern living room with large, open, bifold oak doors that looked out onto her back deck and the valley below.

"Marco sent you." She sat down in an armchair and looked out towards the small sliver of the lake that could be seen from the chairs. I was almost visibly startled out of my skin when I saw a pale man who looked like an older version of Marco sitting in one armchair.

His eyes fixed on the book sitting on the end table beside him, a book he'd never be able to pick up unless he was an exceptionally strong ghost. It had to be Marco's brother and Bailey's deceased husband, Herb.

I glanced over at him as though I was just looking around the room. There was no need to let Bailey know.

Did she even know he was there?

"Yes," Cory said. "I'm Cory Corvin and this is my associate, Dexter Lacy. We rep—"

"I know you're working for Dunn based on his surname." She pointed a short but carefully manicured nail at me.

"We've had a report that you are in possession of a forbidden creature."

"Neither of you are the normal team for this, are you?" Bailey said.

"Dexter is being trained and I have the skill for this position." The word "skill" shot out of his mouth like a bullet but somehow managed not to sound rude.

"I see." She poured herself a glass of dark liquor from a crystal decanter on the table under her large television.

"Isn't it dangerous to drink from leaded crystal?" The words left my mouth before I could stop them.

She fixed me with her stern blue gaze. "It was rude of me not to pour you some."

I watched as she poured a shot into another glass for me. She looked at Cory, who shook his head. I had the feeling "no" wasn't an option for me. I looked down at the glass of brown liquid and tried to keep my expression neutral as I followed her nod and picked up the glass. She poured herself another glass, met my eyes again and slowly raised the glass to her mouth.

I took a deep breath and followed suit.

Someone had to do this, right?

I closed my eyes and poured the liquid into my mouth; I gagged as the bitter fluid hit my tongue and burnt my throat.

About a quarter of it leaked from my mouth down my chin and neck before I could force my mouth closed. I closed my eyes and swallowed, my face burning as tears slid from my watery eyes. I couldn't even look at Cory. God, that was embarrassing. I was gagging on hard liquor like an inexperienced teenager. I kept my eyes closed to steady myself as the buzz of the alcohol hit me. Bailey chuckled as she placed the lid back on the glass decanter and gave Cory a satisfied look.

Thankfully, Cory and Bailey were focused on each other when I noticed the ghost still sitting in the chair. My eyes widened as I took the sight in.

That wasn't alcohol!

What had she given me?

Was it just the flavour and the placebo effect, or was it some kind of potion? It had to be some ploy to lull Cory into a false sense of security.

Would a normal mage try to use their magic if they thought they'd drunk alcohol? Gran told me it could be deadly to use magic with alcohol or drugs in your system. Some mages didn't even take allergy pills or basic pain relief, only specially formulated potions. No mage my age would try at risk of having an aneurysm. They would also assume she, an older woman, was at a disadvantage. Only I didn't have the self-control over my magic a typical mage would. I'd subconsciously used my magic because I lacked the control not to. I felt lightheaded, darkness dancing at the edge of my vision as it started to go fuzzy with my rapid breaths. I realised how much danger I'd been in every time I drank alcohol in the past. I knew the feeling, I was on the edge of a panic attack.

I had to pull myself together.

Calm down.

Doctor Bailey still had her full power.

She was the danger here not my past mistakes.

I had to warn Cory not to try anything. I hoped he wouldn't attempt to hurt who he perceived as a helpless older woman to abduct a child. Cory had to know something was up based on my body's physical responses; he used it to basically read my mind.

Why would he stop now?

Were we technically trying to abduct a child?

My stomach curled as the realisation set in. Yes, we were.

"What's so interesting about my bookshelf?" Bailey said.

"I like books," I replied.

"Let's cut the bullshit." She crossed her arms over her chest. "You're here for Thomas."

"We have been asked to rehome him," Cory responded.

"Rehome! He isn't an unwanted dog. He has the intelligence of a human child two years older than he appears," Bailey said.

"If I'm right about my assessment, he's feeding off your life force," Cory said.

"It's worth it to give a lost child a safe home. I've lived a long life."

"I'm trying to save you."

"I don't need some kid puppet of the Agency playing hero. Not everyone wants to be saved."

Cory blinked rapidly as though this information was hard to take in. "I can't leave here without him. It's been reported. Someone else will come."

"And you can't leave here with him, either," Bailey said.

"Where is the boy? If you don't give him up willingly, I will use force to retrieve him. You are now a criminal keeping an illegal creature against the will of Nate Island."

"Force." Bailey raised an eyebrow and chuckled.

I had to warn Cory not to push it.

Surely, he knew she wouldn't make herself vulnerable like she'd pretended.

I had to force myself not to shake as the look she gave Cory darkened.

She was going to kill us.

Out of the corner of my eye, I could see her desk. On the edge of the desk was a spiral bound notebook. The sharp end of the metal spiral was poking from the bottom.

I backed towards the desk with fear; I didn't have to fake it as Cory and Bailey circled each other, each sizing up the threat before them. Cory's left hand was at the top of his right glove, ready to pull the glove from his hand. Bailey pulled a small vial of bright pink liquid from her pocket. I pressed my right index finger into the sharp piece of wire behind my back. I used my thumb to push it into my flesh and didn't stop pushing against it until it was firmly wedged in my finger and I felt the first drop of blood run down my finger. I had a second before the blood and biological magic users in front of me noticed. I started drawing the same sigil I used to control the Short Street ghost. Magic required concentration, and someone couldn't do it if their eardrums had burst. I hoped Cory would forgive me for doing it to him a second time.

"Leave, or I activate the poison in your fuck toy's stomach," Bailey said.

I almost lost focus on the shape I'd started drawing on the desk. She'd drunk the same liquid I had and could use that connection to do what she wanted. She could use the right spell to turn the contents of my stomach into poison.

Cory didn't say anything, only looked at her.

Were they too focused on each other to see or smell the blood?

Maybe they didn't see me as a threat?

Fuck that.

I closed my eyes to focus my will power into the spell.

I didn't have the same connection to this ghost, but I'd manage.

I had to.

"Dex." Cory's voice was sharp. "What you're about to do will kill you."

"It wasn't alcohol," I said.

"The only thing that ghost is going to do is attack you to get to the life energy you tempted it with," Cory said.

My hand went limp and I pulled away from the desk as though it had burnt me.

"Don't fuck with magic you don't understand," Cory spoke through clenched teeth. He looked at the sigil and waved a finger. The blood moved as though a breeze had hit it, drops blowing across the dark, wooden desk and destroying what I'd drawn.

A part of me I didn't even realise was there wanted to cry. I'd never seen him this angry before, especially not at me.

It hurt worse than a slap across the face.

Why the hell did I care so deeply about what this prick thought of me?

There was a chance he was the Templar who'd hurt Eli, White Suit.

I barely had time to scream before the boy was in front of me, its pure black eyes focused on mine.

"Are you bleeding?" Thomas spoke with a voice that sent shivers down my spine. It sounded like a child's voice but was closely followed, almost to the point of overlap by a loud, deep echo of the same words.

I let out a sob.

This thing was going to eat me!

"Tom, could you please leave my friend alone?" Cory said.

"Okay." Thomas stepped back and gave me a sharp look.

I swallowed and relaxed slightly as the thing—the boy backed away. He kept looking at me as though it was my fault his mother was upset.

Cory looked back at Bailey. "Do we really have to do this, Liv?"

"He's only a child." Bailey fell into her chair, all the strength fading from her body as she held her head in her hands and started to cry.

"I know." Cory walked over to her and placed a hand on her shoulder.

"You know her." The accusation left my mouth without permission as I looked between him and Bailey.

"Yes," Cory said.

"Marco is going to keep escalating this, isn't he?" Bailey said.

"Unfortunately. I can't guarantee the next person who comes after him will be as lenient as I plan to be." Cory knelt down beside her.

"He'll be looked after?" Liv wiped her tears from her eyes with the back of her golden yellow sleeve.

Cory nodded.

Liv nodded in response with agreement she couldn't verbalise.

Cory looked over at Thomas. "Would you like to live with other boys and girls like you?"

Thomas stopped staring daggers at me and looked at Cory. "Will Liv come and visit?"

"Yes."

I noticed Cory couldn't meet either Liv's or Thomas' eyes as he said the simple word. I looked down to where I'd been rubbing my bloody finger against the side of my suit pants.

The boy gave Cory a smile that transformed his cold, dark eyes into something almost comfortable to look at. I stood shocked as Cory took Thomas' arm and led him from the house towards the car.

Liv's eyes narrowed as she took a step towards me. "One day soon, all of this is going to fall apart. Whose side are you going to be on?"

I looked down at my shoes and the bloody finger marks on my grey pant leg. "I don't know."

"There are several sides to everything. Remember that while you're stewing over your guilt."

I nodded and quickly left the house without looking back at her before she changed her mind about burying Cory and me in a flower bed.

Soon? It would be decades before anyone in my generation would be powerful enough to defeat magic users like Liv Bailey.

What part could we play?

The established order would use people like us as disposable pawns.

The car ride became surreal as the opening lines of *Bohemian Rhapsody* filled the car as we wound our way along the thin gravel road from her property.

Cory angrily tapped his fingers against the steering wheel as he drove down the empty gravel road. Thick scrubland speckled with farmland surrounded the thin, rough road on either side. Thomas sat on the back seat with a chocolate bar Cory had given him.

"What happens now?"

Cory touched a sigil on the seat behind him before he spoke. "Sometimes, the appropriate thing isn't pretty."

Thomas had noticed Cory cast a spell but didn't seem to hear what he'd said. He looked at us for a few seconds before he looked out the window again.

"I won't like this, will I?"

"You need to know."

"What's that supposed to mean?"

"I can't tell you."

"You said you'd be honest with me."

"Sometimes it's best for your own safety if you see things the way Nate Island intends. The Templars have members who scan people's thoughts."

"Is everything going to shit?"

"Not if we all play our part."

"What are our parts?"

"Your part is protecting vulnerable people from supernatural creatures."

"Thomas doesn't seem like much of a threat."

"He's draining Liv's life force."

"He doesn't seem like an unwelcomed threat." I forced the words through my gritted teeth. Liv was an old, powerful mage who'd lived a long life. If she wanted to give the last years of her life to a supernatural child, were we in the right to stop her? If Marco was to be believed, she'd always wanted a child.

"Where do we draw the line? If a seventy-year-old woman can let a creature drain her, why not a sixty- or fifty-year-old woman?"

"That's being pedantic."

"You are here to follow my orders." Cory clicked his tongue.

I shut my mouth, my teeth clacking together. I put my tongue between my teeth and pressed down slightly to prevent my next words from leaving my mouth, looking away from him.

Maybe it would be okay.

But who was I trying to fool other than myself? The place we were going to would have a sickly dark underbelly like every other corrupt institution under Nate Island's control.

Gran had been right and I needed to talk to her without Mason.

Mason, who was so loyal to the Nate Island cause because he was a Templar himself. A member of a secret society created to push their power even through illegal means. There was no way my oldest brother would take my side.

How could I talk to her with the Templars and detectives tailing me? I couldn't sneak to Mason's house. Not to mention she'd never be left alone at the house, even though she could look after herself for a few hours; no one was going to trust her alone.

14

I bit my lip and blinked back the tears that formed in my eyes. The demon who'd almost killed me was a creature that acted on instinct and looked like a cross between a bear and a wolf, while Thomas was a thinking, feeling being with the cognitive function of a human pre-teen boy.

The long dark lashes that framed his black eyes were rimmed with tears when his head snapped up and he met my eyes in the mirror. My mind flashed to my younger brother at that age.

I'd helped abduct someone's child.

I'd been employed to abduct someone's child.

My eyes were fixed on Thomas' and I found myself unable to blink even as they stung from lack of moisture.

I closed my eyes and focused on taking steady, careful breaths. This was how it was and I couldn't change it.

Not alone.

I didn't want to be here in this place anymore.

The seat belt cut into my chest and neck as the front of the car crashed into something hard.

The airbags wacked into my body.

I opened my eyes as I screamed.

My entire body shook. My breaths came out in small, panicked gasps. I looked over at Cory, who slumped in the seat, unconscious.

Blood ran from his nose and down his neck onto his perfectly ironed white shirt collar.

I tried to pull off my seat belt, but it wouldn't move. I was stuck, pushed back against the leather seat. I looked around the car and saw

Cory's keyring had one of those tools on it that broke car windows and cut seat belts.

My shoulder and elbow screamed at me to stop as I reached out to grab the keys. I managed to get my fingers around the tool and pulled. It detached from the keyring so quickly it almost slid from my shaky fingers. I didn't know if Cory would be happy about what I was going to do, but whatever we'd hit properly totalled the car anyhow. I cut the belt and freed myself.

I reached over and carefully moved Cory's head so his neck wasn't crushing his windpipe. The air bag had been deployed and he likely hadn't broken anything, but I'd heard people had died in accidents like this from not being able to breath because of their slumped heads. I just hoped he didn't have a neck injury.

I checked his pulse at the same time. I had no idea what a normal pulse rate should be, but it did seem a little too fast.

I looked out the cracked front windscreen. We were in a paddock filled with long, dry grass.

What we'd hit was below the bonnet of the small SUV, so I couldn't see it. The cool breeze on the back of my neck reminded me of Thomas.

I turned around and looked at the empty, glass-covered back seat. He'd broken the back window and escaped.

Fuck.

I hoped he went back to Liv Bailey and got the hell out of town. Cory had likely told the prison he was heading towards that we were coming and would have to report this.

I slowly opened the car door and walked around to the front of the car.

We'd hit an old, grey tree stump. The front of the car had been low enough to be crushed by the impact. I looked back at Cory in the car. I had no idea who to call apart from Eli. I looked around the paddock we were in and at the tracks we'd carved in the grass from the wire fence we'd crashed through. I wasn't one hundred per cent sure where we were. I pulled my phone from my pocket and only realised I had no reception after I tried to call Eli.

Cory came to with a loud, ragged breath as he stared around the car. I ran to his door, pulled it open and cut his seat belt off, careful of his body. He seemed to have come to enough to notice Thomas was missing. He said something to me that I didn't understand.

He pulled himself from the car and I had to rush to catch him before he fell.

"What if you've broken something?" I said.

"We need to report this," Cory said.

"There's no phone reception here, so we'll walk back to the main road."

"Main road" was a relative term, as we had still been on a gravel backroad.

We carefully walked back to the road and I sat him down on some soft, short, green grass under the shade of a eucalypt tree.

He used the white silk handkerchief he carried in his suit jacket pocket to wipe the blood and sweat from his face.

I sat down beside him and waited as he called the Agency and a tow truck.

"What would they have done to Thomas?" I said.

"You don't need to know any more."

"I want to know," I said. "The *lesson* you wanted to teach me isn't finished."

"Jesus Christ, Dexter. What do you want from me?" His voice rose.

"Answers. I'm sick of this 4D chess shit you have going on. You promised to be honest with me," I said. "You said Thomas was a child with human-level intelligence. What were they going to do to him?"

"If you do another runner, I'm not chasing after you. I'm done with that behaviour. I forgot what you could be like."

"Stop talking like that, it's confusing and it just makes it worse," I said.

"Sorry." He leant against the eucalypt that shaded us, fine pieces of bark flaking off onto his red, green, and black tartan suit.

I blinked back the tears that had formed in my eyes and met his. "You know Liv Bailey."

"Yes, but I'm off the Christmas card list after what I just did."

"You've met Thomas before."

"Yes."

I waved a hand towards him. "That case wasn't a red one, was it?"

"It was classified at a green level with the potential to become blue if Liv or Thomas had become agitated."

"We're not remotely qualified to tackle that. I can't imagine you got any high-level demon-hunting experience when you trained to be a doctor; a pathologist, at that."

He just stared at the grass under us.

"You could have gotten us killed," I said.

"I handled it."

"I think you were serious about what she could have done to us and barely talked her out of it."

"I had to do this case by the book before someone else. If it were anyone else, someone would have got killed."

"We almost got killed! Why would you purposely put me in that kind of danger?"

A look of total devastation washed over his face. He closed his eyes, took a deep breath and relaxed his features. "I didn't think it would get that far."

"You took away her child."

I expected Cory to argue; instead, he let out a loud, shaky breath. "I had to do this by the book for their safety. If she killed one of our coworkers, they both would have been hunted down and executed."

"That doesn't make it right."

"We've been over this before," Cory said. "You know my stance on it."

"They've got you properly leashed like the bitch you are."

Cory laughed. "Dramatic, much?"

"You're a cunt."

Cory walked back to the car, rubbing his temples. "I will not be on the receiving end of the serve I'd get if I leave you out here."

"Are you going to get into trouble for this?" I said.

"Yes, but I've got a member of the board who'll protect me."

Grandfather.

Cory had drugged me, thrown me over his shoulder and delivered me to him.

I pushed my head backwards hard against the tree trunk as I gritted my teeth. Why did I have to be attracted to this guy? Eli was only making it worse by giving me permission to seduce him. I hadn't seduced anyone in my life, or at least anyone I knew of. I felt the gaps in my memory like invisible walls and wanted to scream.

"Are you okay?" Cory carefully scanned my body with his eyes.

"No," I said.

"They imprison and brainwash human-like demons to work for them. They also force them to breed when they reach maturity. Their children are blank slates for Nate Island to have perfect agents who are raised to follow their order. Cannon fodder that can go into situations unsafe for humans," Cory said.

"That's beyond fucked up," I said.

"You wanted to know." Cory didn't look at me this time.

"I can't believe you were going to sell out Thomas just to teach me some kind of lesson."

"Are you serious? Not everything is about you. I wasn't trying to teach you some kind of lesson about the Agency. I was trying to do my job. A job I have to do to protect myself."

"It was me you almost got killed today," I said. "Am I just cannon fodder too? As a criminal? A mage that went *wrong*. A person who didn't learn my place and be a good little mortal like I'd been told?"

"Dex."

I turned my back on him and pulled my phone out to send a text to Eli. Cory had told the tow truck driver where we were.

Eli took me in his arms without speaking when we arrived home. Just one look at my expression, and he knew it'd been a bad day. After a long shower together, we sat on the bed and watched a comedy.

I couldn't deal with anything dark at the moment.

I didn't speak a word until I'd drunk enough of the gin and tonic he made to loosen my tongue. I told him the whole sordid story, the look on his face becoming more troubled with each word.

He didn't speak until it was clear I didn't have anything else to say. "That's fucked up."

"You honestly didn't know?"

"No. I doubt it's common knowledge. The vast amount of people wouldn't stand for this." Eli didn't really drink outside of social occasions, but he reached over to the nightstand and downed a few mouthfuls from the gin bottle. He pulled away from the bottle as the liquor stung his throat and caused him to cough. "Demons imprisoned as breeding stock so they can create an entire generation of slave creatures who'll unquestionably follow Nate Island," Eli said.

"Cory didn't seem as concerned as he should have been," I said.

"That's because he thinks if he can be a good little kid and play along, he can change things from the inside. It's why he gets along so well with your grandfather," Eli sighed. "It doesn't work like that."

"How does it work?"

"You change things from the outside."

"I want to know how!"

"You don't need to do anything. I'll let the right people know and they will solve the problem."

"I hope Thomas finds Liv Bailey and they get out of town before the Agency catches up with them."

"Are you sure that's safe?" Eli said.

"Yes," I said.

Eli kissed my forehead and held me close as I fell asleep in his arms.

I was safe for what felt like the first time that day. I couldn't believe Cory had brought me into that situation. Even if Liv Bailey was hesitant to kill him, I was a stranger to her.

15

I woke suddenly in the night. I was about to roll over and go back to sleep, but then I saw the shape at the end of my bed.

My stomach clenched when I realised it was a person. Someone was in my room! It wasn't Eli. He'd told me he was going to leave and talk to someone about Thomas and Liv Bailey after I fell asleep.

I tried to scream, but a hand sealed over my mouth before more than a muffled squeak could escape. I froze in terror as the assailant put his weight on my body and pushed me down hard against the bed.

Had Siegfried decided he wanted his revenge after all?

I managed to slip my arm free and fumbled for something, anything, on the nightstand. My fingers curled around a long metal pole. Before I could pull at the lamp, I felt a spark of pain go through my arm.

"Stop struggling," the man holding me down hissed.

Ralph? I relaxed and stopped moving. I forced my panicked body to take deep, relaxing breaths.

He was going to keep the pressure on me as long as I struggled.

What the hell was he thinking? Eli would have attacked first and asked questions later.

Why was Ralph here?

I spoke as soon as the hand was removed from my mouth. "What are you doing here?"

"Have you seen Gran since Mason took her?" Ralph asked.

"Only at a dinner party the other night. I didn't talk to her."

Ralph growled and ran a hand through his dark hair before he took a seat on the bed beside me. Even in the dark, I saw mud slip off his boots onto the carpet as he aggressively crossed his legs at the ankles. "We need to save her. Mason's too far gone to be near her."

I had no idea why he'd become so angry after the relaxed conversation we'd had at the lookout.

What had happened between now and then?

"I just need you to get in contact with Gran and make sure Mason isn't giving her a hard time."

"Why would our brother give her a hard time? He loves her just as much as we do," I said.

Ralph grabbed my hands and looked me in the eyes. "Promise me, Dex."

"Promise you what?"

"When I tell you to run, you run."

"Excuse me?"

"I know that Corvin arsehole is trying to worm his way back into your life, but I won't let that happen." Ralph stood up and started pacing around the room. "We've done too much to have everything ruined because you can't keep your dick in your pants."

It took me a second to recover from the words 'dick in your pants.' Sometimes Ralph affirmed my gender so aggressively it startled me.

Corvin back into my life? I didn't know Cory until a few weeks ago and I sure as hell hadn't had sex with him. "What are you even on about?"

Ralph looked around the bedroom and let out an exaggerated sigh. "I know you probably thought it was a good idea to ingratiate yourself with a prominent family, but the whole marriage thing was a little much, wasn't it?"

"You're not making any sense." I stood up and grabbed the front of his shirt in anger. "What is going on? Why are you acting like this?"

Ralph looked at me, shocked, as though he only just realised I was an adult a couple of inches taller than him and not some child he could manipulate.

He pulled himself back from me and straightened his shirt. "It doesn't matter. The plan has gone to shit because you couldn't keep your head down. They're going to kill Gran after a sham public trial designed to humiliate her."

"People are not as stupid as you think they are. They knew Gran and Pop taught me magic."

"I knew we should have told you," Ralph said. "Not let you wander around Dunn vulnerable and oblivious to your past. Pack your bags. I'm pulling you out now."

"Excuse me?"

"Excuse me, excuse me, excuse me. Stop saying that, you sound like an offended middle-aged woman who wants to speak to the manager."

"You know what? I really would like to speak to your manager because the service is up to shit." I took a step towards him, and he stepped backwards.

Fuck this arsehole.

I would not do what he said just because he was the precious big brother I'd always idolised. I wasn't a little kid anymore.

"Get your things." Ralph poked me hard in the chest, his voice dark. "It's not a request. It's an order. I won't let you be their puppet."

I moved around him so the door was to my back, careful to look like I was moving towards the large wooden wardrobe.

He seemed to relax as though he thought he'd won.

I really was a pushover.

"I'm not going anywhere. You are going to leave the way you came." I spoke sharply and carefully, ensuring every word was clear.

Ralph let out a bitter, mocking laugh. "Forget your shit. Get out that window before I make you."

I punched him in the nose, my resolve almost crumbling when I felt something break under my fist.

I'd punched my older brother who was accused of multiple murders in the nose.

Hard enough to break it.

Ralph flew backwards from the impact.

I'd punched my potentially innocent older brother in the nose. The guilt hit me like a wave of sickening dizziness.

He looked up at me, the shock, rage and anger in his eyes solely directed at me.

I dived for the bedroom door, kicking him as he lunged towards me. I yanked open the door and screamed, "Get the fuck away from me!" I ran out into the dark wooden panel hallway and crashed into the opposite wall. I recovered just quick enough to avoid Ralph, who rushed from the bedroom intent on crushing me against the wall.

I let out the highest pitched scream I could and yelled, "Help!"

I tripped at the top of the stairs as Ralph grabbed my ankle. I managed to kick him in the face before he grabbed both of my feet and rolled down the stairs.

I landed at the feet of Viola, who had yanked her bedroom door open just as I'd landed at the bottom. She looked at me, shocked and angry at the noise.

Ralph was walking down the staircase, illuminated by the moonlight that shone in the large windows lining the stairs.

He spat out a mouthful of blood and fixed his gaze on me.

He didn't see Viola; she was in a blind spot. I didn't look at her, not wanting to give her away. She wouldn't let him take me, right? "I'm not going anywhere with you."

"You are," Ralph said. "But I'm going to make you regret what you did to my face first."

Viola dived out from her bedroom threshold, used magic to jump over me and stood between Ralph and me. She used her own Telekinesis Magic to push Ralph out of the window. "Leave him alone."

I heard the rest of Eli's family rush towards us as Ralph flew from the window. It wouldn't be enough to seriously hurt him, but would it be enough for him to give up and leave us alone?

I didn't want him to get hurt.

I pulled myself to my feet, my entire body shaking as I watched the window and waited for him to jump back through it.

"Where's Eli?" Viola inquired.

"Out," I responded.

"What happened?" Lacy Senior demanded as he ran into the hallway with the rest of the family.

"Ralph," Viola said.

I didn't relax until Viola had reached the window and said he was gone.

Lacy Senior pointed a finger at me. "What happened?"

"He broke into my bedroom and started talking crazy. He wanted me to come somewhere with him and got violent when I refused." It sounded weak when the only sign of injury on my body was the bloody scratches on the leg he'd grabbed and bruises from rolling down the stairs.

I was the one who'd got violent first.

I'd pushed him to the end of his rope.

"Where is Elijah?"

"Out with friends," I answered.

Lacy Senior looked at his watch. "It's one a.m."

I shrugged.

Did he want me to attach a tracking collar to him or something?

Eli was my husband, not my property.

Part of me knew I was supposed to be the property in Lacy Senior's eyes as far as this arrangement went. I was someone he allowed his grandson to fuck. He could easily get rid of me and probably would have sooner if my grandfather wasn't his friend.

We spent the rest of the night sitting downstairs in the living room together in silence.

Around three a.m., Eli came home and endured a lecture from Lacy Senior about going out late.

Kat slid the business-sized yellow envelope across her glass dining table towards me. "This is the person you used to be."

I placed the glass of water she'd given me down on a coaster, picked up the envelope and unwound the string that held it closed.

"I managed to talk Aubrey Quinn into letting you owe her a favour," Kat said.

I looked down at the pieces of paper that I'd slid from the envelope. They were photocopies of newspaper articles about Nox and his crimes from before February 2016. There was a period at the end of 2015 without any articles.

"Why aren't there any from late 2015 if I turned up in Dunn without my memories in 2016?"

"You were missing for a couple of months at the end of 2015."

"And no one thought to mention that?"

"Look. You were likely caught up with this stuff near the end of high school, then you left for a year after you graduated. A year later, you came back and started studying online. Then you went to Perth for graduation and stayed there until you suddenly turned up in early 2016 honestly believing you'd spent the last few years in Perth," Kat said.

"What happens now?" I said.

"I thought you knew that. You know all the information I have," Kat said.

"You wrote some of these articles."

"I didn't know you were Nox until we were talking to him and his brother."

"I was seventeen when Nox was created." I laid the pieces of paper out on the table in order. "I've got a lot of this information from people telling me different pieces."

"I just thought you might want them," Kat said.

"It will help," I said. "I need a timeline to try and discover who did this to me and why the Agency is trying to frame me for this new string of crimes."

"Are you sure they're framing you? What if it's Ralph trying to frame you?"

"I trust him," I said.

"I don't. Odd how Nox and Dark Matter have been connected to a group of kids who didn't have the ability to open a portal to let a demon in," Kat said.

"You think Dark Matter opened that portal?"

"Yes."

"Why? Ralph has a reason for taking that spell book but no reason to kill those kids."

"I didn't say it was on purpose. They may have taken on more than they could handle," Kat said. "But that email sent to Eli connected Nox with the situation."

"I think that was because I went there," I said.

"What if that's not true?" Kat's heels clicked on the blue and white checked lino floor as she walked over to the sink to wash up the cups. She wore simple sandy pumps, a tweed knee-length skirt, tan stockings and a white button-up shirt with a waistcoat that matched her skirt. Her mousy brown hair curled in loose perfect waves, carefully held back from her round face with conservative hair pins. She looked more like a traditional journalist than usual. She leant over the sink and contemplated the idiot she thought I was.

"Am I keeping you from work?" I said.

"It's my lunch break." She tapped her French tip nails against the edge of the metal sink.

I nodded, even though she couldn't see me.

"I don't know what you're trying to prove, Dexter."

"Prove?"

"This is all making me realise we never really knew each other. You were always closer to our other friends, caught in rivalry between them over who was your best friend. Sometimes I think I was only your *friend* because I'm your cousin."

"I'm trying to find out what was done to me and why," I said. "Prove I'm not Nox and save my gran. I know she's not related to you, but Ralph is. I'm pretty sure he isn't doing the darker things Nox is currently being accused of."

"The murder, you mean," Kat said.

"Yes," I said.

"Want to learn about the local vigilante crowd? Have a frank discussion with your precious husband." Kat grabbed her soft, white pea coat from where she'd folded it over her chair. "Or maybe June. She's probably an easier mark."

I looked Kat in the eyes. "I was your friend as a kid because I liked you. I don't get why you're still obsessed about who was best friends with who when we were twelve." I left the house without another word.

It shocked me she was pretending we would have stayed close friends when she was keeping magic secret from me.

16

I had to visit Gran to talk to her without prying ears and tell her my side. Knowing she hated me was killing me.

I'd wait until everyone in the house was asleep. Gran would be on the lower floor, with everyone else on the upper floor and opposite side of the house. The biggest challenge would be sneaking down the stairs.

The instructions Pop left were clear.

It had to be a safe place I could easily picture in my mind.

Capture all five senses.

Nowhere else downstairs held the importance the tiny secret room connected to my childhood bedroom did.

I was sure it used to be a storage space when the house was originally built. When I was a kid, it was empty and the perfect secret paradise.

At midnight, I downed half the teleportation potion; the only thing on my mind was the safety of my secret room.

The worn oak floorboards, white wallpaper with blue stripes and tiny pink roses. The crown-moulded ceiling with intricate rose borders that matched the wallpaper. A room that smelt like old books, even though the space wasn't large enough for a decent-sized bookshelf. Dust so thick I could taste it in the air, in my head, the smell of a clean, well-kept old book was almost orgasmic. I was pulled from my thoughts as I landed flat on my back, my gaze on the roses carved into the white textured ceiling as soon as I opened my eyes. I could just about make out the shapes in the half-moonlight that shone in the small window above my head. I pulled myself from the dusty floor and held my nose as I almost sneezed. No one knew I was here and sneezing was the best way to announce my presence. Mason was the strong, protective type and a light sleeper. I'd noticed as much when I lived with them between moving back to town and marrying Eli.

I carefully walked down the hall to the stairs; thankfully, I didn't need to pass Mason's room to get to the staircase. I just hoped none of his kids woke up.

It was easy to find my way around my childhood home in the dark, every step I needed to take to sneak downstairs without waking the household ingrained in my muscle memory.

I walked into Gran's room and watched her sleeping for a minute, trying to figure out how I'd wake her. Her eyes opened, and I had to clamp my hand over my mouth to muffle a scream. A squeak escaped between my fingers.

"Dexter," Gran whispered.

It wasn't a question; it was a statement. She knew who I was. She confirmed my suspicion she was stronger than she claimed to be.

"Yes," I said.

"Go home."

"Excuse me?"

"Leave the way you came."

"We're alone. No one's here. We can talk openly and privately." I sat down on the carpet beside her bed and tried to take her hand. She pulled her hand away from mine and pinched my fingers when it was clear I didn't get the message and tried again.

"Please tell me how I can make this right," I said.

"You can't," she replied. "There's no making this right."

"I'm sorry." I forced myself to breathe slowly to hold back the sob that threatened to escape my throat, glad she couldn't see the tears that framed my eyes.

"You told them our secret."

"Grandfather found out," I said. "Please believe me."

Why had Ralph thought this was a good idea?

"There's nothing I have to say to you. You've made your bed at their feet, and now you have to lie in it."

"I had no choice but to work for them."

"Great for you. You're still young enough to be useful." She paused so long I almost thought she was done speaking. "I'm not."

"Please don't say that," I said.

"It's the truth."

"I don't want it to be the truth."

"I didn't want to be in this position. Yet here we are."

"Gran."

164

"Go, before I alert Mason to your presence," she said. "I'll scream and he might attack first and ask questions later."

"I'll come and see you later."

"Tell Edwin his way won't work. He was at that dinner party the other week," Gran said. "Arrived at the same time as that Cory."

She said "Cory" like it was a dirty word.

"What has he done?" I said.

She let out a bitter laugh. "Cory's nothing but his puppet. A kid so desperate for a parental figure they'll cling to anyone who offers them a snippet of kindness. That one is Edwin's to the bone."

"What do you mean?" Did she mean what I thought she did? Grandfather seemed hostile to Nate Island and if Cory was on his side, that meant...

He was what?

A double agent?

As soon as the words sunk in, I wanted to forget them.

Would he be in danger by proxy if I knew?

Or was Gran wrong, and Cory had been thoroughly brought into the folds of the mage community?

It felt like something that was dangerous to know.

Cory being a double agent was too good to hope for.

Had she told me this to fuck with me?

If the wrong mage read my mind, it would get him killed or imprisoned regardless of the truth.

"Tell Edwin that playing within the rules and wishing hard won't get him the outcome he desires," Gran said. "He was always as much of an idealist as Dorian and look where that got him. Though Edwin always played the dumb blond well for a man when we were young."

"You're not very nice," I said.

"Don't see this as an excuse to fall into their arms again."

Their? Was she still talking about Cory? She had to be, right? She'd been using that pronoun for Cory.

"It's not as bad as the Lacy boy, but we both know the truth of that," she said. "It was always women before he came along."

I walked out of the room without another word, hot tears running down my face.

It cut to the bone every time someone didn't take my relationship with Eli seriously.

What if the words got to him? What if paranoia wormed its way into his heart and soiled the love he had for me?

"Did you get what you wanted?"

I yelped as Mason walked out of the room beside Gran's and into my path.

"Did you hear all that?" I said with a faint voice.

Shit!

Would he hurt Cory?

Mason placed a single finger on my lips and forced a small vial of potion into my hand. He led me across the house and into the sunroom. "If you know what's good for you, you'll forget everything you learnt here tonight."

I pulled back from him and gave him a dirty look. "I'll do what I like. From what I've heard, you have a vested interest in the situation."

"Who told you that?"

"It doesn't matter."

Mason leant close to whisper in my ear. "You forget that they're my grandparents too. I was almost an adult when Pop died. I knew him better than you ever will."

The reminder curdled my stomach and clamped down on my heart.

"She whispered violence in one of my ears while he whispered idealism in the other. I was their first experiment, first contest," Mason said. "But as the oldest male magical heir of Edwin Arkwright, I only had one destiny. Do you think I had a choice regarding my life path?"

"No." The truth had never tasted so bitter in my mouth. I wanted to hate Mason for being a Templar, but he didn't have a choice. With Kat's father dead, Mason was the oldest male in the family with magic, apart from Grandfather.

"I couldn't pass it on to Ralphie or you with your illegal magic, and Ned was always so young, the baby brother."

"What does this mean for your sons?" I asked. "Are you going to repeat the cycle and sentence Dante to the same fate as you?" He'd reached out to wipe the tears from my face with a handkerchief, so I felt him stiffen. Mason had the incredible skill of making me feel like a little boy, always found a way to make me need him, want him to care about me the way Ralph did. As a kid, I'd been confused by one distant and one overly attentive older brother and desperate for Mason to love me like I loved him. Now Mason seemed to be making up for lost time while Ralph pulled away.

"Have you ever loved me?" I said.

"Dex," Mason said.

"All I wanted my entire life was for you to love me."

"You're my brother."

"I don't want some obligatory 'you're my brother of course I love you' bullshit. I want you to actually love me," I said. "Help me. What they're accusing me of isn't fair."

"I know it isn't fair. None of this is fair. It kills me that this happened to you. That they did this to you." Mason spoke through clenched teeth. He rubbed my neck where the bruises Siegfried left had been. He slid to the ground and ran a hand through his dark wavy hair. "Who hurt you?"

Hurt me?

Thanks to Cory's magic, they had faded as though they were never there.

Mason had seen them at dinner the other night like everyone else.

"Who did it?"

"Siegfried Thornton."

"Why?"

"Kat and I broke into his house."

"What would possess you to do something like that?" He looked utterly panicked in the dim moonlight. I looked into his eyes when I spoke. I wanted an indication of what he knew. "To find information about the Agency framing me and him for the current Nox's crimes."

"You are so naïve." Mason shook his head. "You remind me of Pop sometimes. That same idealistic naïveté, so sure there's someone or something out there that will live up to your expectations of how the world should be. How you want it to be. The world doesn't work like that. People are selfish. The ones who aren't out for blood are the ones who get gutted."

"I just want to live a happy, safe life on my terms in a world where no one is hurt unjustly," I said.

"Take that potion and forget tonight. For your safety and the safety of me and your *friend*," Mason said.

"Why did you say 'friend' like that? Are you talking about Cory?"

"Yes." Mason gave me an exasperated look as he stood up to walk from the room, done with the conversation. "Dex?"

I looked up to see that he'd turned around.

"I do love you," he said.

"Then show me you care about me."

"I'm sorry for the way I treated you growing up. I was an idiotic teenage boy who didn't want to share his parents' attention with another sibling. Ralph took to being an older brother so easy it made me jealous. I took my anger out on you and I'll never be able to forgive myself."

"I want to believe you, but I'm not sure I can. I'll never be able to forget the way you hurt me."

"I know. I just—" He left without another glance back towards me.

Just what?

I wanted to scream.

I took a heavy breath.

I waited until I heard his door close before I drank the remaining half of the teleportation potion to return to the bedroom I shared with Eli.

17

I was pulled from a late morning half-sleep by a hard knock on my window. When I opened my eyes, I met Thomas' dark voids.

He smiled at me, all sharp teeth, a predator that had caught his prey. He wasn't done with me.

I jumped from the bed and grabbed the door handle as the window smashed behind me.

I screamed as a body hit the floor. I felt the disrupted air from him lunging at my ankle as I ran from the bedroom.

It was the middle of the day and no one would be home. Even on a weekend, the other people who lived in the house had places to be.

I ran down the hall with the knowledge that any gains I made were him playing with his *food*.

Floor plans of this house wouldn't be hard to find if he wanted them.

No matter how safe I thought I was, it was all a lie.

"I called Cory and told him what I'm going to do," Thomas said. "By the time he gets here, I'll have your head ready to greet him on the front gate. First, I'll let you suffer a little. By the time I got back home, the Agency had taken her. My mum is rotting in a jail cell or worse. Cory ruined everything."

There had to be a way to distract him until Cory came.

I ran into Eli's father's office, locked the door and climbed out the window onto the lower part of the roof.

I slipped a couple of times on the mossy tiles, cutting my bare feet and hands as I made my way towards the side of the house that overlooked the pond.

Cory was on his way; he had to be.

I turned around on the edge of the roof and faced Thomas where he stood a couple of feet from me.

He raised an eyebrow. "Do it. I dare you."

I let myself drop backwards off the roof, hopefully into the pond where Eli and I spent hours skipping rocks as kids. We'd taken turns telling each other about the horrors that lay under its surface.

I knew it was deep, but fear wrapped coils around my heart.

Would it be my grave? If no one knew I fell in there, would they ever find my body?

I didn't brace myself against the impact; hitting either the ground or the water like this was going to hurt. I hoped the water would hurt less than the lawn.

How high did I have to be before the surface was hard enough to kill me?

The last thing I saw before I hit the water was Thomas' disappointed face as he looked over the edge of the roof.

Guess he didn't know me as well as he thought.

Pain overtook me as my body slapped hard against the surface of the water. The air was wrenched from my lungs in the short seconds it took me to sink.

The murky water was deeper than I assumed.

I was locked in a surreal moment of frozen time. A stranger in this alien space that had likely never seen human life. I panicked trying to find the surface.

I was going to die!

My head pounded as the edges of my vision slowly darkened. I swam towards the direction I hoped was up.

This is why Thomas had let us go.

He wanted revenge against Cory.

The realisation was like a lead weight that drained the energy from my body.

All I'd wanted to do was put some distance between us.

My body moved instinctively, desperate for air, and I sucked icy water into my lungs.

I woke as I coughed water from my lungs. I tried to push the person above me away in a panic as I fought for air.

"Dex. Hey, hey, it's okay."

I realised the person who rubbed my back was Cory.

He sounded like he was crying.

I looked at him. He was soaked with dirty pond water, a fresh cut on his bare left hand, his eyes red and damp.

Another sob left him.

He brought the shaky, bloody hand to his mouth as though to silence the sound.

"Cory?" I said.

"I thought I'd lost you again."

"I'm okay." I let the tears form in my eyes.

I was alive.

We sat there in each other's arms and ugly cried.

His tears were anguished, but mine happy.

I was alive.

I wanted to scream victory, but I kept the smile from my face.

Cory still looked like he was seconds from his entire world ending, like I was going to suddenly keel over and die. Seeing him like that hurt more than expected.

"What happened to Thomas?" I said.

"I wounded him and he ran off." Cory moved away from me and wrung some water from his dark, wavy hair. It was matted where it sat above his shoulders. He pulled a somewhat dry handkerchief from his pocket and tried to wipe the mixture of tears, snot and stagnant water from his face.

"I'm sorry."

"You're never really sorry."

That stung, but I kept silent.

"What do we do now?"

"I don't know. Sometimes I almost forget," he said.

I wondered just how involved the two of us had been in another life. The life I'd been made to forget.

He narrowed his green eyes at me. "How do you know?"

I stood. "I need a shower. I stink."

"A bath sounds safer. You almost drowned, Dex." Cory's expression was stony as he stood. "You need to rest. Sit or lay down."

I looked him in the eyes. "Knowledge is dangerous, but we could pretend things are as they once were for a while… if you wanted."

"That's a dangerous proposition." His pupils dilated. His face displayed an emotion somewhere between sadness and desire.

I forced back the urge to kiss him and gave him what I hoped was a sexy smile instead. "There's plenty of other bathrooms, but I'll leave my door open."

He swallowed. I could see a thousand thoughts flash through his mind, his green eyes displaying an array of emotions.

I walked off towards the house, my heart beating rapidly in my chest.

The version of Eli that existed in my head reminded me of every lewd thought I'd refused to allow myself to think about Cory.

I didn't look up at Cory as he walked into the bathroom seconds after I'd sunk into the tub. I listened as the pieces of his clothing hit the floor one by one; each built upon my arousal. I hadn't thought about the logistics of how two people around six feet tall would both fit in a bathtub together.

"Are you sure this is okay?"

"Eli gave me permission."

"Explicit permission?"

"Yes."

"The two of you talked about you having sex with me?"

"Him as well," I said. "He's always on. If you know what I mean."

"Eli and I have," Cory said.

"Have what?"

"Had sex."

"Okay." I was slightly shocked. That hadn't been what I expected. It made things slightly more complicated. It also explained a lot. Eli and Cory knew each other more than they were putting on.

Why hadn't Eli mentioned that?

I was sick of them treating me like a delicate wilting flower who couldn't handle things as they were.

"Before you and him," Cory said.

I turned to face him. "Was I wrong in assuming you and I —"

"No."

I took a moment to scan his naked body. Long limbs, well-muscled stomach, legs and arms that spoke of hours in the gym. A light dusting of carefully groomed dark hair covered his skin.

"You really are something to look at," I said.

He met my eyes and raised an eyebrow. "Turn around."

I obeyed him. A shiver of arousal passed through me as I waited for him to take the lead.

Cory slid into the tub behind me and sat, his legs on either side of my body. I felt a jolt run up my spine through the points where our bare skin connected. Cory's nipples were pinpricks against my back as he rested against me.

"Close your eyes and mouth."

"Okay." I closed my eyes and waited in anticipation for what he'd do. I felt water fall onto my scalp and drops slide down my face. Before I could speak, he had grabbed shampoo and started to lather it into my hair. I knew from the smell it was Eli's.

This was a whole lot more intimate than I pictured.

Cory came across as someone who wanted a boyfriend rather than a fling. Not the type to sleep around and that had me off balance.

Had I loved this person carefully washing my hair once?

Had he loved me?

Did I break his heart?

Is that where this angsty, sad act came from?

I could almost feel his sorrow leak into me. Each kiss he trailed under my chin, down my neck and onto my shoulder burnt with it.

I wasn't the person he loved anymore.

That version of me was dead... erased.

I was someone else wearing his ex-boyfriend's skin. After we were clean and dry, I led him into the bedroom, my hand wrapped firmly around his.

Cory rolled off me to lay in a relaxed heap of long limbs. He lay on his back and stared at the ceiling, wide-eyed, as he caught his breath. He ran a hand through his incredible hair, which had been thoroughly mussed by the activity.

I took a moment to take him in. His long, muscled legs were even more delicious without clothing covering them.

He was covered in a layer of sweat; we'd have to have a shower.

Why was this enchanting, attractive person interested in me?

Was he interested in me, or had this been another manipulation tactic?

I looked over at him. He'd enjoyed himself, right? He seemed into it when he thrust his body against mine. When he pressed me down onto the bed and had his way with me.

I had no idea why I genuinely wanted him to desire me.

I wasn't the person he wanted me to be.

I was a broken reflection of that man.

He winked when he noticed me staring and met my eyes. "Was that how you wanted it?"

How I wanted it? No one had ever asked me that before, and Cory was far from my first.

"Dex?"

"Yes."

"Good." He pushed my fluffy hair back from my forehead and kissed it. It was almost startling how gentle and caring it was.

His eyes so close to mine, I could see flecks of brown in the green and the disappointment when I froze as his lips met my skin.

"Cory, I…"

"It doesn't matter." He let out a shaky breath. "Sometimes I forget. I have no idea what I was thinking."

"Forget what? What aren't you telling me? What is the secret everyone is keeping from me?" I knew what was coming, but I wanted him to say it. Wanted confirmation that Siegfried hadn't got to me. That I wasn't paranoid. It wouldn't be real until someone I cared about told me.

Cory didn't know I knew.

He sat on the opposite side of the bed, his back to me. "I can't tell you."

I sat up and curled my legs under me. "I'm sick of people lying to me."

"If you're honestly in the position you claim, the less you know, the better it is for your safety. If they think you know anything, they'll strip your mind bare. You're nothing but a tool to get to more important people."

"Has my memory been erased?" I said.

"Parts of it," Cory said.

"Why pretend to care about me if you're working for people who want to hurt me?"

"I'm not. Not really."

"Stop all this political shit and be honest with me."

"I'm watching you under the order of someone who cares about your safety. I was asked to prove you didn't know anything and that you were honest about your memories being erased."

"Grandfather?"

"Yes." He turned around to face me.

"Why?"

"I respect Edwin. He's been my mentor since I started."

"Are you trying to tell me my grandfather is a Templar?"

"Are you surprised? He was the Arkwright heir like Mason is. It would be remiss if a board member, ex-mayor, and part-owner didn't know about all the inner workings of the Agency."

I forced him to make eye contact with me. "I feel like I've known you far longer than I should have."

He didn't say anything.

"Were my memories of you collateral damage?" I said.

"I think so, but I had nothing to do with it," Cory said.

"Were we in a relationship?"

"Dex."

"People don't kiss people like you just did casually," I said. "You said we'd fucked before, but it's more than that, isn't it?"

"Don't call it that," Cory said.

"Fucking? What would you like me to call it instead?" I said.

"It doesn't matter. We haven't been together in over two years."

"How did I know you?"

He looked away from me again, his mouth a thin line.

"Did Grandfather ask you to look out for me because he knew?" I asked.

"Knew I cared about you? Yes," he replied.

"You're only telling me this because it's the least dangerous thing I forgot."

"It's been eating at me not saying anything."

"Did you love me?"

I saw his eyes widen as he looked fully away from me. "It's been two years and you're with Elijah. This was a momentary lapse in judgement."

"I'm a lapse in judgement."

"You were here, I was emotional and let my guard down," Cory said. "I thought you were dead when I pulled you from that pond. I was just so happy you were alive."

"I liked it. What we just did."

He let out a bitter chuckle and ran a hand through his hair. "I promised myself I wouldn't fall for this again."

"Fall for what?"

"Your bullshit," he said. "When someone tries to pull away, you bring out the guilt trip and charm."

"I'm not that person."

"Sometimes it's hard to accept that."

"Did I hurt you?"

"You have no idea," he said.

"How long were we together?" I said.

"Almost three years."

"Why would they have given me fake memories?"

"If you learn the truth, you can't tell me. Even people who want to keep a secret are a danger to each other. If you have a dangerous secret, you can't tell Eli, me or anyone you think you can trust. It adds extra minds to be spied on."

I nodded and pretended not to notice how he brushed off the fake memory question.

"No one can ever know we had sex apart from Eli. I can't expect you to keep it from him."

"Didn't your handlers want you to seduce me?" I said.

"They wouldn't want me to actually have sex with you. Not after how close we got the last time," Cory said.

I had to fight back the tears that formed in my eyes.

"I was a naïve and sheltered twenty-two-year-old nerd who'd just gotten out of a long-term relationship with the only guy I'd ever been with. You saw the empty space inside my heart and crawled inside. They thought letting me date Trevor for four years was enough experience for me to do what they wanted."

I looked at his face and made him meet my eyes. "What does 'let you date' mean?"

"They forced him to break up with me for the sake of our positions within the Templar. Queer and reasonably pretty in a feminine kind of way, they had plans for me from the start. They let me date Trevor to get *experience*. I'm supposed to be an irresistible, gender-bent temptation who will bend for any willing cock they need on their side."

"Did they know?"

"That I fell in love with you? Yes. I was reeled in, not the other way around."

"Why did they let you approach me this time?"

"I'm the only one willing to do it. It doesn't matter how well I perform the magic side of my job, to those at the top of the ladder all that matters is I'm able to bite pillow for the sake of the organisation. I made the mistake of letting them see that in me. No one said this was going to be easy."

I felt sick as I looked at him. "Have they made you do things you don't want to do?"

"It's their job to make me do things I don't want to do," he said.

"Why?"

"Why?" He raised a dark eyebrow as he spoke.

"Why did you decide to work for the Templars?" I said.

"Magic needs to be kept out of the hands of the masses who could misuse it. I've seen what happens when a community rebels against the rule of Nate Island and it's not pretty."

Eli walked into the room and smiled when he noticed us. He walked into the closet, stripped his clothes off and pulled on a clean pair of tight, short boxer briefs. He turned around, took a couple of minutes to slowly run his eyes over both of our bodies then flopped backwards between Cory and me.

"That was hotter than I could have ever imagined," Eli spoke.

My head spun as I realised Eli had watched us and what he'd been doing to need a change of pants. "I heard you moan."

"Fuck. It was hard to keep quiet after I saw how you reacted to what Cory can do with their tongue."

"Why do the two of you think it's appropriate to swear like that?" Cory asked.

"It didn't bother you so much when Dex was begging for it." Eli threw his head back against the pillow and let out an exaggerated moan. "Fuck me! Yes, harder. Fuck! Just there."

The obvious hit me then.

Cory, who could sense other people's heartbeats from a distance, would have known Eli was watching us and exactly what he was doing.

"Don't be jelly, Dex." Eli licked his lips. "I let you have your share, now it's my turn."

"I'm not," I said.

Eli winked at me, pulled himself onto Cory and started making out with him. It was hard to push past the little voice in the back of my brain that said I shouldn't be enjoying the sight before me as much as I was. I was supposed to be jealous, but this was one of the hottest things I'd ever seen. There was a knock at the bedroom door. I yelped and almost fell off the bed. I grabbed the nightstand to steady myself.

"Eli, it's family game night, remember?"

It was Eli's mother.

Cynthia was on the other side of the door and we were on the edge of having a threesome.

"We're changing," Eli said. "Be down in a minute."

"Dinner is on the table. There's a plate out for your friend too," Cynthia said.

"Friend?" Eli said.

"We have security cameras and I can sense their heartbeat on the other side of the door." Cynthia walked off. She, Viola, Lacy Senior and Barton had seen everything that had happened outside. It wouldn't be hard for her to guess what we were doing in here either.

"I hope you're hungry." Eli pulled on a pair of loose sweatpants.

Cory laughed and stood up. "Do you have clothing for me to borrow, Dex? Mine smell like pond water."

My mind went to the pile of wet clothing on the bathroom floor. Putting it in the washing machine had been the last thing I'd cared about. Hopefully, Cory thought my life was a worthy price to pay to lose a custom magic suit. Even though I was apparently a lapse in judgement. The pang of sadness I felt at that thought shocked me. The people who erased my memory had broken me, stole parts of me and left the remains piled in a corner. I could never forgive that. Even if I'd agreed to this, I couldn't have any real idea what it would be like to be a jagged reflection of a person.

I grabbed a tee shirt and sweatpants from my closet. There was no chance in hell any of Eli's clothing would fit Cory.

Eli pulled me into a hall cupboard and closed the door and I watched as he cast a silence spell. "You have to understand if I haven't told you something, it's for your own safety. If one of the Templar agents sees the wrong thought in your head, it will be all the excuse they need to rifle through your mind. They won't care about being careful. They will do damage and hurt you."

"Okay," I spoke the word slowly. Siegfried hadn't cared about that. Maybe that was a concern. Maybe everyone was right about him and, by extension, Wyatt. I knew he was going to tell me something I should have known a long time ago. That warning was similar to what Cory had told me when we were in bed together.

"There's something you're going to find out about Cory and I know you'll freak out about it after what happened between you."

"Just tell me," I said.

"Cory's the White Count," Eli said.

My ears rang as I leant against the wall behind me to keep on my feet. Cory was the White Count, and Eli, who'd encouraged me to have sex with him, knew. The person who'd broken his nose and ribs. My skin crawled at the memory of Eli kneeling over as he was punched in the stomach by Cory.

"He didn't hurt me," Eli spoke almost too quickly. "It was all an act until you used that ghost to burst everyone's eardrums."

"An act?"

"Your grandfather heard what they were going to ask Cory to do to me... to us. Cory and I put on an act," Eli said. "I was surprised he agreed to it, I thought he was angry after what I did."

"That attack was about me, wasn't it?" I said.

"They thought you'd do something to save me if yo—" Eli cut himself off as though he only realised he'd have to explain something I wasn't supposed to know.

"Still remembered being Nox."

Eli took a step backwards and crashed into the wall behind him. "How?"

"Siegfried." I looked at him, shocked at how quickly he'd tried to put distance between us. "You don't think I'd hurt you, do you?"

"I'm sorry," he said.

"Are you scared of me?" I said.

"Never."

"You just jumped back like I was a live wire." I realised my fingers were wrapped through my hair. I removed my fingers before I could pull at it.

"How much do you know?"

"Little."

"Never think about any of this at work or in public, even for a second."

I nodded. "You and Cory know each other."

"Yes."

"Why did you think he was angry at you?"

"I stole you."

"Stole me? How could you steal me? I'm a person."

"You were with him, and the moment you claimed memory loss, I strode in and stole you," Eli said. "Don't look at me like that. I did steal you. It used to be him shared between you and me."

"That was two years ago."

"You were together longer than we've been."

I gave him a small smile, though I had no idea if it was sad or to reassure him.

Eli said, "I let him fuck me. You had an open relationship because you were only supposed to be using each other for magical politics. It was always in a dark bedroom and I didn't know him as Cory."

"How long have you known who the White Count was?" I said.

"He wasn't the White Count back then, just another foot soldier."

"Should I want to date a guy who has sex with the criminals under his care?" I said.

"I initiated almost every time. It was really hot. I wasn't even captured ninety per cent of the time," Eli said.

"What the fuck is wrong with you?" I said.

"I'm young, dumb and full of c—"

"I don't need to hear it."

"I'm the ultimate switch and I wanted to see what it was like to be dominated by someone powerful."

"He still had sex with someone he considered a criminal. Someone he had authority over." I dug my nails into the wrist I held.

"He doesn't have authority over me. I don't answer to the Agency off the clock. That's not how this works. The only power they have is gained through force." Eli slowly ran his tongue over his bottom lip. "He's easy. Like you. I really like easy men; a few targeted words and they're dropping their pants and spreading their legs."

"Doesn't that make you easy too?"

"I take advantage of easy people."

I nodded my head and hummed. Yeah, that made him easy too, despite his protests.

"Hearing you and him together today appealed to parts of me I didn't even know existed," Eli said. "There's just something about the two of you over the other guys I've been with."

"You are the crudest little prick I know."

"You married me." His smirk made my stomach flutter.

I gave him a small smile.

"Shit." Eli ran a hand through his hair.

"What?"

"Siegfried ruined everything by telling you. I was told just saying it could cause you psychological damage," Eli said.

"Why are you so scared of him, anyhow?" I asked.

"He's blackmailing half the town. He has a lot of power."

"Does that include you?" I said.

"Let's just get downstairs. I don't want to leave poor Cory alone with my family for too long," Eli said.

I didn't argue.

18

I looked at the message for a long time.

I need to talk. You'll want to hear this. Come alone. - ST

Siegfried Thornton, it couldn't be anyone else. I almost let the phone slip from my numb fingers as I collapsed back into the chair I'd been sitting in.

I had to go.

I stood up again and grabbed my shoes and car keys.

The burger joint he directed me to was located on the southern outskirts of Tallow. A locally owned twenty-four-hour hole in the wall across the road from a large rest area frequented by truckers, road trippers and backpackers hitching their way to Sydney or Brisbane.

At nine p.m., the place was mostly empty, which would give us privacy.

"What do you want?" I avoided eye contact as I sat across from Siegfried.

"A conversation. You give me information and I give you information."

"A conversation? You threatened to assault me."

"I was honestly trying to scare you out of trying something like that again. The world is filled with worse fuckers than me, and you need to learn respect, or you'll get killed."

"Oh, yeah. I'm fucking sure of that."

"I thought that was behind us. I was angry because I thought your brother killed the love of my life," Siegfried said.

"Why would Ralph do something like that?"

"If he did it? He's Nox. He didn't like me blackmailing him and decided to make me pay."

"So you thought you'd hurt me to make him pay?"

"I thought I was angry enough, but I couldn't go through with it," Siegfried said. "You remind me too much of my brother."

"What do you want from me?" I said.

"I need you to tell me where Ralph is."

"I don't know where he is."

"I found out who killed Greyson. They're about to make a move on you and Ralph." Siegfried fell silent as a worker brought food to the table. I thought he'd picked this place because it was transient without table service. Had he paid them extra to do that? "Seeing as Ralph is the current Nox, he is in the most danger. Someone needs to warn him. They might come for you first as the weak link and arrest you, but they will kill him on sight."

"Who told you this?" I said.

"I have my sources," he said.

"I need more information than that."

"They saw you on a security camera talking to Ralph at the lookout, drinking with him. You both looked pretty chummy."

"I decided to hear his side after our meeting," I said.

"Then there's Mason, who isn't very good at keeping his pretty little head shut."

"They read his mind?"

"They have Mind Mages who scan people walking in the front doors."

"He was worried about them reading my mind. Gave me a potion to forget," I said.

"Best you don't damage those brain cells of yours with any more shit like that." Siegfried's complexion paled a little, and he placed down the fork he was going to use to eat his gravy-covered chips. "Sorry. The thought of giving my brother or sister a potion like that if they'd gone through what you had makes me feel physically sick."

"It did damage my trust with him." I took a big bite of the burger he'd ordered for me to try and settle my stomach.

"With those two things plus the Thomas situation, they have enough to arrest you for working against the Agency."

"I didn't do anything there. Hell, he even came to the house and tried to kill me," I said.

"The only witness they have to the crash is Cory. He had a head injury and doesn't remember."

I remembered what Wyatt had said his job was then. "Wyatt's your source, isn't he?"

"Yes. They tolerate him because they wanted a Thornton talented at Mind Magic working for them. Our family has always had an affinity for it, like the Gerstle family with Death Magic. Magic isn't hereditary, but some people seem to have a genetic disposition for certain skills."

"Did the Templars have your Greyson killed?" I lowered my voice when I spoke.

"I'm pretty sure. They want me to do something that would give them an excuse to get rid of me," Siegfried said. "No one but the leader ever knows who the current Trigger Man is. I've gathered that neither of them like my control over Wyatt."

"Trigger Man?" I said.

"Their top-level assassin." Siegfried picked at his chips.

"Who's the current Templar leader?"

Siegfried wide smile lit up his eyes. The genuine joy he was about to have floated off him. "Barton Lacy Senior."

And I'd married his wayward grandson. As an ex-vigilante, puppeteered by Evelyn Patton and Edwin Arkwright who would never bear Eli's children even though I had the *ability,* forcing him to make Viola and her eldest daughter Megan, the primary Lacy heirs.

What had he been planning to do with me before this? I was supposed to be the second chance at a perfect Lacy and Arkwright union before anyone but Eli realised I was a man. There was so much damage Barton could do without Eli even knowing if he wanted Eli to produce an heir. I was reminded of my IUD, as though I could feel it as a physical presence in my body; I'd had thoughts of physically clawing out my uterus growing up.

He'd realised I wasn't going to play along like his family and wanted to clean his hands of me.

He had to do it without pissing off Grandfather. I called him Grandfather, but it was more a sarcastic nickname mocking the idea of the man he should have been. We'd always been close growing up; he'd spent every spare moment he had with his family. From what I'd gathered, his own grandfather had been a powerful, abusive man. His own parents were passive victims of it until he broke the cycle. Lacy Senior reminded me of my great-great-grandfather, even though I'd only ever heard stories. Grandfather had fought back when he planned to kill him for being gay and to get rid of his baby sister for being a girl instead of a replacement male heir. Even though Kat's father was the eldest son and had magic, he'd wanted a do-over.

Both Lacy Senior and Grandfather had been in their mid-twenties then. They'd been raised in that culture by men like that. If Lacy was painted with the same brush, were Viola and Eli in danger too?

Now more than ever, I felt like the puppet of older powerful men and women.

In that moment, I could understand why Siegfried, who was only in his mid-thirties, had decided to use his abilities to burn it all down rather than participate in the system.

Remind these people of their dues.

I was about to speak when Hawking burst through the door with a gun pointed at our table.

"Hold it. You are under arrest!" Hawking said.

Siegfried swallowed a transportation potion before anyone could react; he was gone.

"You try it and I'll shoot," Hawking smiled at me, a hunter who had found its prey.

I stood still, let him cuff my hands and throw a black cloth hood over my head.

Once we arrived in the holding cells, Andrea attached cuffs to my ankles, chaining them together and me to the ground under the bench, then took the cuffs off my hands. "You have one call; I suggest it's to your lawyer."

I didn't have a lawyer.

Eli didn't have the power to help me and I didn't want to ruin Cory's career if I called him. I had no guarantee anyone else would help me, even Grandfather, if they found out where I was and why. There was only one person who I wanted… needed. I dialled Mason's number and felt tears well up in my eyes when he answered.

"Mason Arkwright speaking?"

"Mase." A sob escaped my throat.

"Dex?" he said.

"I'm in real trouble and I need you."

"Dex! Where are you?"

"The holding cells under the Agency." I wiped the tears that ran down my face with the back of my wrist. "They've arrested me and want to do a memory probe."

"I'm coming. Just hold on." He hung up the phone.

As soon as I placed the phone on the hook, Hawking re-cuffed my hands. "I've been asked to do a *thorough* search."

I felt a shiver run down my spine and settle as nausea in my stomach as he pushed me down the hall, his rough grip tight enough to bruise my arm.

He spoke as though it would be his pleasure to make me as uncomfortable as possible.

"Don't think anyone is going to care if you scream. Dominguez hates your kind just as much as I do. Wealthy spoiled brats of Agency *golden* families who need to be taught their place." He pushed me into the hard metal door frame as we walked from the hall. My face took the brunt of the blow.

I felt something wet run down my face. It tasted metallic rather than salty when it ran into my mouth.

My whole face hurt and I couldn't tell what was bleeding. "I've been framed."

He cut me off with a hard kick to the stomach. He gripped the front of my shirt and forced me to stand as my legs threatened to crumple under me. He grabbed me by my hair and pulled hard enough that I felt a handful of hair come away from my head when he let me go. He threw me to the cold hard concrete below our feet.

"You're fucked in the head." I wondered how much I could take. If I made him angry enough to really hurt me, Mason had to tell Grandfather, and this prick would be done for.

He slammed his foot down on my ankle.

I screamed in pain.

"You privileged members of legacy families think you can tread all over the rest of us and play by your own rules. Get away with everything while the rest of us have to play by Nate Island's puppet strings. You go on a criminal rampage for five years and you're just a wayward son in need of guidance. If I even thought of doing something like that, I'd be executed without a second thought."

"You don't scare me." I hissed through my pain as I pulled myself from the ground, met his eyes and spat the blood from my mouth into them. "Cunt."

He hissed in anger and backhanded me across the face.

I closed my eyes and took a deep breath; if I was in control, this would be okay. There's no way he wasn't through after hurting me like this, I'd make sure of it. How many other people had this arsehole hurt? I'd be the last one after my injuries were exposed. He had to hurt me in a way that couldn't be hidden.

I was pulled from the ground by my neck, both his hands around my throat.

My air was cut off as he tightened his grip, his sharp blue eyes fixed on mine. With my arms cuffed behind my back, I couldn't do anything to stop him or even struggle. "Your brother killed the kids in that house and you helped cover it up. My sister was there, but no one cares about her because a Carson brat was killed."

I felt his spittle hit my face as my vision started to darken at the edges. I really hadn't thought this "make him hurt me" idea through.

I struggled to take a breath.

At the movement, he squeezed tighter.

Where the fuck was Dominguez?

He was going to kill me!

"What the fuck?"

He let go.

I dropped to the floor as Hawking was pulled back by someone who had their arm around his neck.

I blinked away the darkness and tears. I forced myself to focus despite the dizziness as I realised it was Cory who had grabbed him and spoken. I watched through unfocused eyes as Cory threw him to the floor and punched him in the face.

"Don't kill him." My voice came out gravelled and faint with fear. Cory couldn't hear me.

If Cory killed him, Cory's life would be over.

"Please." My throat felt like it was being stabbed by a thousand daggers as I struggled against the cloudiness of my brain. It'd be so easy to give into the call of sleep… Exhaustion racked my body.

Cory punched Hawking for a fourth time as he struggled under him, trying to get an advantage.

"Shit! Stop!" Andrea screamed and grabbed Cory by the back of his collar.

Cory spun around, anger in his eyes, but stopped short of hitting Andrea.

"He tried to kill Dexter." Cory pointed at me.

Hawking spat out a mouthful of blood and hopefully a few teeth. "He provoked me."

"Get out of here and go to sick bay, Hawking."

Hawking struggled to his feet and walked out of the room.

Why the hell was he investigating this case?

Andrea pointed towards Cory. "Search and heal him. I need to get that idiot seen to."

"Idiot? More like homicidal maniac," Cory said. "It's people like that who give us a bad name."

"His sister was one of the kids killed by that demon." Andrea just shook her head at him and handed him a grey shirt, matching track pants and slip-on sneakers. Cory accepted the bundle, and I let him sit me on the couch in the back office past the concrete room and slowly peel my soiled clothing from my body. Someone working on our floor must have told Cory what happened.

Against my better judgement, I let myself relax into his touch as he healed my body.

"Did you provoke him?"

"He thinks I helped kill his sister, when I was almost a victim of that thing too," I said.

I was sitting beside him, head buried in my hands, when Andrea returned with a stern look on her face. She looked at me, smiled then turned to Cory as she slid a thumb drive from her jacket. "I have something you might like to see. The reason why he's here."

Cory looked at her then nodded. He stood aside as she cuffed me and walked me to a holding cell.

I placed my head in my hands and tried not to cry. I watched them walk into a back room together.

When Cory walked out of the room, he didn't look at me and left the area with another word.

What had they shown him?

Was there something Siegfried didn't get a chance to tell me?

"That's what you get for fucking with things you don't understand." Andrea folded her arms across her chest and smiled. "Privileged fucker like you has so far to fall."

Privileged? I wanted to laugh. She was the one married to the Dominguez family heir. How was her position different from mine?

Was Andrea a Templar?

I didn't think Hawking was; with his anger issues, it would be too much of a risk.

Mason walked into the area and gave Andrea a hard glare, his usually tan face bright red. "How much to bail him out?"

"I have forty-eight hours left to question him. He's not going anywhere for all your family's money," Andrea said. "We have him on aiding and abetting at least five murders."

"What?" Mason said the word so quietly I could barely hear and he looked like he could be knocked over with a feather.

"Please, you have to help me. The people who don't like Grandfather have it out for me. Please look at me, one of them just tried to kill me. Ask Cory."

"Shut up." Andrea slapped the bar next to my head.

Mason took a long, hard look at my still-visible bruises. "If one of you touches him again."

"You'll what?"

"I'm coming back for him in forty-eight hours and he better not have any more damage. If he does, I will end your career and have you exiled. You have nowhere near the power I do, and I will use it to my full advantage to protect me and mine. Understood?" He spat the word "understood" at her, and for a split second I swore I saw her twitch slightly, as though she was about to smile.

"Fine," Andrea said.

My heart sank as I watched Mason walk off after he gave me a nod and reassuring smile.

I didn't feel reassured.

Like always, Mason had done nothing but think he had authority over anyone else in a room. As though everyone he spoke to was just going to follow his orders. They might have respected him slightly more than me, but they saw him the same as me. A spoilt son of a founding family. Only in some ways, Mason was worse because he actually did wave his Arkwright-sized dick around.

I was given a potion to null my magic when Andrea walked back to the cell. She brought me to a room with a steel table in the middle and chained the handcuffs to it. I was thankful Hawking hadn't come back; I knew the next time I saw him, I was dead. I hoped they wouldn't let him back until Mason could get me out.

"Talk." Andrea sat down after she turned on the monitoring devices within the room.

"About what?" I said. "Why should I present myself for a dangerous memory probe when you got rid of your only leverage?"

"Me allowing you the freedom of choice was me being nice."

"I'm sure my family will like you damaging my brain," I said.

"Your family has already damaged your brain," she said.

I swallowed, unable to respond.

They were still trying to blame Gran and Ralph? Did she know the truth, or was she in on it?

"Different family, but that doesn't change the result."

"Ask me what you need to know," I said.

"We'll start with the library and the books stolen from the Lacy vault," she said.

"It was Nox and another man called Dark Matter," I said. "Dark Matter opened a hole through the wall and they let themselves in."

"And you didn't mention this earlier?"

"They threatened to kill me."

"You claim that Nox, the current Nox, is another person?" she said.

"Nox is another person," I said.

"Cory Corvin has handed in his evidence against you. He claims that you admitted to being Nox prior to 2016 but had your memory erased.

We've spent the last couple of years trying to decide if this claim was true. Then you married into the Lacy family and the investigation was fast-tracked."

I understood why he had to do it, but it stung to know he'd put things I'd told him in confidence in a report. Had the last couple of weeks all been a ploy to get revenge or do his job? Maybe he was lying about not being allowed to sleep with me too. To make me feel like I was special. He told me he was ordered to sleep with me when I was first being investigated as Nox. Had the whole "jilted lover who'd gone too far in his mission" thing been a lie too?

Had Cory been playing me this whole time?

"He's been playing you."

Was Gran's assumption about him being Grandfather's creature wrong? Was he playing him, or pretending to on behalf of Nate Island? I'd given into him because I thought he was Grandfather's. Maybe it was worse... Had Grandfather forgiven Nate Island for what they'd done to him? He must have done something for them to allow him to become mayor of Dunn.

If Cory was working for Nate Island, what did that mean for Eli? For Eli, Cory and me?

"Playing me?" I said.

"Dr Corvin was given a very sensitive deep-cover mission."

So deep I knew who he was working for and why. Didn't everyone know he was the White Count? Why had I been so easily fooled into thinking he was a double agent?

That I was the exception?

That explanation didn't support Grandfather involving Eli, who was rumoured to be a vigilante himself. Several people had hinted at it, particularly Kat and Siegfried, who would know.

"What is your story? The defence you're going to give?"

"Should I be talking to you without a lawyer?" I said.

"Maybe you should have called one instead of your brother," Detective Dominguez said.

I didn't respond.

"Are you going to talk? You've already submitted to questioning without a lawyer by responding to me and not asking for one sooner."

I frowned at her. Did it actually work like that? Last I heard you should have a lawyer present the moment the cops tried to question you.

Did it work differently for magical crimes?

This obviously wasn't going through mundane channels.

Was this situation even legal?

It didn't matter.

They weren't going to let me leave or supply me with a lawyer.

Part of me wanted to tell her about Cory's connection to Liv Bailey. That he had dragged me into a situation that could have gotten me killed. If they hadn't arrested Liv, I would have suspected Cory crashed the car on purpose.

Where was Liv, anyhow?

Why hadn't Thomas come back again the moment I was alone to try and kill me again?

Had he lost his reason to hurt Cory?

Had they let Liv go?

I bit my tongue to prevent the angry admission from leaving my mouth.

I wasn't going to ruin his life like he had mine.

I was a better person than that.

Wanted to be a better person than that.

"Tell me about the demon attack," Dominguez said.

"There's not much to tell. It was an accident," I said.

"You just walked into a house with several dead teenagers, and it was a coincidence?"

"Yes."

"That creature could have only been let into this dimension by someone like Dark Matter, who is one of Nox's close associates."

"I didn't have anything to do with that. I was just doing the book collection job the mayor gave me," I said.

"Why did you crash the car Cory was transporting the demon known as Thomas Bailey in?" Dominguez said.

"I didn't."

She hummed.

"I didn't." I looked down at the table, not caring when I went cross-eyed.

"I almost think you'd be safer here. Dr Corvin did state he pulled you from a body of water on the Lacy property after Thomas tried to drown you."

"Thomas was angry at Cory for taking him away from Liv Bailey and I was an easy target that would upset him," I said.

Andrea laughed. "Dr Corvin wouldn't be upset if anything happened to you. All this lovey-dovey stuff was an act. Maybe you are as stupid as you claim. Who knew all you needed to spill your guts was a good *screwing*?"

The way she said 'screwing' made me feel dirty, like I'd been used and taken advantage of.

I had been used.

Cory had used and taken advantage of me, knowing I'd be an easy mark.

Did Eli know?

I felt like I desperately needed a shower.

I took a breath.

There was no way I was going to cry in front of this woman. Why hadn't Eli come for me yet? Surely he knew or had missed me by now.

I'd been here for hours.

Had Eli known and was just taking advantage, getting his fill? I was silent as I was led back to my cell by Dominguez and shoved in. I walked over and sat on the bed, curled in a ball that hid my face between my knees so anyone watching the CCTV couldn't see me cry.

I was pathetic.

This was pathetic.

I couldn't believe I'd let myself think people like Cory and Eli could actually love me.

At some point I drifted off into an uneasy sleep against the wall. I woke to a commotion outside the cell as Dominguez and another cop rushed up to the bars.

"What the hell is this?" Dominguez held a photo up for me to look at.

My stomach twisted when I realised what I was looking at: a photo of Hawking, his body limp and tied to the statue in the centre of town, a note with the words *'you hurt him, and I hurt you – Nox'* written on a white piece of paper pinned to the front of his dress shirt. He was still in the work suit I'd last seen him in.

"I don't understand." I took a step back away from the bars.

"Someone really wanted to send a message," Dominguez said. "As far as we can tell, he was forcefully drowned by someone with water-based powers in a process designed to take hours. We're lucky we found him in time."

"I guess you're going to accuse me of that now, from a holding cell."

"Oh, fuck off," Dominguez said.

"You hate me and just want me to go down for something," I said.

"You're lucky I don't hit you," she said.

"That sounds like the bare minimum of treatment in this place. Maybe you're why people don't like Nate Island and not people like me."

She hissed at me then left with her colleague.

Who had tried to kill Hawking?

How had they found out what he'd done to me?

I slid to the floor.

Had Mason or Cory told someone?

If one of them had let it slip, it could have been anyone.

Wasn't the obvious answer Mason?

I didn't want Mason to be the person who had spoken to someone who would have done that.

If Hawking wasn't a Templar, would they have done this as an excuse to go after Ralph officially?

I didn't know anyone with Water Magic.

At least I didn't think I knew anyone with Water Magic.

The lawyer Mason hired came soon after, and they were forced to release me.

As I pulled off one of the prison shoes, a piece of paper fell from it. I slipped it into my pocket and didn't look at it until I was a good distance from the holding cells. *'They showed me doctored footage of the crash.'*

The note was written in Cory's small, neat handwriting.

19

I screwed the piece of paper up in my hand as I walked from the Agency building towards town.

My conviction grew as I distanced myself from Dominguez's magic. She'd shown her hand; I knew she had the ability to read and manipulate emotions. My mind was clear now she wasn't using my darkest fears against me.

The most direct path was a short trail through the small reserve between town and the Lacy-Thornton Hotel. I wasn't ready to go home without talking this over with someone. I didn't trust Cory enough to see him yet, and I didn't feel safe enough to sleep in a house with Lacy Senior. I didn't have any friends of my own, and I didn't have any family in town who wasn't neck deep in the whole situation.

My phone was flat and I couldn't contact Eli.

I didn't think it was safe to go to Gran's parents' house in Tallow. Any move that looked like it was ordered by her and they'd be on me again.

Somehow, I found myself in front of June's apartment, which was in one of the handful of small apartment buildings between the newer and older parts of the centre of town.

She opened the door and looked me up and down. "Do you need a drink?"

"Something that will get me halfway drunk through one glass," I said as she moved aside to let me in.

"Eli's been looking for you." She crossed the small studio apartment to her kitchen pantry. It looked like it had once been a carefully crafted vintage wardrobe but was now painted pale blue to match the tiles above her sink and on the floor.

"Neither Cory nor Mason told him I'd been arrested?" I bit the inside of my cheek as I sat down. "Neither of them told my husband what had happened to me?"

"You were arrested?" The bottle of white rum she pulled from the cupboard clinked a little too hard against the plastic cup she was pouring into.

"I think they did it to lure Ralph in, but he didn't take the bait," I said.

"Why?"

"I think Lacy Senior wants to get rid of us," I said.

"And pair Eli off with a nice girl?" June laughed. "He may identify as bi, but that doesn't mean he's attracted to every gender. He told me he's attracted to masculinity rather than any particular gender."

"Masculinity?"

"So even if he found a woman he's attracted to, she wouldn't be one Lacy Senior approved of," June said.

I waited until she'd placed the cups in front of us and sat down before I asked the question I really wanted to know.

"Why didn't you say anything about my memory?" I downed half the contents of the geometric plastic cup, a mix of white rum and lemonade, in one go as I waited for her to speak.

"By the time I realised what happened, Eli warned me against it because I'd come to him confused about why you didn't acknowledge me the same way you used to. You looked at me like I was a stranger and I was worried I'd done something wrong."

"You were working and living in Beckham then." The thought hit me as the buzz of the alcohol started to sink in.

"I missed the drama," she said. "I was working for a magical embroidery company that was little more than a sweatshop."

"Is that why you quit?"

"We were being underpaid, but the boss also had an eye for valuable magical items. She stole an irreplaceable object from a kid fresh out of school who came to do an internship. It put a friend of mine over the edge, and I followed her."

"That's why you came to work at the library a few days after the wedding," I said.

"I was almost late for the wedding because I was helping get the object back," June downed a mouthful to match mine. "Had to quit after that."

"Sorry."

"It's not too bad doing grunt work at the library. I'm just glad I didn't have to move back in with my parents and be the perfect Dalton daughter. Marry a son of my father's business associates like my older sisters."

"Because we're either useful tools or making new ones," I said.

"You have a rare magic and you need to make yourself a useful tool. Change Lacy Senior's mind on getting rid of you," June said.

"Most people say the job will kill me within a year," I said.

"Fuck that! Most people don't have rare magic and don't learn new magic or hone their skills after they leave high school. Even those working for the Agency."

"Templars aren't chosen to advance, they're trained into it," I said.

"Bingo. That's why so many people let themselves get drawn into radicalisation. It's a path to learn magic from the most powerful mages in the country," June said.

I was silent as I let that sink in.

"I rejected the Agency and spent twelve hours a day working minimum wage sewing enchantments into cheap clothing made by someone paid shit-all in the third world," June said.

"Does what you do even have an application at the Agency?"

"I would have been enchanting the Templars' uniforms," June said. "My father is a Dalton and mother a Chesterfield, so I had a good job planned out for me the moment I showed skill in a certain magic."

"Jesus," I said.

"Someone let me know what I'd be doing there and I left to find a job in the garment district of Beckham the next day," June said.

I decided to get the conversation back on track now I felt more comfortable with her. Now I trusted she hadn't been close enough to purposely participate in the conspiracy of keeping my mental state a secret. Most people outside of the Dunn Agency gossip mill mightn't have known or noticed I had changed. Part of me wondered if I had friends from that life who now had no idea why I was ignoring them until they pieced it together.

"Eli and I sort of got together with Cory," I said. "It's early and I don't know what to call it, and now there's all this drama."

"Let me guess, Cory did something," June said.

"Detective Dominguez said that Cory was manipulating me and none of that was real," I said. "But he saved my life twice and seems really bothered about my memory loss."

"You and Cory used to be together."

"He told me," I said.

"I think you broke up or had an argument just before you vanished

195

for a couple of weeks and came back like the last few years hadn't happened," June said. "Eli said it was like you'd been living this other life in Perth."

I handed her the note Cory had left in my shoe.

"Do you think he's Nate Island's?" June said.

"I think he and Eli are my grandfather's. He should be working against Nate Island, but if he became mayor, he must have done something to get back on side."

"From what I've heard, Edwin Arkwright is the most powerful Empathy Mage anyone has seen. I heard my dad and uncle drunk once talking about how it proved the idea of breeding strong mages with each other correct."

A shiver of disgust went through me at the idea. Why were these people so obsessed with eugenics?

"I think it's actually years of generational trauma, eventually leading to people who need to become more and more skilled to survive," June said.

I bit my tongue; she had no idea what my grandfather had to survive when faced with a family patriarch who didn't want him. "But he hasn't broken the system. Ralph and Gran are sure it can't be done from the inside."

"I'm no rebel. I'm just trying to survive," June said. "Eli is playing both sides of the card. Only people like Lacy Senior know that, which means he will never be allowed into the roots of power like your grandfather and Cory." June downed the last of her second drink.

"What should I do?" I said.

"Like I said, you need to find a way out of your current situation, then make yourself irreplaceable. A tool Lacy Senior thinks he can use."

"Did you know he was the head of the Templars before I told you?"

"No, but it makes a lot of sense," June said. "Even though he's only my cousin's grandpa, he's always wanted to have control over my life. As though my choices reflected on him, when I'm a Dalton and most people forget that my mum and aunt used to be Chesterfields."

"You think I should talk to Cory?"

"I think you and Eli should talk to Cory." June smiled at me and looked me in the eyes. "I'm here as an ally if you need me."

I nodded.

"You can sleep here if you don't want to be in the same house as the man who wants to kill you," June said. "But I am going to tell Eli you're here."

"Don't let him come and sleep here," I said. "It might make Lacy Senior angry. The other night Ralph tried to abduct me. Now I see that it might have been a misguided attempt to keep me safe. The point is, he was angry when he discovered Eli wasn't home."

June's eyes widened.

"Like, unreasonable anger about him not being where he was *supposed* to be." I ran my finger over the layer of perspiration on the outside of my cup.

June walked over to the window to call Eli, then she brought back a blanket from the cupboard and helped me unfold her sofa bed.

Cory's house was a two-storey cottage-style house with an attic down a short dirt drive. It was at the end of an outer street and was almost encroached on by the state forest. The only thing separating the land was the standard chain link fence with metal wrapped around the bottom at the edge of the property line. To get into his yard, I had to walk through a gate built into a tall white picket fence. The outside of the white weatherboard house was overgrown with vines that reached the edge of the red-tiled roof. I didn't know Cory's work hours, so I had sat around June's house until after five.

I knocked on Cory's door.

He opened it a crack and I shook the bottle of whiskey I'd brought so he could see it.

He unlocked the door, and I was shocked to see him wearing a loose grey tee shirt and matching track pants. It was a jarring change from his usual eccentric collection of suits that were almost certainly custom-tailored.

"Can I come in?" I smiled at him.

He smiled and moved aside to let me in.

In the kitchen, I poured both of us a glass of the whiskey, topping it up with ice and Coke when he gave the go-ahead.

"You should start." Cory grabbed his drink and took a long sip.

"Eli told me that fight in Main Street was fake, and you're both on my grandfather's puppet rack," I said.

"He's my direct boss and mentor. I respect and admire him," Cory said.

"But he asked you to look out for me because we used to be involved."

"He trusted me to do what was best without hurting you."

I took the first sip of my drink, wincing from the over-appliance of whiskey. "You better start talking."

"Against my better judgement, I care about you," Cory said.

"Against your better judgement." I tilted my glass so the ice clinked against the edge.

"You weren't a very good boyfriend," Cory said. "It's like someone has placed a person I could actually be with in the skin of my shitty ex."

"Did I hurt you?" I said.

"You weren't abusive, just an arsehole."

I laughed as I felt the buzz of the alcohol start to affect my mind. "This whole situation is fucked up."

"I wasn't supposed to fall in love with you," Cory said. "It's happened twice. There are two different versions of you in my mind, even though you're technically the same person."

"Which one is better?" I said.

"You, as you are now. He wouldn't have cared about Thomas," Cory said.

"He didn't ask to exist, just like everyone else."

"Liv is the only friend of someone I care about." Cory looked down at the last mouthful in his glass. "I wanted to get on top of her and Thomas' situation before someone else did."

"That wasn't a red case, was it?"

"No. I warned you of the danger she possessed, but I had faith she wouldn't hurt you or me," Cory said. "My parents abandoned me to my aunt and uncle when I was eight. After Nate Island decided it was done with the town I'd learnt to call home, I was shipped off here."

I looked up and met his damp, green eyes. "You were forced to come here?"

"I was given a choice of five places, or I thought it was a choice... at first. I chose Dunn because my grandma was here. I was never close to her like I am her wife. I didn't know her very well, because she lived here. Her wife was the first person who truly made me feel like a heard and whole person since I lost my parents. Then I realised they wanted me to spy on her and friends of hers, like Liv." A sad, bitter laugh escaped his mouth.

I didn't know how to respond.

"You and I connected because we were both outcasts, viewing magical society through a double-sided mirror but never able to truly touch it. I've spent my entire life learning to pretend to be normal and you made me realise I didn't have to. You loved me for my weird self. I needed that: a person who saw me. I know the Templars didn't intend for me to actually fall for you, but I don't think I can ever fully be the person they desire me to be."

"I still want to," I said. "Love you."

"I'd be taking advantage."

"We already had sex. I think that ship has sailed," I said. "Eli didn't have the same reservations. You're a good person, Cory."

He actually let out a sob this time, his eyes filling with tears as his body shook just enough for me to notice. "I want to be. Nate Island will have me killed. Every other kid they took from my village was under ten; I was a gamble. A risk they wouldn't have taken if they knew how I spent the first eight years of my life. My uncle hid my origin from official records. I did love my aunt and uncle; they took me when no one else wanted me."

"There's something I have to tell you." I grabbed his hands and met his eyes.

"Ralph is the current Nox, isn't he?" Cory said.

"Yes," I said. My stomach dropped when I realised the words "isn't he" were bluntly added to the end of the sentence as though they were an afterthought. "The Agency framed him for the summoning in that house. They're using me to get to him. Siegfried said it was two birds with one stone because Lacy Senior wants to get rid of me."

"Have you talked to Eli about this yet?" Cory said.

"I haven't seen him."

"He needs to hear this." Cory pulled away from me and pulled his phone out of his pocket.

I sat on his couch as I waited for him to finish talking to Eli. As I waited, I took in the house for the first time. It looked like something that belonged to an eccentric scientist uncle in a middle-grade fantasy novel. The house was close to one hundred years old with an interior that hadn't been updated since at least the sixties. The smell of books permeated the air so strongly it almost certainly had to be artificial. I was sitting on a soft green, Victorian high-backed loveseat framed with dark wood. On the matching end table beside me was a decorative silver vase filled with an arrangement of dry native flowers and peacock feathers. They sat beside a lamp with an elaborate, black and green fabric shade with a beaded fringe and heavy gold base. The bookshelf across from me was stacked with sleek hardcover books, the majority leather. My eyebrows disappeared into my hairline when I noticed the perfect specimen of a stuffed male peacock that sat on top of the shelf. I knew Cory was eccentric, but I didn't think he was quite weird enough to have dead animals in his house.

Maybe he was.

The decorative centrepiece of the wall behind me was a collage of small frames with dried butterflies. It honestly felt like the house simultaneously belonged to him and someone else.

All the wood in the room was the same well-kept dark wood, including the floor under my feet, apart from the large green patterned rug under the couch, matching armchairs and coffee table. The coffee table held a handcrafted white teapot and mug painted with flowers. I reached out and touched the teapot, which was still warm, beside an open copy of a trade paperback. I marked his place and flicked through the book, quickly realising it was gay erotica. The burly shirtless dude on the cover should have alerted me to that. I placed the book back down in the same spot.

I suddenly felt like I had invaded someone else's private space.

The only other object on the coffee table was a scented candle, which joined the others around the room, casting a dim, warm light. I sniffed the candle as a suspicion slipped into my mind. I almost laughed; he had a book-scented candle. A tiny voice in the back of my head wondered if he'd notice it missing or care if it was me who took it.

I pulled back from the candle as he walked back into the room.

"Having fun?" He raised an eyebrow.

A heavy blush crossed my face as he walked across the room and came to sit beside me. My brain reminded me of the erotic novel I'd discovered.

What the fuck was wrong with me?

I'd had sex with Cory. For God's sake, why was I blushing over him reading a sex book?

I read sex books—well, erotic fanfiction, but there wasn't much difference.

"Do you like the reading material?" Cory smiled slyly as he placed a bookmark in his novel.

"You have a house."

"Yes."

"It's very you." Even though I'd said that, it still felt like he was squatting in someone else's house, someone who was at least seventy years older than us.

"Most of this stuff belonged to my uncle," he said.

"Oh."

"He was offered a job here in the fifties," Cory said. "My grandma came out here to visit him twenty years ago and never came home."

"Is it invasive for me to ask what happened to your hometown?"

He looked down at his long, ungloved, scarred fingers. "A civil war between those loyal to Nate Island and those who weren't. I was seventeen. Once the dust settled, Nate Island took all the surviving kids and split us up. I have no idea what they did to the adults, but even the loyalists were taken as prisoners of war. I'm almost one hundred per cent sure they were executed."

I felt sick. "Why are you a Templar? It sounds like Nate Island ruined your life."

"Because I learnt I have to toe the line or die. I chose not to die. I spent a year on Nate Island training to become a Templar before I came here," Cory said. "My choice was simple."

The centrepiece photo above the neglected fireplace to our right was a large photo of a man, woman and girl in the early twentieth century. "Is that your uncle?"

"Yes, and his family," Cory replied. "My cousin in the photo is still alive, but I don't really talk to her. She doesn't live in Dunn and couldn't take the house."

"Your mother's family aren't mages, are they?"

"No," Cory said. "My cousin and her family live in a remote community. I have no idea where, it's an illegal magic community."

"Illegal magic community?" I said.

"There are small magical communities outside of the Nate Island mages and the Morse Bay alchemists. You should know, because you'll have to deal with people from there sooner or later. Unaffiliated magic users don't last long. If you don't have magical allies, you're an easy target."

I was about to respond when Cory stood seconds before there was a frantic knocking on the door.

What had Cory told Eli?

Eli walked into the room ahead of Cory and sat down beside me. "My grandpa's behind everything?"

"Yes," I said.

"What's the next move then?" Eli said.

"We compromise with him?" I said. I honestly had no idea. June's idea of getting out of this then making myself a valuable tool was easier said then done.

Cory yawned. I looked over at the standing grandfather clock near the bookshelf; it was almost midnight.

"We should go," I said.

"You can come to bed," Cory said.

"I don't really feel like sex right now." I looked down at my hands.

"I was talking about sleeping. It's late," Cory said.

"Isn't that attention you don't want? I'm pretty sure your bosses are going to assume we're fucking if we spend the night," I said.

"Hide the cars," Cory said.

"You drive a hard bargain. I'm in." Eli stood and pulled his keys from his pocket.

Cory rolled his eyes. "You aren't the one I needed to talk into staying."

Eli winked at Cory and blew him a kiss before walking from the room.

I followed Cory to the end of the main hallway. He opened the door to let two golden retrievers inside. I stood in the doorway to the room, shocked he had dogs.

"What are their names?" I asked as one ran over to me, looking for a pat. I smiled down at her and provided the pat in question.

"Atlas and Comet," Cory said. "Comet is only a couple of years old, but I've had Atlas for almost ten years."

The dog he was patting had a lot more white on him than the one who was bouncing at my feet.

Cory gave Atlas a pat behind his ear.

The green wallpapered hall was narrow and lined with wall lamps that reminded me more of gas than electric lamps. This house had to be the oldest in the street; it wasn't a massive stone or brick mansion, but it wasn't a post-Second World War prefab, either.

The rest of the houses in the street, apart from one new house on the far corner, were all post-war three-bedroom prefab houses, likely filled with so much asbestos that they should have been condemned.

The stages of construction in the town told a long tale of its struggles and prosperity.

The houses in the newer parts of town were light-bricked and tile-roofed, apart from in the new housing estate that had just been built, which was filled with flashy rendered houses out of reach to most people who weren't city arrivals who had high-powered jobs and wanted a 'tree change,' as though living out here was a lifestyle rather than a life. A sick sadness built in the pit of my stomach when I thought about the people who'd never be able to afford to leave this place, stuck in their families' prefab houses or farms.

How would it be living here with a less accepting family?

There was a reason I hadn't come out as trans in high school; it would have been stupid and dangerous to come out at Tallow High in 2012.

Yet people used that as an excuse to gossip about me as though I couldn't be interested in men if I'd been with a woman. Even Eli hadn't been out at his high school, and he had a boyfriend during his final couple of years. Part of me wondered if Cory had been out in high school.

"Were you out in high school?"

"Okay. That's a weird change of topic," Cory said. "Sometimes I wonder what goes on in that head of yours."

"It's just people getting to me, forget I said anything." I ran a hand over my face, my eyes sore from the fatigue that had slowly crawled into my veins once Cory mentioned the time.

"I wasn't out in high school. I was the unschooled, weird-looking, fat, goody two-shoes, nerdy kid who was learning Blood Magic after my hippy parents abandoned me. If anyone found out I was queer, it wouldn't have ended well. I was a virgin until I was nineteen and started seeing my ex, Trevor."

"Unschooled?"

"I spent the first eight years of my life in the back of my parents' van, travelling from the top of Canada to the Darien Gap."

"Why?" I said the word without really meaning to.

The more I found out about this person, the more interested I was in him.

How did his mind tick?

Which side was he really on?

Who was he truly loyal to?

Was it Nate Island?

If it was, would it be without the threat of death?

"There was no 'why' with my parents. I have no way to contact them and have no fucking idea if they're still alive. You know what hurts the most? My uncle reported them missing when they never came back for me and the cops closed the case because they found my parents alive, well and voluntarily open to giving me up."

"I'm sorry."

"It's almost been twenty years. I'm over it. They stopped visiting and trying to play happy families for a week a year when I was thirteen." He closed the door and brushed past me without saying another word.

The way he spat the last line, he didn't sound over it, but I wasn't going to press the issue.

What could I say?

The idea of just sleeping in the same bed as a person I was romantically interested in seemed even more intimate than sex.

I felt relaxed for the first time in days as I lay in the early morning light and watched Cory sleep. Eli was pressed against my back, arms around my middle, his morning visitor firmly pressed into the back of my leg.

Cory looked so peaceful as he slept, his face and body fully relaxed.

Although Eli's snores ruined the atmosphere, he was too short to do it right in my ear.

The only thing that made me uncomfortable regarding Cory's house was that he'd decided to set his large bed up in what had to have once been a conservatory or greenhouse. I had no idea how I'd feel about sexy sleepovers here. I was glad I hadn't decided to have sex without seeing the bedroom first. The glass-walled and -roofed room held an almost absurd number of plants. The only furniture was the massive bed, a soft modern couch and a bedside table that held his glasses, retainer case, a glass of water and a copy of a book that didn't look like erotica. It had to be cold in here during the winter, but it was oddly beautiful, even though the idea of having sex here felt awkward. I shouldn't have felt awkward about it; the neighbours couldn't actually see us at the back of the house.

I pulled myself from Eli's arms and managed to get out of the bed as carefully as possible. The bathroom was on the other side of the house because this wasn't an actual bedroom.

I decided to see if Eli had brought us a change of clothes when he arrived the night before.

A page from a newspaper was wedged under the windscreen wiper of Eli's car. I grabbed it and almost ripped it in the process when I saw the edge of a grainy black and white picture of Nox. The heading read, '*Beloved Arkwright Son Wanted Criminal Nox.*' I looked at the byline and saw it was written by Kat. I knew which Arkwright son was taking the blame when I saw a colour photo of Ralph in the middle of the article. A photo of him in a nice maroon blazer and white button-up shirt, his dark curly hair cut short and carefully styled. The image had been taken from one of my university graduation photos. Mason, Ned, and I were cut from the photo to leave Ralph as I'd last seen him before the start of this business. Someone had brought a copy of one of my graduation photos to use against Ralph. My stomach curled, revolted at the horror that she had named me as the previous Nox. I screwed up the paper and threw it onto the gravel drive.

This was the last thing I needed.

What the hell had I done to Kat to deserve this?

I brought up Kat's social media pages to see where she'd checked in last because she was that kind of idiot to bask in the fame her job brought her. Desperate to be a local celebrity.

The diner.

She had checked in at the diner ten minutes ago.

I ignored Cory calling after me as I hopped into the car and drove off.

This was something I needed to do alone.

I hated that so many people were using me against my family as some type of twisted revenge.

20

Kat was cutting into her pancakes when I sat across from her and hit the table between us.

"Morning." She calmly continued to cut her raspberry pancake into small, neat pieces.

"What did I ever do to you?" I said.

"Nothing," she said.

"Why did you throw me under the bus with that article?"

"I know Ralph is Nox."

I let out a shaky, angry breath.

"And you decided to throw me under the bus too?" I said.

"I've heard things about you and I know where I stand," Kat said. "Your coworkers at the Agency should know who they're working with."

"After this, Katrina, I know where I stand. I'm going to do you a favour and forget I know you. Forget I ever cared about you." I waved off the menu the waitress tried to hand me and walked from the diner.

I sat in the park across the road on a park bench made of rotten wood under a tree that dropped its tiny orange leaves on me. My thin, dark grey hoodie did nothing to ward out the cold breeze.

The smell of wet grass and rotten leaves was strong as the cold air numbed my nose, the slight metallic tang of the dust under my feet mingled with it as I dug a hole with the heel of my boot. I'd broken through the thin wet layer of dew-soaked dirt to the dry ground beneath.

I needed to talk to Eli and Cory.

I felt like shit for storming off like that.

I had no idea what to do or how to go forwards.

I lay on the bench, my head hanging upside down off the end.

I didn't think anything of it when a council park maintenance van pulled up beside the bench I was on. They were such a common sight in the town's parks. The only odd thing about it was it had driven across the park and left deep tire marks in the damp, pristine grass. I moved a second too late as a person jumped from the van, wrenched my head up and shoved a chemical-soaked rag over my face and nose. I choked out a startled breath before I realised what I'd done and the world faded.

My stomach dropped as I realised where I stood: Siegfried Thornton's house.

I pulled my limbs closer to my body as I realised we were in the hall with the suits of armour.

Fuck.

If they woke, it would be like something out of a cartoon. Only the bad guy wasn't pretending and monsters were really real.

The idea felt ridiculous, but the axes the knights held looked sharp and well-maintained.

The monsters were real. I blinked away the thoughts and looked back over at a Templar who had a gun trained on me. This wasn't a kid's cartoon. Those axes and that gun were real and could kill me.

Fuck.

"I heard you've already been here. Bet that pissed him off." The voice was muffled and I couldn't discern the gender of the person who took me.

I knew it was the Templar's Trigger Man.

I watched as a short, red-suited Templar opened a portal and pulled a tied-up young man from the hole. A young man who was a mirror image of myself.

Trigger Man grabbed it—him.

Trigger Man was holding a living, breathing copy of me by the collar.

As I looked into his panicked eyes, I saw real terror. He wasn't working with them, he was a prisoner as good as me.

If they hurt him, would anyone care?

I swallowed two mouthfuls of vomit and it ran out of my nose before I just gave up and let it happen then and there in the hall, much to the dismay of everyone else.

If they hurt him, no one would care.

The red Templar gave me a sharp look, and I knew she was the one who had pulled me back into the car when Eli was attacked. "God, that's fucking gross."

"It adds to the theatre," Trigger Man said.

Theatre? I met the other Dexter's panicked eyes again.

Trigger Man smiled as they looked at me. "Don't worry, it's only a construct."

Trigger Man handed the gun to Red and used a gloved hand to pull a knife from their jacket. They slit the throat of the doppelgänger before I knew what had happened while I was making eye contact with him.

I felt like part of me faded as the life left his eyes.

I let out a sob as I wiped some of the warm blood from the side of my face.

A deep, metallic smell joined the room's odour of vomit, dust and old wood.

Somehow, they'd managed to do that without setting off the alarm and waking the suits of armour, but what other alarms had they set off?

"Sorry, I didn't realise how messy that would be."

"What the fuck?" I screamed at him, my voice cracking hysterically. I took a step towards him and felt the heavy keys in my pocket move. I knew how to walk home from here.

I was the closest to the door.

I knew how to escape this house and get to safety.

"Take a chill pill, Dexter," Trigger Man said. They turned to have a whispered argument with Red.

I slowly wrapped my hand around the keys in my pocket. I pulled them out and threw them at a suit of armour near the Templars. I bolted as the suits came to life and the two were distracted. I felt the air disrupted behind me as I dove through the door at the end of the hall and locked it behind me.

A suit of armour had swung its axe at me.

I ran from the hall, making sure to avoid the traps Kat had mentioned. Even if I'd set off others, I hoped to be far from the mansion before Siegfried turned up this time.

Halfway up the incline into the bush surrounding the house, someone crash-tackled me to the ground. I rolled down the hill as I scrambled for purchase and came back with only dirt under my fingernails. By the time I recovered, Trigger Man had their knee against the small of my back.

"You are done with that bullshit," they yelled from above me as they twisted their knee a little, just enough to hurt me as they put pressure on my spine.

Could I throw them off without causing damage to my back?

"You shouldn't have gotten involved in the magic community in the first place," Trigger said. "Why couldn't you stick your cock in a non-magical arse? I thought your taste in women needed work, then I met the men you fuss over. Good God, you have fucked-up taste in sex partners.

I'm surprised you didn't spread your legs for Siegfried, he'd be right in your fucked-up ballpark."

"We need to go, Siegfried will be here any minute," I said.

"I made a distraction that will keep him occupied and not provide him with an alibi."

"Shit." I didn't mean to say the word out loud, but it spilt from me when I realised what Trigger Man was trying to do. The Agency was trying to frame Siegfried for my murder. Everyone who still loved me would think I was dead when they found the construct's body.

Cory, Eli, Mason, June and Kat would lead a push against Siegfried because they knew he had a motive to hurt me. Trigger Man probably planted evidence, and with Mason backing him up, Cory had more than enough influence to convince Grandfather it was Siegfried.

No one would come looking for me because they'd think I was dead.

I felt a wave of red-hot anger towards Trigger Man but forced myself to push back the urge to throw them off and punch them to within an inch of their life. They may have been shorter than me, but they were stronger and fitter with dangerous magic. They wouldn't hesitate to hurt, maybe even kill, me if it was going to derail their plans.

"You are going to follow me to the car I have parked on the main road and not fight against anything I say or do," Trigger Man said.

I nodded and let them take my hand to help me to my feet. I looked into their piercing grey eyes. "I understand."

I recognised those eyes.

The Trigger Man was Andrea Dominguez.

I didn't think Red was Hawking. The Red Templar was too short and sounded like a woman. I was sure Hawking didn't have that kind of magic; he'd also still be in the hospital.

The car sat in the same rest area Eli and Cory had stopped at after they rescued Kat and I from Siegfried.

"Let's get out of this hell hole," Dominguez said as she fixed her mask in the car mirror.

I nodded and hopped into the car. As the adrenaline fled my body my eyes grew heavy and I found it harder to keep them open.

I was jolted from my light sleep by Dominguez taking a sharp turn that caused my head to smack against the car window.

"Hell!" I yelled at her without meaning to, angry and in pain.

She snarled at something on the paved road we had turned off. We were currently on a narrow gravel road, surrounded by trees on both sides. I saw the moon reflect off water through the gaps in the trees as the left side opened to a creek that ran close to the edge of the road. We had to be on someone's drive. How long until we reached a house? I couldn't see any lights in the distance.

What had spooked her on the main road?

She was forced to slow the car as she navigated the thin, dark road.

The air shimmered a good hundred meters in front of us and a tear opened in a large tree trunk to reveal Nox and Dark Matter, who walked out onto the narrow asphalt road ahead. I realised where they were as they stepped from the portal. Dark Matter held out an arm as Dominguez drove towards them.

"Those fuckers found a good spot to stand," Dominguez smiled.

She was going to run them over.

They couldn't defend themselves if I was in the car.

I pulled off my seat belt, opened the door and tucked my head in to protect it.

I rolled out of the car.

Pain shot through my body as it hit the bank of the creek, a sharp whack on the back of my head as gravity carried me down the embankment off the side of the road.

My mind returned to drowning in the Lacy's pond the moment I hit the cold stagnant water of the creek.

I wrapped my hands around the grass above me and pulled myself out of the creek. I coughed up water as I found stable ground.

I could smell and feel the blood running down the back of my head and into my shirt. Everything spun as I placed one foot in front of the other on the gravel path.

This had to be the way, right?

"None of that." An arm wrapped around me and I was spun around to face Nox... Ralph.

"None of what?" I hissed. My head spun as a wave of pain overtook me, my legs shaking as I struggled to keep standing.

Hell, I wouldn't have kept standing if Ralph wasn't there to steady me.

"You have a hole the size of Tasmania in the back of your head. I need to get you to a hospital to check for brain damage and you're going to need stitches. Do you understand what I'm trying to say?"

"A little."

"I'm not letting you have some weird concussion and ego-driven bad-arse moment that ends with you keeling over in the bush somewhere. Do you have any idea what I went through to find you?"

I started crying.

Ugly, loud, wet crying.

"We need to go." I looked around for Dominguez as I came back to myself and realised I'd been crying into the dark fabric of Ralph's shoulder. His silk suit was damp with my tears.

Even though it was dark, the full moon lit up the area outside the shade of the trees like a beacon without any artificial light pollution.

"Dark Matter sent her through a portal," Ralph said.

"Portal?" I said.

"She should be in the middle of Sydney." Dark Matter visibly shook as he walked over to us, his voice faint.

"We need to go to Siegfried Thornton's house," I said.

"Why?" Ralph frowned.

"She killed a... a..." I didn't have the words to describe what I'd seen. "A construct that looked like me. Said she was going to frame him for my murder."

"She's probably already got someone who is going to go to the house to 'bribe information from Siegfried' when you're reported missing," Ralph said.

"I would have been. The last time anyone saw me was this morning," I said.

"People are looking for you, but I don't think they trusted the authorities to care," Ralph said. He pointed at Dark Matter, who slumped against a nearby tree, a layer of sweat covering the pale skin exposed by his emerald green silk mask. "I think he needs a rest."

I pulled my phone from my pocket; it was in a zipped pocket of my hoodie and still seemed to be working. "Do you know where we are?"

"An hour east of Tallow," Ralph said. "Tell whoever you're calling to meet us on the highway near the Reed Road turnoff."

I nodded and pressed Wyatt's name in my contacts.

"Hello?" Wyatt dragged the word out slowly in a cautious tone with a hysterical edge.

"I think you've found the present Detective Dominguez left your brother," I said.

"Dexter?" Wyatt said.

"Yes."

"Thank God," Wyatt said. I heard the muffled bump of fabric against a hard surface on the other end of the phone. I imagined him leaning against a wall for support.

"Are you okay?" I said.

"I was supposed to be preparing a dinner for my sister when she came home from university for the weekend. Now I'm cleaning up a mess before my brother returns with her." Wyatt's voice hurt my ears when he spoke, his voice high-pitched and tinged with fear.

"I can help," I said.

"Help? I think you've done enough helping," Wyatt said.

"Dominguez is the Templar Trigger Man, she was going to kill me," I said. "She decided to frame Siegfried for it."

"I have no idea why she would do this to me," Wyatt said. "What does she think happens to my reputation at work if my brother is arrested for murder?"

"Just keep it together. I'm going to get a lift to the Agency and get them to call an emergency board meeting," I said. "Get the hit on me and Ralph called off."

"I'll tell Sig what happened," Wyatt said.

"I'll try and do something about that too," I said.

"I have my own patron on the board who won't be happy to hear about this. I'll call her now," Wyatt said.

"Okay." I hung up and dialled Grandfather's number.

After the call, we started the slow walk back to the highway. Ralph supported me and Dark Matter stumbled beside us in a daze.

Ralph and Dark Matter hid in the long grass of the paddock beside the highway as we waited for Grandfather to pick me up. I knew he would be able to sense them with his Emotion Magic, but if he couldn't see them, he'd overlook it.

21

Grandfather pulled up beside me in his small SUV. Both Eli and Cory sat in the backseat. When they had a good look at the condition I was in, Eli hopped in the front seat and Cory pulled me onto the back seat to lay with him as he worked on healing me.

I just wanted to rest and knew I probably had a concussion, but I had to stay with it long enough for Grandfather to get me out of this situation. One day I'd be strong enough to save myself, but now I needed his help. I hoped Wyatt's benefactor would help.

"What happened?" Grandfather said.

"Barton Lacy tried to have me killed so he could frame Siegfried Thornton for my murder," I said.

"Do you have any proof of this?" Grandfather said.

"There's the body of a construct at the Thornton House," I said. "Wyatt's there alone and found it."

"Fuck," Grandfather hissed.

I was startled to a sitting position. I'd never heard him swear before.

"He's a good kid and didn't deserve to see that," Grandfather said.

"You know him?"

"His mentor is a close friend of mine," Grandfather said. "An actual close friend. I've worked with the kid before, and he doesn't deserve that. He's a genuinely nice person. I'm not sure where it comes from, given he's half Thornton, half Dominguez."

"What?" I could barely speak through the shock.

"Your Detective Andrea Dominguez is Wyatt and Siegfried's aunt by marriage," Grandfather said.

I shouldn't have been surprised. If Lacy Senior could order my execution, then Siegfried's aunt could frame him for murder.

"He needs a hospital," Cory said.

"I'm not going anywhere controlled by the Agency until I know I'm safe," I said.

Grandfather sighed. "This car isn't going anywhere near Morse Bay."

I froze and looked at him.

"Yes. I know you brought Eli there," Grandfather said.

"I went with Eli there," I said. Viola had brought us there, but I wasn't going to say it.

One more memory to be used against the both of them.

"How did you get hurt?" Grandfather said.

"I jumped out of a moving car being driven by Dominguez acting in her role as the Trigger Man. I thought I could land in the water, but it didn't quite work," I said.

His eyes widened and he gritted his teeth together before he spoke. "Please don't do anything that reckless again."

"I'm fine," I said.

"I'm pretty sure the back of your head is cracked open," Cory said. "You get the staples again. Lucky you keep that part of your head shaved."

"I'm going to take you to a long-term recovery hospital," Grandfather said. "You should have been sent there after the demon attack."

"What do you mean?" I looked at the car door in front of me, tempted to jump from this car.

"I have a plan and it relies on you being there until your gran's trial," Grandfather said. "Cory is going to stay with you in his official Templar role to protect you until I can sort things out."

I nodded.

"We send workers there after they have experienced trauma," Grandfather said. "The team you will be working with is currently there. It might be a good chance for you to meet them."

I looked out the window and watched as the stars drifted by. A headache had a stranglehold on my brain, but Cory wouldn't let me close my eyes.

The facility I'd been brought to clearly had the same architect as Dunn Town Hall. I felt a strange sense of déjà vécu after I'd been patched up and was finally allowed to wander freely. The drugs had worn off, and I felt a dull throbbing in my head as I walked down a hall that made me feel like the last few weeks had all been a dream.

I walked out the back door and crossed the backyard, which held a

214

few strangers reading alone, talking in small groups, or playing a large, casual game of croquet. I walked down the backstairs to the beach behind the building. On the outside, the building reminded me of something out of a movie based on an Agatha Christy novel. Somewhere sunny the wealthy English went on holiday at the turn of the century. A square flat-roofed building with white render and blue window trim. It reminded me of pictures I'd seen of Greece. This place looked like a resort, but on the inside, it was a piece of authoritative government architecture. I slipped my shoes off as I walked onto the sand from the tall staircase that wound its way down the cliff from the Agency's recovery facility.

I physically had to hold back the urge to dive into the ocean and swim away from this place. It was safest to sit still until I was allowed to leave. If I ran now, Gran, Ralph and I would be labelled as traitors with no more chances. I sat on the beach, disregarding the risk to the cleanliness of the white shorts and light blue polo top they'd given me to wear. I looked at the deep blue water to the horizon and took a long breath of the salty but fresh sea air.

I no longer had an axe over my neck, but I was still their prisoner in all the ways that mattered.

"She's not going to let it go." Alexander Hawking sat down beside me, sunglasses propped on his thick, messy hair. He wore a loose button-up shirt with a tropical flower pattern made of garish mismatched colours. Only two of the buttons were done up, exposing most of his muscled torso, which was covered in a thick but well-groomed layer of hair.

I bit back the surge of envy I felt as I looked at him. Even with top surgery, I'd never have a body like that. I looked down at the sand, reminded of how out of place I felt in my own skin. "Andrea?"

"You either humiliated her or killed her. Seeing as you aren't dead, you humiliated her," he said.

"Yes." I clenched my jaw. Why did this prick have to talk to me?

"Her handler isn't going to let you forget it either. None of the Templars will like you much. Most of the time you don't know who they are but have to work with them." He clicked his tongue against his cheek.

I looked up at him and gave him a sharp look.

He made a lewd gesture with his long tongue. "If you keep tonguing your Templar, it's going to be even worse for them."

"Tonguing, seriously?" I said.

"Well, what else do you do when there's no dicks involved?"

"None of your business," I said. "You don't need to be a creepy prick while you're threatening me."

"Don't worry. You're too easy," he said.

"Because I'm polyamorous?"

"Couldn't pay me to do it." He smiled. "I've got a target lined up. A real challenge, that will piss the right people off."

Why in the fuck was Hawking trying to do weird objectifying men's locker talk with me?

"Best part is he'll think he convinced me," Hawking said.

"Why are you doing this? Did you lose a few brain cells when they tried to drown you?" I said.

"It was more a waterboarding, actually," he said. "People underestimate me because I'm not from a fancy founding family."

"Maybe they didn't want you dead."

"They wanted to point at your precious Ralph and say he did it. I was going to be collateral in the fucked-up chess game your grandparents and their peers are playing with this town." His hands curled into fists. "Too bad I have friends."

I felt sick at the thought. That would have thrown Mason under the bus because he was the only person who could have told Ralph about Hawking hurting me.

"I'm coming for you, your brothers and your peers. Another generation isn't going to grow old to play sick games with the rest of us."

I bit my lip hard to force myself to stay quiet as I felt his spit land on my face with his last line. He wasn't the only person who'd suffered at the hands of Nate Island. I didn't respond as he stood up and kicked white dry sand into my lap. I expected him to purposely spit on me, but thankfully he was polite enough to refrain from that.

SUBSCRIBE to my fortnightly author **NEWSLETTER** to receive the latest news, sneak peeks and bonus content. It's also a great way to keep in touch as you can respond to each email.
Find it at my website geekaflame.com

If you enjoyed this book, please consider leaving an honest review where you purchased this book or on your favourite website.

ACKNOWLEDGMENTS

I'd like to thank my mum, dad and sister for their lifelong support of my ambitious dream of being a storyteller. Mum and Dad, even though you don't quite get it sometimes I'm grateful you never discouraged me from working towards this dream.

The members of Wordsflow writers' group who talked me into the idea of actually publishing my writing one day.

My editor Skylar Noble Bray who tolerated my odd grammar choices and helped me turn a 150,000 word draft into a trilogy where all of the storylines I wanted to explore can shine. My cover designer Fantasy & Coffee Design who created a cover better then I could have ever imagined. Eliott of EliottDesigns for the interior design and formatting work that turned my word doc into an incredible looking book you can hold in your hand. Nicholas Taylor for proofreading the final version of this book to ensure it is the best quality I can produce.

Emily for copy/line editing the original web novel version of this story.

Lastly my readers on Tapas.io who supported me and continued to read the web novel version every week.

AUTHOR BIOGRAPHY

Ashton K. Rose writes Australian paranormal, urban fantasy and mystery fiction filled with LGBTQIA+ characters.

Ashton currently lives in sunny Queensland able to enjoy the best of the Australian bush and beach.

Ashton spent their first fourteen years being raised on a remote farm shaped around the remains of an old mining town. Surrounded by the skeletons of past lives and their matching ghost stories, Ashton developed a love for fantasy, horror, and dark fairy tales from a young age.

Carrying a love of ghost stories into adulthood Ashton started writing novels about magic, vampires and ghosts. Ashton decided to set The Southern Magicks in a world heavily inspired by the backdrop of the Australia bush/beach and the speculative fiction Ashton has consumed over a lifetime.

Keep updated on Ashton's writing at geekaflame.com or find them on social media using their linktree - linktr.ee/geekaflame.

Printed in Great Britain
by Amazon

15756760R00135